The Dogwood Days
of Summer

The Dogwood Days of Summer

The Southern Isles

Laurie Beach

TULE
PUBLISHING

Dedication

For Bill Lokken
with thanks for all of the summer days
spent boating on the Tennessee River
and gratitude for the kind of love
only a father can give.

Chapter One

"MARRY THE MAN who loves you more." The advice had stuck with Brooke Warter like a clamped-on tick since middle school. "If he loves you more, you'll never have to worry," her mother said. "If he loves you more, you'll be stable your whole life." For years, Brooke saw the concept as not only annoying but potentially dangerous. At the very least, the idea was out-of-date. *Marry a man who treats you like an equal*, she thought. *Marry a man you don't want to live without.*

It took one terrible night to recognize that her boyfriend of seven years did not, in fact, *love her more*. Brooke sat in her pajamas on the iron balcony of their Savannah apartment as a hazy sun peeked above the horizon. The balcony was off the master bedroom, and she'd thought it was so romantic when they rented it. To her right was their evergreen tree in a big black pot—the first thing she bought when they moved in. She'd wrapped it in twinkle lights with visions of Gates waving to her from below, shouting at her to join him at the pool, or telling her he'd be right up. There were two chairs and a bistro table next to it, perfect for romantic wine nights and stargazing in bathrobes. None of which happened. Not even once. Instead, they forgot to water the tree, and it'd been crispy and brown for years, the lights hanging unplugged and filthy, half of them on the ground.

She'd spent the day before cleaning the living room and bathroom, making appetizers, and even creating a bespoke cocktail out of Gates's favorite flavors—tequila, Cointreau, orange soda, and a splash of cream. She called it The Gateway and was proud of herself for thinking of it. His friends held plastic cups of that orange drink while hiding and giggling behind her overstuffed white couch and faux-marble kitchen bar, ready to pounce. "Shhhh," she'd said, straining to listen past the aggressive thumping of her heart. "I think I hear him." She waved to everyone. "Get down!"

There was a knock at the door, which was strange, because Gates had a key. She swung it open to a collective groan. No one was there, just a tiny brown box with the Amazon swish. She snatched it and shut the door. At least the new brown leather wallet she'd bought for him had shown up.

An hour later, no one was interested in hiding anymore, the meatballs were cold, and all of the ranch dip had been eaten. Several of his friends had tried texting and calling him, and no one had gotten an answer. Brooke was beginning to wonder if she should start calling local hospitals.

"He's at The Whistling Pig," someone finally said. Brooke felt her neck turn red and splotchy, and she wished she hadn't worn a button-down blouse. What was he doing at a bar? "My brother's working tonight," the guy said. "He said Gates has been sitting there for hours."

"Alone?" Brooke asked.

The guy nodded. "Maybe he had a bad day at work."

Brooke exhaled. "Maybe he did." He'd never done anything like that before, bad day or not. Especially on his birthday. She scanned the apartment filled with men dressed in shorts and polo shirts and women with heavy party makeup. Not one of *her* friends was there. They were all his closest friends, and she'd never had a meaningful conversation with any of them. Their groups of friends had never intermingled. It was like they'd kept their lives separate despite living together. Who were these people who'd known him from childhood, or college, or work, where he'd maybe, but probably not, had a bad day? "Should we all surprise him at the Pig?" she asked.

"I'll check the vibe," the guy said, texting.

Brooke put the meatballs in the microwave and pulled the tin foil off the fruit skewers. "We might as well eat all of this."

"Um." The guy shot Brooke a look of pity while all eleven guests listened intently to what he was about to say. "He doesn't seem to be doing well. My brother says something is definitely off, like negative one hundred."

Gates's favorite cake—chocolate with whipped cream frosting—was still chilling in the refrigerator. Brooke pulled it out. "Then we might as well eat this too."

By the time she cut the cake, most of the guests were either eyeballs deep in their phones or saying their goodbyes. No one was hungry, and no one wanted to stick around for Gates to come home. "Thanks for coming, y'all," she said with too much perk. "He's gonna be so sad that he missed his own party." A weird noise escaped from her. It was supposed to be a carefree giggle, but it sounded more like a trapped cat. Embarrassment and disappointment had a stranglehold on her throat.

That was at six o'clock. Gates didn't come home until well after one A.M.

He went straight to her, not even noticing the colorful balloons in the corners of the room or the melting cake on the coffee table. "I can't be turning twenty-four and still in the same place I was in high school," he said.

"Same place?" Brooke tried to keep the anger out of her voice.

"We're living in an apartment, Brooke. I'm still working at the bank."

"But we're young. This is our work-hard era. You're smart, Gates. You're—"

"Stop trying to comfort me."

"I'm just pointing out that we're doing well. These things take time."

"And suddenly you're a cheerleader. You're not Jessa, Brooke."

"Jessa? Why are you bringing up Jessa?" She didn't try to hide her anger that time.

"Because you're pretending to be sweet. You're not sweet, Brooke. You're nice."

She stood from the couch, fists clenched and nostrils flaring. How dare he bring her best friend into the discussion. "What in the ever-lovin' hell is the difference between sweet and nice anyway? They're the *same*." She stomped toward the bedroom, then turned back to face him. "I had a surprise party for you tonight, and you never showed up!"

He didn't even flinch. "I know."

"You *know*?"

"A bunch of my friends came to The Whistling Pig."

That stung. Her guests left to find him and didn't invite her. "Clearly, I'm not *nice* enough for your friends to like me." Her face burned and her stomach hurt. Who was this man she'd spent seven years with? Who was *she*? "It's over, Gates."

"Yes, it is." He was solemn as he said it. But firm.

"You take the couch." She shut the bedroom door.

There was no coming back from a day like that. She knew with clarity the next morning that her relationship with Gates would never be the same again. As the sun rose higher in the sky, she wanted to call Jessa. But in that moment, even her best friend felt like an adversary. Her hands shook as she remembered what he'd said: "Jessa is sweet. You're nice." She typed into her phone, *What is the difference between sweet and nice?*

There was nothing. But what she did find was the difference between nice and kind. Generally, niceness was superficial. It was saying you felt badly for someone when you really didn't. It was empty words without real feelings behind them. But kindness, well, that wasn't superficial at all. Kindness meant action. It meant bringing a casserole to a sick friend because you cared, because you *wanted* to help them, not because you wanted to look good or because you wanted them to like you.

That's who Jessa was. Naturally kind or, as Gates said, *sweet*. It felt like such an affront. Especially when Brooke had just slaved over and paid for an entire party for him. She'd gotten all of his favorite things. Everything was to please him, not to be *nice*. Right?

Although she had to admit that she was hoping he would reciprocate and do something special when her birthday rolled around. So, maybe she wasn't pure in her intentions. Maybe she was just pretending to be nice. If she was honest, she'd actually been a little resistant to buying him that darned chocolate cake, because her favorite was vanilla with buttercream frosting. She even considered pretending to forget that he liked chocolate and buying vanilla instead. Buying a cake for herself on someone else's birthday was exactly what her mother would do. Brooke shivered at the thought. Was she like Cornelia? Was she actually bitchy underneath a veneer of niceness?

Brooke pulled her knees up to her chest, chilly in the early morning air. She couldn't remember the last time she and Gates had kissed. Not just a hello and goodbye peck, but a *real* kiss. At least, without several cocktails first. The fact was, they'd been acting more like friends for a couple of years now. His sense of humor was childish, his style of dress was nerdy, and every one of his hobbies required him spending time away from her. All of it made her mad. He should want to spend as much time as possible with her. He should tell her that she was pretty more than just every once in a while. He should take her feelings into account when he made Saturday night plans without her or hung his dumb red Corvette poster in their family room without asking. He should...

She covered her eyes from the glare of the sun. Everything rang so hollow. Maybe she was the problem after all.

She had to fix her life. And she would start by forcing herself to be sweet.

Chapter Two

THEY SAY HAIR holds memories, so Brooke cut hers off. She did a cheeky little spin next to the marble-topped kitchen island. This would steam up her mother hotter than the coffee in her hand. Years of learning had taught her that it was a better strategy to hit her mother in the face with what she'd done instead of trying to pass it off quietly. Cornelia's anger lasted longer when she thought someone was trying to trick her.

Just like the split ends and bleached blond mistakes that currently lay on the floor of a nearby salon, Brooke's old life was a thing of the past. Her new life of being genuinely sweet and lovely to everyone was about to begin. Her hair sat blunt above her shoulders instead of tangling down to the small of her back, and already she felt wiser, more mature. All she needed was to wash in a box of brown dye to match her outgrown roots, and she'd be a whole new person.

Brooke's mother was less than thrilled that her daughter had moved back home, and the new hairstyle served to make it worse. If Cornelia didn't have a mouth full of hot coffee, she might've said a curse word. Those, of course, were to be saved for the most extreme situations. It had always been that way—anything unsavory in Cornelia Callaway Warter's life was to be pointedly ignored. Therefore, she continued to sip at the spot on her mug where her lipstick stained the rim, and refused to look at her daughter. Cornelia firmly believed that girls with blue eyes must have blond hair. She'd been paying to have her daughter's hair professionally highlighted since the tender age of four.

"It's much better now, isn't it, Cornelia?" Brooke said. "Don't I look classy?" Brooke would never tell her that one of the reasons she'd gone to the salon was because she hadn't washed her hair for a week—unless rinsing it in ocean water counted as clean.

Her mother said nothing, but her lips were pursed with wrinkles appearing all around them like a sunburst.

Finally, after Brooke ate an entire biscuit, egg, and sausage breakfast in silence, Cornelia spoke up. "You fixed the sheets on the guest bed?" Almost everything the woman said sounded like a question that should end in *right*?

"Yes, Cornelia. I made the bed." The same bed she'd slept in for eighteen of her twenty-three years was now the guest bed. Instead of a frilly pink comforter and stuffed animals piled in the corner, every piece of her childhood, including her collectible concert posters and school awards, had been taken off the walls and replaced with watercolors of magnolia flowers that perfectly matched the green-and-white bedcover.

Brooke walked out of the kitchen, past the double staircase, toward the extra tall and wide front door. There was no *Have a good first day of work*, or *It's so nice to have you home*. Brooke yelled "Goodbye" because she knew she'd be in trouble if she didn't. There was no answer. It was just as it always was with Cornelia—orders and judgment. All the time.

If she'd had a choice, Brooke would have happily stayed a two-hour drive away in Savannah. But since she'd abruptly left her job, her apartment, and Gates, that was no longer an option. Her little white Audi was parked by the front door where she'd left it when she arrived last night. It was still filled to the top with everything she owned, right down to the bathroom trash can. It had all been festering and stinking in there for a week. A week she took for herself. A week she didn't plan to tell anyone about.

There was no guessing how long her parents, Cornelia and Trigger, would let her stay. But none of that mattered now; all of her focus needed to be on her new job at one of the only businesses on the island aside from Salty Dot's food truck and Fred's old gas station. The Saltwater Winery had been open only a few years and was already a big draw for tourists in their rental cars, driving all the way across Goose Island to the very tip by the oyster beds. A retired couple had planted grape vines years ago, and there'd been pushback ever since. The locals would call her a traitor, but she needed a job, she wanted to be near Jessa, and the Saltwater Winery was hiring.

She'd driven about twenty yards down the long driveway when she spotted a white-haired woman in a blue bathrobe moving barefoot and apparition-like among the Spanish moss-draped oaks. Brooke rolled down her window and waved. "Nana!"

Nana had always been spry. She practically skipped over to the car. She may have been in a bathrobe, but her eyebrows were drawn on and her cottony hair was pulled back into her signature black-ribboned short ponytail. "Who are you?" she asked, leaning down to look Brooke square in the face.

"You know who I am, Nana."

"I don't believe I do."

"I'm your granddaughter—Brooke."

"Hmm. Let me get a good look at you." She squinted in at her, while Brooke smiled sweetly. "Yes, you do have a familiar face."

Brooke shook her head. Nana was not truly forgetful, she was just having the time of her life pretending. "I'll see you at supper, Nana. I've got to get to work now."

"Well, all right, then. Welcome home, sweetheart." Nana reached in and touched a small, misshapen hand to Brooke's shoulder. "It's meatloaf night."

Even though her best friend was the manager, Brooke was still shaky with nerves as she walked past the wooden picnic tables and cornhole games to the low-slung tin-roofed

11

building of the Saltwater Winery. She wore her best jeans and a tank top, knowing that she'd be given a branded winery T-shirt. Today she was supposed to shadow a coworker and learn the different types of wines. With a deep breath, she knocked on the locked front door. It was nine A.M. and they didn't open until ten. No one came to the door, so she knocked again, wondering if she was supposed to find an employee entrance around the back somewhere. A male voice yelled, "We're closed!"

"I'm Brooke Warter," she said into the crack between the double front doors. "I'm the new employee."

The door opened and an unsmiling older man said, "I don't know where Jessa's at."

Brooke didn't ask his name. He didn't seem open to conversation. "Is it okay if I come in?"

He left the door open and walked away. That did not bode well. Jessa failed to mention that they would be working with a rude, unfriendly grump. Brooke stood in the middle of the gift shop in the dark. The man had disappeared so fast, she didn't see which way he went.

"Jessa?" Brooke called, walking past a huge metal tree with empty Saltwater wine bottles slid onto each limb. Against the rustic wooden walls were shelves lined with bottle openers, T-shirts, and charcuterie boards. It smelled musty, with a lingering light floral aroma of women's perfume. Had it come from the grouchy man wearing dirty jeans and a ball cap? She'd caught a whiff of honeysuckle, or maybe jasmine, as soon as he walked away.

"Jessa?" she called again, her voice more urgent. There was no answer. Not one piece of her wanted to walk farther into that building where she might be confronted with the old man again, so she turned around and walked back out the front door.

Jessa had told her that their coworkers were great, that they'd all be friends, and that they were going to have an epic summer working together. It was supposed to be the adult version of their old days at Camp Dogwood, where fun was planned from sunup to sundown. The winery even had cats roaming around, which was a reminder that it was a more casual, farm-like winery, not the kind that refused entrance without a coat and tie or at least a platinum American Express card. Outside, there was a large sign with a photo of people holding wineglasses and dancing under the stars. It was pasted to the side of the building inviting everyone to MUSIC AMONG THE VINES every Friday night. To the left of the building, swings hung in the old oaks just barely longer than the airy moss draping the limbs, and wine-barrel cocktail tables dotted the grounds next to picnic tables and an assortment of tall, colorful metal bottle trees. There was cornhole, bocce, little slant-roofed outhouses, and even an overflowing fenced-off garden with a sign above the gate that said AMELIA'S PATCH OF HAPPINESS. The grounds had grown and blossomed since she'd last been there, as if the place were getting comfortable with itself.

The more Brooke looked around, the more she forgot about the rude man who smelled like flowers.

As she neared the corner of the large, low building, Jessa's voice rang out. "Watch out, here they come!"

What was coming? Guests? She didn't even have her SALTWATER WINERY T-shirt yet. She heard the scratchy scuttle followed by a cacophony of clucking. From the backside of the building, running at full speed, came a brood of the fluffiest Silkie chickens she'd ever seen. It was a chatty blur of feathery feet and crested heads as they ran right past her to their favorite pecking grounds and immediately went to work. Jessa wasn't far behind.

"Oh, good! You're here!" Brooke ran up and gave her old friend a hug.

Jessa had always been the pretty one. Carolina Jessamine was her name, after the South Carolina state flower. She could have won any state beauty pageant and, if there was a contest for sweet, she could've won that too. To look at her was to believe she had it all. But Brooke knew better. If it weren't for the fact that Jessa didn't, in fact, have it all, Brooke would probably hate her.

"I'm gonna introduce you to Skip and June before we get started with the wines," Jessa said, leading the way toward the acres of vineyards.

"Is Skip the guy who opened the door for me?" Brooke asked.

"Is he missing a leg?" Jessa asked, laughing. "He does get

in every now and then."

"No, I don't think so. He wasn't very friendly—"

Jessa chuckled. "Was he black and white?"

They were almost to a white-fenced area where Brooke saw clearly what Jessa was talking about. A handmade wooden sign on the gate said SKIP AND JUNE, and inside were two friendly goats. One was black and white and missing a front leg. "That must be Skip," Brooke said.

"Yep."

"So, who was the grumpy guy who opened the door for me?"

"Had to be Duke," Jessa said. "You haven't met him before? He's the owner. But don't worry, we usually don't see him. He tries to leave before the guests arrive."

Brooke leaned against the fence. The place was beautiful, but it was—a lot. "Jess. I don't know if I can do this."

"Aw, honey. You're just pouring wine for guests. It's easy. All you have to do is smile and pour." Jessa put a skinny arm across Brooke's shoulders. "And in between, we'll have fun. Just like our old camp days."

Brooke left Camp Dogwood, or as they liked to call it "The Dog," long ago, taking with her the one thing she should have left there. Gates Lancaster. She had no business trying to go back in time. But the truth was, she hated being alone. Since she left Savannah, she'd been weepy and filled with regret. So what if Gates didn't feel like the man she should spend her life with? At least he'd stuck with her. He might have even loved her. Maybe that's what love and marriage was—simply choosing someone who was willing. The whole idea of soulmates might very well be a hoax.

By the end of the day, Brooke had learned to describe the varieties of muscadine and scuppernong wines by their intended purposes: Porch Pounders, BBQ wines, picnic wines, dinner wines, and dessert wines. Just like the grapes, the scuppernongs were white and the muscadines were red, but it was going to take forever to learn the details—which wines paired best with warm brie and pears, or lamb, venison, or pheasant, which had notes of caramel and butterscotch or dark cherry, vanilla, violet, elderberry, or loquat. It wasn't long before her new white T-shirt had splash stains of red, as did her formerly clean tennis shoes. But at least she'd survived. Watching people enjoy themselves on that early summer day had been a great distraction. She wasn't on her phone looking back on photos of Gates Lancaster from the past seven years or stalking his newly cleaned up Instagram page—the one that no longer included photos of her.

"You wanna come eat supper at the truck with me?" Jessa asked. "Mama parked out by the Baptist church today."

"Can't. It's meatloaf night. Cornelia would kill me." They were walking to the dirt parking lot together, her feet throbbing from a day spent standing. Even though it meant sitting down, she still dreaded getting back into her over-stuffed car. She couldn't be bothered to unload everything when she'd just have to pack it up as soon as she found an alternate place to stay.

"You know my mama is dying to see you," Jessa said. "She's been talking up a storm. Said she had a vision of you as a hot dog. That woman has officially lost her mind."

Brooke stopped walking. "Dottie saw me as a hot dog?"

"Street meat is actually what she said."

"Jessa." Brooke shivered. "I dressed up as a hot dog for Halloween." It had been a mistake, one of her many regrets. "I thought I was being funny. I didn't want to be a sexy nurse or devil or, you know. Anyway, Gates hated it. Said I embarrassed him."

"Do you think that's why he broke up with you?"

"He didn't break up with me, Jess. We both ended it. Well, me more than him, but it was still mutual."

Jessa looked back toward the winery, like she was checking to make sure no one else was around. "What happened?"

"I had a surprise birthday party for him." Brooke was tired of thinking about it. "He knew about it, and he didn't come home. He left me there to be humiliated."

"Who was the girl?"

"There wasn't a girl. He just didn't want to spend his birthday with me. He was literally sitting alone at a bar."

"I have trouble believing that."

"It makes sense to me, Jess. We didn't want to be together anymore." The loneliness that had been living like a brick in her chest moved to her stomach with a nauseating shift.

Who was she, if not Gates Lancaster's girlfriend?

"It's sad," Jessa said. "I thought y'all were it since The Dog days. Figured I'd be carrying flowers at your wedding."

"Well, I guess I'll be carrying flowers at yours."

"Very funny. You know I hate men."

"Still?"

"What I have is a lifelong affliction." Jessa motored on, leaving Brooke standing there. "You can't trust any of them. Not one."

Brooke knew she'd hit a nerve. Jessa had a daddy-shaped hole in her heart that would never heal. Not only did she not know who her father was, her sister, Tulip, didn't either. Dottie made no secret about the fact that she chose her baby daddies based on what kind of kids she wanted—Carolina Jessamine was born to be beautiful, and Tulip was born to be smart. Brooke feared that Dottie didn't even realize that she got so much more. Her daughters were not just smart and beautiful, they had the kind of grit that comes from knowing on a cellular level that the only person they could truly count on was themselves. They had Dottie, each other, and several years ago, they gained their uncle Fred when he moved to the island. But that was it. And, having only three family members in all of the world probably felt like one big wind could knock them over.

"Thanks for giving me this job, Jess," Brooke said. "I mean it."

"You know, if Libby wasn't working marketing, I'd have

given you that job. But with only a week's notice, I didn't have much available."

"I'm just happy to have a paycheck." Brooke had been using her social media management degree back in Savannah. She shook her head at the irony. She was great at crisis management until it came to her own life. "Hold up. Jess, did you say *Libby*? Please tell me you're not talking about Libby Trotter."

Jessa nodded, opening the door to her car. "Y'all are good now, right?"

"I mean, I haven't seen her in like ten years."

"Well, she's still Libby, but not as bad as she used to be."

Brooke walked two cars over to her jam-packed Audi, spewing words under her breath that would make her mother faint clean away.

"I just can't fathom that she'd bug you anymore," Jessa said. "Y'all are grown-ups now."

Ah, but there were no real grown-ups. People over the age of eighteen were just varying levels of child/adult hybrids. With just the mention of Libby Trotter, all the feelings of a bullied little girl came rushing back. "Right. Okay." She climbed into her car. "See you tomorrow." She hoped she'd sounded sweet as she sat in stunned silence.

So, Libby Trotter was back in her life. If she'd known that was going to be the case, she might have fought to stay with Gates.

Chapter Three

GATES LANCASTER WAS the best-looking guy in all of Camp Dogwood. Even in the fourth grade, there were distinguishing features that set him apart. The way he carried himself was probably the biggest. He didn't have to worry about sitting alone at lunch because people clamored to be near him. He was chosen first for every team, every skit, every outing, and every girl's crush. His parents redshirted him to give him an advantage in his youth soccer career, so he was a year older and three inches taller than everyone else, but he would have been the leader either way.

Brooke knew that leaving him and coming back home would be difficult, but she thought the hard part would be her parents. She hadn't accounted for the memories that kept infiltrating her brain like a computer virus. She'd been the quiet girl, the under-the-radar camper, picked somewhere in the middle for sports teams, and completely dependent on her one friend, Jessa, to be her life preserver. When Gates Lancaster chose her, it was like Elvis Presley choosing a random fan from the audience. Out of a hundred girls at camp, she was the lucky one.

Brooke pulled into the long driveway, keeping an eye out for a sprightly old woman in a blue bathrobe. Nana very well might run out in front of the car. She'd done it before. The curtains were wide open in the dining room, and she could see her mother setting the table. Cornelia was of the generation that considered it rude to have your drapes drawn. Even setting the table was a show, whether someone was watching or not. People should be allowed to see into your home from the street. It was simply the gracious and neighborly thing to do. Brooke sighed and put her car into park. It was so much work to pretend like things were perfect all the time—exhausting to act like they had nothing to hide.

"Anna Brooke! Are your shoes on in this house?" Cornelia yelled when Brooke opened the front door. "And do not leave them by the door. Take them with you to the guest room." The guest room—Cornelia's code for communicating to Brooke that she was not allowed to overstay her welcome. It was an emotional sting every time she said it. "Wash up and come straight downstairs."

The only people who still called her by both names were from her childhood. She wasn't a little girl anymore. She'd ditched the name Anna back in the sixth grade when she learned it was given to her in honor of one of her daddy's many ex-girlfriends. Cornelia only allowed it, and then held on to it, to be a martyr. Brooke renewed her decision to leave all of her belongings in her car. She wouldn't be staying long.

Nana traipsed her way to the main house from her backyard cottage promptly at six P.M. She wore a pink terrycloth house dress and bright pink lipstick to match. "Nana," Cornelia said with a tone of surprise, "you look very nice tonight." It was a definite improvement from some of her other ensembles.

Nana sat at the table and pulled the rubber band from her hair. "The elastic in this hairband is shot." She threw it and its corresponding white hairs onto the middle of the beautifully set table. Her thin hair now stuck straight out on the sides like she'd used an entire can of hairspray.

Brooke knew from Cornelia's tight expression that she was hoping no one could see her mother-in-law's hair from the street. Brooke grabbed the rubber band and stuck it in her pocket. Dinner was the usual stilted questions about Trig's day at work with surface-level answers and too much silence. Every now and then, after a small and well-chewed bite of meatloaf, Cornelia would look toward the front window and smile widely in case someone happened to be looking in. No one seemed to remember that Brooke had a day at work that she might like to talk about too.

It didn't matter that she was surrounded by family or that she had Jessa nearby, Brooke was alone. And it was going to be her first summer alone in seven years. After clearing the table and doing the dishes, she left Cornelia, Trig, and Nana in the den with their cocktails and evening news. "I'm going to Jessa's," she said. Cornelia flinched but didn't make eye contact.

Trig gave her the thumbs-up.

"Bring me back a tub of Dottie's tomato gravy," Nana said. "I'll have it on my biscuits tomorrow morning."

"I think the food truck is closed, Nana."

"I thought you said you were going to her house," Cornelia piped in.

"Yes, but I'm not going to ask for tomato gravy when she's not working. I'm just going to visit Jessa."

"In all of these years—" Cornelia shook her head and took a self-righteous sip of her gin and tonic. "Twenty-three years and have you learned one thing?"

"Please don't start with me."

"Get your grandmother that gravy. It doesn't matter one lick if you inconvenience *Dottie Boone*." She said it like the woman's name was a swear word.

It was a fight Brooke knew she couldn't win. "Yes, ma'am."

Nana waited until the conversation was over before saying, "I don't believe I want that gravy after all. I'll have myself some blueberry pancakes instead. See to it, Cornelia."

Cornelia's face went stone cold. She stared daggers at Trig, like he'd done this to her. Which, in a way, he had. Trigger, named for Roy Roger's horse, was Nana's oldest child and therefore in charge of her well-being whether his wife liked it or not. He also happened to be the wealthiest. And, he had only one child—Brooke—unlike his other two brothers who had four children each. Nana had been his responsibility since his daddy died going on eight years ago.

Brooke remembered when Nana moved in. Those were the days when Brooke would go straight over to Jessa's house after school. The tension at her own home was too much. Cornelia didn't take well to having her mother-in-law under the same roof. It took less than a year for Trig to build Nana a house out back. After all, it was his responsibility to keep Cornelia happy too.

On the way to Jessa's house, Brooke visited Fred at the old gas station and bought a pack of bacon, an onion, and two cans of diced tomatoes. Fred's name used to be De-Wayne, but when he quit his job as a corporate lawyer and bought the falling-down station to be near his sister, Dottie, the former owner left behind a dark blue jumpsuit with a stitched-on nametag that said *Fred*. It became DeWayne's new uniform. Somewhere underneath his beard, inside the baggy coveralls, and behind the toothpick he always kept in his mouth was a decent-looking middle-aged man. Most people never knew his real name. He was just Fred, the gas station owner, sandwich maker, secret-keeper, animal rescuer, and romantic target of every available older woman in two counties. He might live on a boat behind a store so old that it still had a faded Sunbeam Bread advertisement from the 1940s painted on the side, but the man was known to have money. He also had a hot plate behind the counter with warm cookies for whoever needed one.

Brooke always needed one.

Brooke was counting on Dottie to have some flour and seasonings. Maybe she and Jessa could whip up the gravy while they talked. Nana deserved to get her tomato gravy. Brooke passed Salty Dot's bright yellow food truck and pulled into the overgrown driveway leading to Dottie's brick ranch-style home. There were cats sitting in the front windows, just like there always were. The sight sent a rush of warm, grateful familiarity straight to her heart. She walked right in without knocking.

"Jess?"

There was laughter coming from the kitchen.

"Dottie? Tulip?"

She wound her way to the back of the house by the family room until she found Dottie, Jessa, and her sister, Tulip, who appeared to have colored her hair a strawberry blonde. This was not unusual for Tulip, who'd already gone through pink, purple, and rainbow hair. They were all laughing around the kitchen table. Everything was the same—the rust-orange couch, brown wood paneling on the walls, well-worn carpets, fading artwork, and metal diner-like table in the low-ceilinged house. It was comforting, right down to the smell of the cat box.

"Hey, y'all!" Brooke announced happily as she dropped her bag of groceries on the Formica kitchen counter. Dottie ambled over for a hug. She smelled like frying oil.

"Let me look at you." Dottie wasn't scrutinizing her to tell her she was pretty or as a happy reminder of her face.

No, she was reading her. She squinted and pulled her bottom teeth up over her top lip. She was missing a tooth. When had that happened? Dottie shook her head. "Your frequency is as off as a derailed train."

"I'm just going through a little something, Dottie. I'll be okay."

"I wasn't born faraway." She acted personally offended. "I know that."

It was wistfully familiar the way Dottie always messed up phrases like *born yesterday*. Brooke looked past her to Jessa at the table. Her smile faded as she realized the other person was not Jessa's little sister. No. It couldn't be. Without warning? Why hadn't Jessa told her? The girl sitting at the table was Libby Trotter. Brooke fought the urge to sprint out of the house. Instead, she did her best to paste the smile back on her face and press down the overwhelmingly big feelings.

"Be right back. Been holding it too long!" Brooke hoped to sound pert and nonplussed, but her voice came out shrill. She practically ran to the bathroom and shut the door. Dottie's house was *her* safe place. She sat fully dressed on the closed toilet. She knew she would have to talk to Libby eventually, but she wasn't ready. There was a knock at the door. Brooke didn't trust her voice to answer.

"I'm coming in," Jessa said. Dottie didn't believe in locks, so nothing in the house was secure. Jessa closed the door behind her. "Don't be mad at me."

"Do you remember, Jess? Do you remember what she

did to me? What she did to Nate?" Brooke's face turned red-hot.

"That was a long time ago. We were kids."

"Make this fast, Jess. I don't want her to know she's bothering me."

"I mean, I'm in the bathroom with you," Jessa pointed out. "It's kind of obvious."

"Dammit." Brooke flushed the toilet.

"I'm sorry. I know she was horrible to you. But it's probably time to move on."

Brooke turned on the faucet to blast the sound of washing her hands. "I will never forgive her." The last thing in all the world that she wanted to do was walk out of that bathroom and face Libby Trotter. Now that she didn't have Gates, she was extra vulnerable. How should she act? Like nothing had happened? "What am I supposed to say to her?"

"Just start with hello," Jessa said.

"I'm past this, Jess. I don't want to go backward."

"You're not going anywhere but out of this bathroom."

"Did she know I was coming?"

"Yes, I told her."

Brooke shot her a look. "What'd she say?"

Jessa's hand stopped on the doorknob. "I can't remember. I think maybe she just laughed."

"She *laughed*?" Brooke caught sight of the horrified look on her own face in the mirror. Whereas she'd felt pretty all day with her new haircut and full face of makeup, the girl she saw in the mirror was much too familiar: alone.

"Actually, it was more like a chuckle," Jessa said.

There was a knock at the door, and Brooke flinched. "Y'all can come on out now." It was Dottie. "Libby said to tell y'all goodbye. Said she's meeting up with some kind of group that gets together to run marathons or some such nonsense. She's got to get up at the butt crack of dawn tomorrow, so she can't stay and play nice."

Jessa opened the door and moved into the hall, but Dottie put an arm out so Brooke couldn't pass. "That girl's hiding something," Dottie whispered so close to Brooke's face that she could see the smattering of gray hairs in her eyebrows. "I feel it all through my nose."

It had been a while, so Brooke needed a moment to remember. When Dottie felt things in her forehead, they were scary and must be taken seriously. When she felt them in her hands, it required action—something had to be done about it quickly. But when she felt them in her nose, Brooke remembered, "It might blow over as fast as a fart in the wind."

"That's right." Dottie put her arm down and stepped back. "But I'm telling you, there's something there."

"Are you getting any premonitions?" Brooke couldn't help but keep glancing down to Dottie's missing tooth. How long had it been gone and why hadn't she gotten it fixed? Dottie caught her looking.

"It's just a tooth, Anna Brooke Warter. If it bothers you

that a person is missing one, that is your problem. It don't mean a danged thing to me."

"Yes, ma'am. I mean, no, ma'am. I think you look great." Dottie's face was wide, rugged, and beautifully familiar.

"Now, I can't see a thing when it comes to Libby. But for you—" She stared square into Brooke's face. "There's a storm blowin' in. Something from your past is about to come into your present."

"Looks like she already did, and she just left," Jessa said. She'd always been highly suspicious of her mother's hit-or-miss psychic prognostications.

"Do you think it's Gates?" Brooke asked.

"Oh, it's definitely Gates. But there's someone else. I see fireworks."

"The literal kind or the love kind?" Jessa asked.

"I can't tell."

They made their way to the kitchen, where Dottie had already unpacked Brooke's bag of groceries and set her cast-iron pan on the stove. "Looks like y'all want some tomato gravy."

Brooke nodded and pulled the can opener out of the drawer. "Nana's got a hankering." She opened the lid of one can. "The fireworks—like, I might meet someone else? Someone who actually suits me?"

"Whoa, slow down there, Smelly," Dottie said. "How long have you been single now? A week? Two? Your heart is in no shape to stick on anyone now. It's as slick as an oil spill."

The truth was, her heart had been empty for years. Not sticky, not slick, but an under-filled balloon with a slow leak.

"You don't have to make the gravy, Mama," Jessa said as Dottie sidled up to the stovetop. "I know you've had a long day."

"I dipped her in corn syrup and rolled her in sugar when she was born," Dottie said, kissing her daughter on the forehead. "That's why she's so sweet." Brooke flinched. Dottie kissed Brooke's forehead too. "I'll take y'all up on that. I'm so tired, my brain is all cottony."

Jessa laid the bacon in strips inside the pan, as Dottie, in her wide-rumped way, ambled down the hall. "So, do you think you and Gates will get back together?"

"If Cornelia got what she wanted, we would. But, no. I don't think so."

Jessa appeared deep in thought as she pressed the bacon down with a fork. "Would you rather talk about Gates or Libby? Which would be more helpful?"

"Is there anything *you* want to talk about, Jess? What's going on in your life? I heard you're building a house?"

"I'm fixing up that old one out by the marsh. Didn't cost too much to buy. But that's boring. I want to talk about you." Jessa should've been a therapist with the way she listened to everyone else's problems. Hers were never of any concern. She never complained. Ever.

"Jess, you're the nicest person on the planet. I mean, the sweetest." Brooke cut an onion in half and peeled off the outer layers. "Like, naturally sweet and caring. Which is why Libby freaking Trotter is now working with us."

"She's actually pretty good at the job."

"Do you know what she's good at?" Brooke chopped the onion into small squares. "She's good at ruining lives. Like mine. And Nate's. God, I don't even want to talk about it."

"Then don't. If those onions don't make you cry, he will." She carefully flipped each hot, spitting piece of bacon. "I'm only saying this because I love you." She paused. "But maybe Libby wouldn't have the power to bother you if you didn't let her."

"I was a kid, Jess!"

"I'm talking about now." She turned off the burner and put a dainty hand on Brooke's shoulder just long enough to calm her down a little. "Anyway, Nathan probably has a wife and baby by now. Camp was a long time ago." Carefully, she set the cooked bacon one by one on a paper towel.

Brooke shook her head, dropping the raw onions into the bacon grease. It'd always been frustrating to her that Nathan Daugherty wasn't on social media. She couldn't find him anywhere. Her phone buzzed in her back pocket, so she pulled it out and saw the name Gates Lancaster on the screen. She hesitated, then clicked decline. "You know what? I could probably let it go if it was all Libby's fault. But you're right. It wasn't. It was mine. I never should have let her get away with what she did. I should have fought harder."

Chapter Four

I T WAS THE Saltwater Winery's annual scavenger hunt for prizes. The Running of the Ducks was created by Libby and Jessa to attract new customers and add a little competition to the usually demure wine scene. She had pulled Brooke from behind the tasting counter to help hide little yellow rubber ducks around the property. They balanced several in trees, floated some in the fountain, taped one to the bottom of every Adirondack chair on the beach, placed several in the gift shop, in Amelia's flower garden, on every corner of the outdoor stage, and in all of the nooks and crannies they could find. It was like an Easter egg hunt for wine drinkers.

"You remember when we hunted for these at Camp Dogwood?" Jessa said. "I was as skinny as a bean pole, and your teeth were too big for your mouth."

"At least I was the duck-hunting champ. Remember?" Brooke pointed at herself victoriously. "Nate and I found two of them." Brooke still dreamed about those ducks sometimes, and each dream involved a little white one still hidden beneath the old creek bridge.

Jessa fiddled with a duck wearing a princess crown and smiled with nostalgia. "I should thank your parents again. If they hadn't paid my fees, I'd never have gone. Some of my best memories are from that camp."

"You know they only paid those because I refused to go without you." Brooke placed a yellow duck in a tall planter that spilled over with pothos and sunpatiens. Truth was, she'd needed Jessa at camp with her. It was always a trade-off. Jessa got all of the attention for her ballerina figure, long white-blond hair, full pink lips, small nose, and perfect skin. So Brooke had to put up with being the *uglier* friend in order to have the positivity, loyalty, inside jokes, and unwavering support of her best friend. "What kind of prize is the winery giving to the folks who find these ducks?"

"Wine, wine, and more wine."

"No pizza party? No movie night? No dance party?" At camp, there were three large teams and three ducks. When a team found a duck, they won the activity that corresponded with the number written on it in sharpie. Some teams won every prize, some teams got nothing. But all of them had a celebration at the end.

"Lame, right? I should tell Duke to step it up." Jessa headed toward the vineyard.

Brooke carried her bag of plastic ducks to the chicken coop, her mind back at Camp Dogwood. Several of the girls got their first kisses during the Running of the Ducks. It was the perfect time to slip off on a hunt with whichever boy was making your heart bubble up like a sugary Nehi soda, and then follow it up that night with what had unofficially become known as *date night*.

Jessa should've been the best at finding things, seeing as her mother knew stuff she wasn't supposed to, but Jessa couldn't find a plastic duck if she woke up to it on her pillow. It was funny how things worked out. Jessa had wanted to be on the duck-hunting team with Gates, which, at the time, didn't matter in the slightest to Brooke. Gates was the guy every girl wanted. Brooke wanted to be on Nathan Daugherty's team. She'd been intrigued by him since he first showed up the summer after sixth grade with a noticeable limp, wearing a ratty old corduroy blazer and a tie. He'd rumbled up in a dented red pickup and jumped out from the passenger seat dressed for church and holding a Walmart bag.

"Bye, man. Thanks for the ride," he said like he barely knew the bearded person at the wheel.

Brooke knew immediately that life wasn't going to be good for him at camp. That boy was about to get messed with in the way that snakes mess with mice. He would get eaten up and spat out. His limp was pronounced. And his clothes were horrible. If he was smart, he would run after that old truck and climb back in.

She felt the old mix of pubescent angst and hopefulness like she was back at camp as she set a yellow plastic duck in a chicken's nest. Carefully, she took all of the eggs she could find for the winery's gift shop. They sold them by the dozen in the refrigerated case, and they could probably use some more. What she really wanted to do was find a private spot and search for Nate online again. No matter how many years passed, he still felt like a big part of her life.

So many events from her childhood were fuzzy, and most were completely forgotten, but she could always pull up memories of Nate like they'd happened just a week ago. The first time she caught his eye and smiled at him, he smiled back. Then she proceeded to observe how she was right—the giggling and pointing began immediately. He was given the nickname Zippy, which was meant to point out his limp. Some boys coughed *loser*, and one knocked into him while walking by. Libby, wide-eyed, loudly questioned why he chose to wear church clothes to summer camp, and then laughed at him before he could answer. But Nate never looked upset, he just sat alone like it didn't bother him, ate his meals like he was happy for the good food, and sometimes, not often, but occasionally, he would catch her eye and smile at her.

Nate was only at camp for two years. That was just two years of him being sweet and tender toward Brooke. To everyone else he was as solid and emotionless as a wall. But when she was stung by a bee, it was Nate who scraped out the stinger and ran to The Doghouse to get the calamine lotion. When she got water up her nose, he was the one who jumped fully dressed into the lake to hold her up so she could breathe. And when she had her period all over her white shorts, he walked behind her like a shield, all the way to the girls' cabins, without ever saying a word. There was something strong about him. Something that made her feel like whoever he allowed into his life would always, without fail, be safe. That second year, aside from being considerably taller, he had muscles and a normal short haircut instead of the grown-out bangs that he used to habitually wipe from his eyes. Plus, he smiled at her, not just sometimes, but every time she looked his way.

Jessa's voice shocked Brooke from her reverie. "So, these aren't camp rules. Here, the person with the most ducks wins," she said. "There are 150 total, and we have fifty-three people signed up so far."

"I'm almost done," Brooke said, exiting the chicken coop that was made to look like an old swamp shack. "I got some eggs too."

"Perfect." Jessa opened her plastic bag and Brooke carefully placed the eggs inside one by one. "Save a few ducks for the bathrooms."

Brooke half expected to see the number three drawn in thick black marker on the duck she placed next to the sink inside the slope-roofed wooden bathroom made to look like an old outhouse. It was the number she'd found when her team won movie night. That was two days before her fifteenth birthday, and movie night might possibly mean a first kiss.

She was stepping out of the men's bathroom when a large wolflike dog nearly sideswiped her, running full out toward the sea. "Buttercup!" A woman in a sundress came hustling after it. "So sorry! She only listens to my boyfriend." She stopped when she saw the duck in Brooke's hand. "Do you work here?"

"Just started."

"You must be Brooke. I'm Allie." She stuck out her hand. "I'm one of the winemakers. Jessa said you were coming. Are you up front with the customers?"

Brooke shook Allie's small, surprisingly cold hand. "For now." She put the biggest, sweetest smile on her face that she could muster. "I just left a job in marketing."

"You're from here, right?"

"I'm not sure I should admit that." Brooke laughed nervously. Allie's energy was so happy, it felt overwhelming to try to match it.

"Sam and I just moved into a new house over on the south side of the island. We should have you over for dinner. Jessa too. You don't mind big dogs, do you?"

"I'd love that. And, no."

"As much as Goose Island has grown on me, one thing this place needs is a good sit-down restaurant."

"I'm happy to bring something. No need to cook."

"I'll get your number from Jessa. I better go find Cuppie, he's working with me today while Sam takes the MCAT."

Brooke wasn't surprised that a girl like Allie was dating a

future doctor. "Tell him your coworker wishes him good luck."

She kept glancing down the sloping lawn to the small beach where her dog looked like a wild wolf running in and out of the surf. "I better go. That rotten dog. She's going to be such a mess."

Brooke was both exhilarated at the prospect of having Allie as a friend and wary. Brooke might be a Warter, one of the wealthiest families on the island, but she felt like a pretender. She'd made no headway in her life. What had taken years to build was gone in the time it took to fill her car with her belongings and drive away. Her whole life felt like the empty bag she held in her hand.

Chapter Five

BROOKE'S LEFT HAND on the steering wheel ached like it was just waking up. She'd barely gotten any sleep the night before, so the rest of her felt equally as out of sorts. The memory of camp, of her first crush, split her heart like a sledge ax. It filled her with so much regret that the biscuits and tomato gravy she shared with Nana for breakfast threatened to come back up. She had to shake the nausea and, most of all, the memories, before she arrived at the winery. She needed to be as strong as possible when she saw Libby again.

Hers was the only car in the grassy, gravelly parking lot that morning. She prayed she wouldn't run into Duke Bradley while she was alone. The front door was locked, so instead of knocking, she decided to walk around back.

"Dagnabbit!" a male voice yelled. "Get out of my wife's garden!"

Brooke froze. She wasn't in the garden, so he couldn't be talking to her. It had to be Duke, and clearly, he was somewhere behind the white picket fence surrounding Amelia's Patch of Happiness.

"Shit," he cursed.

The gate flew open, and there he was, staring at Brooke.

"Where's my shovel?" The question was directed at her.

She shrugged. Was she supposed to know where he kept his gardening equipment?

Duke trudged past her and threw out, "Copperhead."

He was going to kill a venomous snake with a shovel? She looked all around at the ground and then up the trunks of the nearest old oaks. Could copperheads climb trees? She was stuck in the same spot when Duke returned.

"I knew I shouldn'ta left that rat snake. Thought he would control the dadgum mice, but the danged thing probably denned up with the copperhead this winter. Now they both have to go."

Brooke didn't know what to say. He'd just spewed more words than he'd ever said to her before. "I'm sorry."

He stopped briefly and looked at her like she was the stupidest person on earth.

She almost said she was sorry again. Did he really have to kill the rat snake? Trig had let one live under their house for years. They didn't hurt anything. Well, except small mice, rats, and the occasional squirrel. They were great pest control.

He closed the gate to Amelia's garden, and Brooke didn't know if she should stay nearby in case the copperhead bit him and he needed help, or run as far and as fast as possible. So she stood, rooted to the spot, horrified.

"Well, hey there, Anna Brooke."

She didn't want to look. *No. No. No. No.* Without a doubt, the bitchiest strawberry blonde in the known world was standing directly behind her. Slowly, she turned. "Hey, Libby."

"How ya doin', sweetheart? It's been a while. Don't you look pretty with your new hairdo."

Brooke knew darn well that when a peer called you *sweetheart*, it was a power play, and the compliment was meant to convey the opposite. They were only a few seconds into seeing each other again, and already Libby was trying to exert her dominance.

"Jessa said you were working here," Brooke said, taking in the upturned nose, freckles, and wrathful eyes that had haunted her dreams for years.

"Yes. I mean, I like the marketing director title, even though I had to turn down so many job offers at bigger and better companies," Libby began, starched and over-perfumed in her monogrammed button-down. "I just have to be near Charleston while I plan my wedding. You know?" Her top lip disappeared when she smiled, making her front teeth look extra long. "There are just so many details to attend to, and James insists on the absolute best vendors, so here I am!" She spread her arms out wide.

"Here you are!" Brooke said. A tiny smile was the most she could give. "Do you know how to unlock the front door?"

"You don't have a key?" Libby feigned concern. "Maybe they only give them to management. I suppose I can let you in."

Brooke walked behind her toward the building. Then she heard a loud *thunk* and turned from Libby to jog back toward the garden. "Mr. Bradley! Are you okay?" She'd almost forgotten he was in there facing off with a venomous snake.

"I'm fine" came the gruff voice as he opened the gate. In his right hand, he held a long, lifeless carcass. "Got him. Gonna leave the old rat snake, though." He walked past her toward the dumpster. "Woulda had to keep the customers away if this bad guy was still creeping around." He looked sad, his eyes red-rimmed and liquidy. "He didn't deserve it."

Brooke's emotions were all over the place. Dead snakes, bullies, locked doors, sad old men. She desperately wanted normalcy. What was she doing here? She stood, staring at the hand-painted sign: AMELIA'S PATCH OF HAPPINESS. There was no happiness for Brooke anymore. She missed her apartment in Savannah and her things in the places they were meant to be instead of festering in the back of her car. She even missed Gates. This was wrong. Being back on Goose Island, near Libby Trotter, at a job that didn't use her college degree. She was better than this. She should be anywhere but there.

"I opened the door for you!" Libby yelled down to her.

For you. As if Libby didn't have to unlock the door for

herself anyway. Brooke sighed. It was a relief to see the tall yellow food truck zooming down the dirt road, kicking up dust. Salty Dot's must be servicing the winery that day, and it was exactly what Brooke needed to feel like she might actually survive the next eight hours. If Libby was the copperhead in the garden, Dottie Boone was the shovel.

Salty Dot's food truck had a chalkboard sign out front that said, TODAY'S SPECIAL: SLOW-COOKED PORK PASTRAMI WITH MUSTARD SAUCE ON A PRETZEL BUN. PAIRS WELL WITH MUSCADINE WINE, and judging from the long line at lunchtime and the trash cans overflowing with paper plates and napkins, plenty of people were happy to try it.

Brooke's day was definitely improving. It was her lunch break. She had the hot pork sandwich in hand, and managed to find an empty Adirondack chair in the shade of a large angel oak. Libby's office was on the opposite side of the building from where Brooke worked pouring wines for the public, so she hadn't run into her again. Maybe, with some luck, she would be able to avoid her completely.

Allie must've been holed up in the lab with the scientists. Brooke hadn't even glimpsed her giant dog since their meeting yesterday. Jessa, on the other hand, was like a birdshot shell discharged and spread around the grounds everywhere at once, giving little pieces of herself to whatever needed her, solving problems and making sure everyone was doing their job. When there was a lull, Brooke watched her best friend smiling and laughing with the customers. The customers' eyes, especially the men's, always followed her as she walked away. Invariably, there were whispers too. People couldn't help themselves when it came to Jessa. She was too pretty not to say something about it.

And yet Libby had chosen to bully Brooke. Brooke was pretty too—she was average height, had straight white teeth and sky-blue eyes. She and Jessa actually looked somewhat similar. Each had the same eyes and the same high cheekbones, only Jessa's eyes were a little bigger, her smile a little wider, and her nose a little smaller. They'd looked more alike before Brooke went back to her natural brown hair color. Why had Libby chosen to leave the prettier girl alone? It made no sense.

The first bite was like Brooke's mouth had just been rescued from a deserted island—only she didn't know she'd been starving. It was life-alteringly delicious. She leaned back into the chair and closed her eyes, taking her time to chew, savoring the mix of flavors. *Hints of honey mixed with yellow mustard*, she thought, her brain learning to find nuances in flavors, thanks to her new job. *Salt with a touch of hickory smoke. Velvety and fleshy, yet delicate.* Dottie sure could cook. She'd been Brooke's savior a million times over the years. Since childhood, Brooke had preferred Dottie's tiny brick house to her own Georgian mansion on the water. Not only was the food better, the people were better too.

Brooke opened her eyes just long enough to take another bite. It was the white hair pulled back and tied with a black ribbon that made her keep them open. "Nana!" She carefully wrapped her sandwich in the wax paper it came in before she wrestled herself up from the chair. "What are you doing here?"

"My granddaughter works here. And I like wine." She was as firm and fierce as a tiny female dictator.

"Did you walk all this way?" It had to be three or four miles, and Nana, while wearing perfectly acceptable blue cotton pants and a matching button-down, had slippers on her feet.

"What choice did I have? My chauffeur abandoned me years ago."

"Nana, you never had a chauffeur."

"I most certainly did. His name was Bob. Bob Ross."

"Like the painter?"

"Exactly."

There was no use arguing. Brooke pulled her phone from her pocket.

"Don't go calling the po-po on me now," Nana said.

"I'm not calling the police, Nana. I'm calling Cornelia."

"Who is Cornelia?"

"Your daughter-in-law, Nana. My mother. I'm Brooke, your granddaughter."

"My Anna Brooke has blond hair."

"Not anymore. I'm just Brooke, and I'm a natural brunette." She knew that Nana was acting, but it was kind of fun to go along with it.

"Now, I need you to put that phone down and start pouring me some wine. I'm thirstier than a beached whale."

It looked like lunch was ending early. Brooke handed Nana the second half of her bottled water, which Nana chugged quickly. "Do you want some of my sandwich?"

The offer was waved away with one flick of a hot-pink-fingernailed, slightly blue, arthritic hand.

Once inside, Nana planted herself at the end of the long raw-edge wooden bar and stayed there until closing time. She had lively discussions with every tourist who sat nearby and even convinced several to buy T-shirts from the gift shop. By the time five o'clock rolled around, Nana was looking peaked. "I had a big day," she said as she hoisted herself from the barstool.

Brooke was bent over, putting the white wine bottles back in the small under-counter refrigerator, when she heard Nana's signature "Mmm." There was something she did not approve of. Brooke straightened.

It was Libby.

"The place is closed," Nana said tersely. "Turn yourself around and go right on back home."

Libby immediately broke into a Mafia-boss smile—all teeth and no heart. "I am the director of this establishment," Libby said, leaving out the word *marketing*.

Nana flashed a look at Brooke before setting her sights on Libby again. "Are you now?"

"Yes, I am. And I certainly don't want to keep you here a

minute longer. I'm sure you have very important things to do wherever you came from." The smile was back, only bigger. "Maybe you have more wine to drink at home?"

Nana nodded, a gleam in her eye. "Well, now. I can see plain as that grin on your face exactly what you're made of."

Libby smirked and walked toward the front door. "Are you catching a ride home, or do you plan to walk there in your slippers?"

"Young lady, the way you are speaking to your elder is beneath me, and I hope, although I have my reservations, that it is beneath you too."

"Where are my manners? I am so sorry." Each word was overly enthusiastic. "Do I need to spell things out for you? Write them down?" Libby held the door open for her.

"I will gladly stand here and give you the opportunity to speak to me nicely," Nana said with syrup in her voice, like she wasn't riled up at all.

Libby shifted her gaze. "Are you paying for the wine she drank, Anna Brooke? Because tastings are only one ounce per glass, and this woman has clearly had much more than that."

"You are not to speak to my granddaughter," Nana said, physically putting herself between the two girls. Brooke almost laughed at how wild and ferocious she looked. Then, just as quickly, Nana changed her tune. "Now, my dear lovely Brooke, let's go home. I have a happy surprise planned for you."

"A surprise?"

"A good one." She winked. "Your mother helped."

Libby allowed them to exit the building then locked the door behind them. As soon as Nana was stuffed into Brooke's cramped passenger seat, she asked, "Who in the tarnation was that?"

"A bully from my past and a coworker in my present."

"She's a snake."

Brooke thought of the poor dead copperhead. Turned out Nana was the shovel instead of Dottie.

"I knew her kind the minute I laid eyes on her," Nana said. "How long have you known that malicious she-devil?"

"Since summer camp."

"Oh, Lord. She's been in your life that long?"

"She had a hand in messing it up."

"Did she do something with Gates? Please tell me that man is not a cheater."

"I don't think he's a cheater, Nana. And no. She did something with, or really, she did something *to* someone else."

"And are you going to tell me what it is?"

Nana must've known by the look on Brooke's face that she was about to talk about a boy.

"What was his name? And I want all of it."

"Nathan." There was pride in Brooke's voice, and it shocked her. She could practically smell the lemon and citronella that the camp counselors sprayed to keep the mosquitoes away, and the warmth of his arm around her shoulders. He'd known she lived on Goose Island, so he'd known she had money. The island has a reputation for generations of inhabitants who owned acres of property and large old homes. But the chasm of wealth between them didn't seem to bother him. "Being back here with Jessa and Libby has stirred up all of these old memories. It's like I've traveled back in time."

"And have you kept in touch with this boy?"

"No." The word was filled with regret. "But I asked him if he would remember me when the summer was over, and he said he would remember me as long as he lived." Brooke felt herself blush. "I believed him, Nana." It felt weird to gush on and on about something that happened so long ago, but at the same time, she needed to say it out loud. "He said it was because I smiled at him. And I did smile at him. He got out of a broken-down truck, and I liked him straightaway."

"Sometimes we just have a sense of folks."

"Yeah. But I also felt so, so sorry for him." Brooke stopped talking as more memories filled her head. It was one of the last times she'd ever seen him and he'd said something that made her wonder. He said his family used to own Camp Dogwood. She was pretty sure he was lying—trying to make it seem like he belonged. She wouldn't blame him for that. He didn't fit in with those rich camp kids at all. Heck, she might have done the same thing if she'd been in his shoes.

Nana put a hand on Brooke's shoulder. "Anna Brooke?

I'm startin' to think you're on drugs."

"Sorry, Nana. I zoned out for a second. All those years ago, Nate said something that I just now remembered."

"Was it important, dear? Sometimes, we tuck away the important things because we don't want to, or can't, deal with them."

"No, it's probably nothing. I think he was just wishful thinking. He said his family used to own Camp Dogwood or something like that."

"Oh, Lord." Nana's skin paled lighter than her pearl earrings. "Was his last name Daugherty?"

Brooke nearly sucked all of the air out of the car with her gasp. "You know him?"

"Nathan Quade Daugherty. His middle name was his mother's maiden name." She stopped speaking abruptly. "I don't want to talk about it."

Chapter Six

"DIN-NER!" CORNELIA'S VOICE broke into Brooke's impassioned internet search like a tornado siren.

"Be right there!" She'd known since childhood that if she didn't answer, she'd be doing extra chores or writing a three-page essay on why daughters must obey their parents.

Even with his middle name, Nathan Quade Daugherty could not be found anywhere on the internet. Was he still alive? She was desperate to know.

She slinked down the wooden stairs carefully, hoping that Cornelia wouldn't notice she was wearing only socks and not her house shoes. When she turned the corner to the dining room, she froze. Cornelia looked furious, Trig looked amused, and Nana sat in her spot at the table dressed in a tall yellow banana costume. Her face, through the hole in the front, looked pleased.

Brooke opted to say nothing, and sat quietly across from her.

"Is nobody going to ask me why I'm wearing a banana costume?" Nana pretended to be exasperated.

Cornelia bit her lips together, her eyes firmly on her

plate.

"Guess we're getting used to you acting crazy all the time, Mama," Trig said. "Long as you don't hurt anybody, it's fine by us if you want to dress like that."

"You people," Nana spat, "are no fun." She scooted out her chair and stood with her hands on her yellow hips. "Ba."

No one said anything.

"Ba!" she said louder, extending both arms out straight to the side.

Cornelia dipped her head and scooped creamed corn into her mouth like it was keeping her from saying something curse-filled and loud.

"What is my name?" Nana asked.

"Grace Sharon Beauregard Warter," Trig said.

Nana made a face at him and turned to Brooke. "Anna Brooke. What is my name?"

"Nana."

"Yes. Ba—"

"Ba-Nana?"

"Finally. Someone with half a brain." Nana sat back down.

"You're not funny," Cornelia said. "Not at all."

"I am not trying to be funny," Nana said. "I am trying to be interesting."

"Is this the happy surprise?" Brooke asked. Her family should be on a reality show. Nana alone could bring in the ratings.

"No. Your surprise informed your mother that he has already eaten dinner and will be here for dessert," Nana said.

Cornelia stared daggers at Nana.

Nana smirked back. "She doesn't know who it is yet, Cornelia."

"My surprise is a man?" Brooke put down her fork with a clank. "Cornelia. You did not."

Her mother shrugged, and answered in a sing-songy voice, "Mother knows best."

"Mother doesn't have the first clue," Brooke said, taking her cloth napkin from her lap and throwing it on the table. "Perfect. Just perfect. Gates is coming over and my grandmother is dressed like a banana."

Gates was the kind of guy who people noticed when he walked into a room. Not just because he looked like an action movie star but because he carried himself like he didn't have the time for or interest in any other living creature. Nothing and no one could touch him. No person could outshine him. He was the Ken doll of human beings.

Brooke wasn't ready to see him. It's not that he'd been mean to her or had broken her heart. No, it was simply that she didn't like who she was when she was with him. Through no fault of his own, Gates made her feel small. When he was around, she was invisible. She was the lesser girlfriend to the handsome guy who could have anything he wanted.

By the time the doorbell rang, Brooke's makeup was refreshed, her outfit changed, and she was more anxious than a freshman on the first day of school. It was silly. She'd been living with the guy since they both graduated from college. She knew that he reverted to a six-year-old when he had the flu and that he swelled up like Violet Beauregarde if he touched anything with wool. But she'd always been nervous around him—like he was the president and she was the intern. He was the lead in the play and she was monkey number five. He won the lottery and she only got one number right.

It was that feeling that created a gap between them. Over time, she began to realize that she couldn't tolerate living her life feeling less than someone. And, Gates seemed to have come to the same conclusion. So why was he suddenly showing up on Goose Island?

"Hello, Mrs. Warter, so nice to see you again." His deep voice gave Brooke the shivers. She couldn't tell her mother's exact words, but she recognized the high-pitched gushing trill. Brooke took each stair slowly, hoping that, given enough time, her heart might calm to a more rational beat.

There he was. Two heads taller than Cornelia and somehow more imposing than Trig. Cornelia looked quite proud of herself.

"Hey, Gates," Brooke said as she stepped onto the landing.

"Hey." He looked down at her like he had forgotten what she looked like.

She remembered her new hairdo. "I cut it," she said. "And dyed it back to natural."

"Looks good."

She couldn't tell if he meant it or not.

Cornelia spoke first. "Nana and I invited Gates here for a little family bonding."

Family bonding with an ex-boyfriend? That was...well, that was just like Cornelia. When she set her mind to something, she was like a hunting dog on a scent—unwilling to give up until she got the kill. And where was the other perpetrator of this crime? Brooke looked around for a flash of yellow, hoping Nana had gone to her cottage to change. It was one thing to feel subordinate to someone and quite another to be seen as flat-out crazy. Or, at least, related to crazy.

"Can we talk?" Gates asked.

"Sure. Out back?" Brooke flashed her mother a stay-away look before leading Gates to the screened-in porch at the back of the house. From there, they could see the sun setting on the marsh, as well as Nana's cute little white cottage off to the left. They sat together on the wicker couch before realizing that Cornelia was right behind them.

"Where are your manners, Anna Brooke?" Cornelia stood like a guard at the door until her daughter complied.

"Would you like something to drink?" Brooke asked Gates. "We have snacks, too, if you're hungry."

"And we have some lovely dessert when you're ready,"

Cornelia said.

"No thank you," Gates said.

"Okay, Cornelia," Brooke said. "You can go now."

Her mother stuck her head fully into the room. "We're so glad you're here, Gates." She gave him a bright smile before finally leaving them alone.

Brooke's phone dinged, and she glanced at the text while she still had a chance. It was Jessa. "*Be here at seven. I downloaded a good one.*" Shoot. She was supposed to go to Dottie's and hang with Jessa in half an hour. She started texting back at the same time Gates said, "I miss you."

Immediately, she stopped. It wouldn't be smart to get back together. He had to know that. "Did Cornelia and Nana bribe you with something? How did they get you here?"

"You think I can be bribed?"

His brow furrowed and she wanted to reach up and smooth the lines while telling him how handsome he was like she used to when he'd get mad. "No. No, I didn't mean that. I just know that they had something to do with this."

"Your mother called me at work to tell me that you hadn't unpacked your car. She said you refused to move into the house because you wanted to come back to Savannah. And then your grandmother took the phone and said that you've been drinking every night and that you're getting really skinny."

"I'm not drinking every night!" And what if she had

been? She'd been home less than a week. Of course, she neglected to count the week in between Savannah and Goose Island. But she wasn't going to bring that period of time into the conversation. That was hers. Just hers.

"Do you want to come back?" he asked.

"I miss you too. I really do. But I think we've both known for a long time that we're just not right for each other. Your birthday proved it."

"You're going to bring that up again?" He shifted in his seat, getting agitated. When she'd first left, it was because he'd been a no-show. She couldn't forgive him for making her look like a fool to his friends who were waiting with her to jump out and scream *surprise*. But during her week alone, she'd realized that their problems were bigger than that. His reluctance to come home was merely a symptom.

"I'm only bringing it up to put it to rest." She thought about reaching over and to take his hand, but again, chose not to. "I always felt so lucky that you chose me. I still don't know why you did. But if I'm honest with myself, I want the person who loves me to feel like they're lucky too. I just don't get that with you. I feel like you're settling. And for that reason I'm not really lucky at all."

"You're talking about luck? How am I supposed to fix that?"

Brooke's phone dinged and she ignored it. "It's my problem. You're not supposed to fix it." She'd always felt like the odd-shaped puzzle piece that didn't fit and no one could fix that but her. "Plus, Dottie said a long time ago that you and I weren't meant to be together."

"Good God, Brooke. Would you stop bringing up that woman? She does not have some sort of supernatural sixth sense. Just ask Jessa. All those years at camp when her mom had her totally freaked out. 'My mama said someone was gonna drown, so I've got to sit here and watch the swimmin' hole every day,'" he mimicked. "'My mama said someone with purple hair might be terribly sad, so now I'm going to stick like glue to that weird girl the whole summer.'"

"And Lance Whiting did start to drown!" Brooke said. "You remember? Jessa sounded the alarm and he was saved."

"He was fine. Jessa's mom just makes stuff up."

"And Suzanna too. She was sad. But we really liked her. She was nice."

"Jessa's mother is a lunatic."

"She said I took something home from camp I wasn't supposed to. Did you know that? She was talking about you, Gates."

"Pretty sure she was talking about The Dog's recipe for mac-n-cheese."

Brooke made a face at him. "I brought two things home from camp—a scar on my ankle from poison oak, and *you*."

Every few seconds there was a zap when a mosquito flew into the blue light of Trig's electronic bug killer outside of the porch screen, and with each flaming death, Gates appeared to grow more annoyed. "What are you trying to say? That all of our time together was wasted?"

"Why did you choose me, Gates?"

"I really don't want to have this conversation."

"You have never been able to give me a good answer."

"No, you just refuse to hear me." He took a deep breath. "I chose you because I liked you. I thought you were different."

"When did you first notice me?"

He rolled his eyes. "At camp. In, like, fourth grade."

"But you never talked to me. I never even saw you look my way. Then all of a sudden, you decide I am the one for you."

"What did you want, Brooke? You wanted my little ten-year-old self to fall madly in love with you? To chase after you and beg you to be mine? I didn't even have armpit hair. It happened when it happened."

Now it was Brooke's turn to roll her eyes, but instead, she took a deep breath and kept her composure. "It was just strange, is all. Never mind. I don't know how to explain it, it's just a feeling."

He leaned back and put his feet on her mother's glass table. "Well, if you want to come home with me, you can."

Movement caught her eye. *Oh, no.* It was very definitely yellow. She leaned in to speak, hoping Gates wouldn't notice Nana moving outside her cottage. "Do you realize what you're saying? If I go back to Savannah with you, we will continue our relationship. Then what? Get married? Do you want to spend the rest of your life with me?"

"I don't want to *not* have you in my life."

Double negatives always bugged her. She glanced toward the yellow figure skipping around an oak tree, and prayed Gates wouldn't look in her direction. "And since it's uncomfortable for you to *not* have me, you're willing to potentially spend your life with the wrong person?"

"Why are you so set on the fact that we're not right for each other?"

"Because we don't fit. I just know it."

"You just know it," he mimicked. "You sound like Jessa's mom."

"Oh, shoot," she said, checking the time on her phone. "I'm supposed to go to her house tonight."

He put his feet down like he needed the ground for stability. "Fine. I'll go to bed."

"Why don't you come with me? I'm sure Jess would be happy to see you." She was already walking toward the door, hoping he wouldn't look back at her crazy grandmother.

His face flushed. "I'm tired from the drive. And your mother has the guest room ready for me."

"I don't feel like it's right to leave you here." She took him by the arm and pulled him toward the house. "I'll cancel with Jess."

"No. Go. Really. I just want to go to bed."

She couldn't read him. "Are you sure?"

"We'll talk more tomorrow." He walked inside without a

hug or a goodbye.

"I have work tomorrow. Meet me at the winery?"

"You have a job here?" He stiffened. They hadn't been talking, so she'd never thought to tell him. He let the screen door slam in her face.

Chapter Seven

BROOKE NEVER ARRIVED at Jessa's house. She made it as far as the driver's seat before she was waylaid by her grandmother, still dressed as a banana. "Is that man gone?" Nana asked too loudly.

"You mean Gates, Nana? The one you invited here?"

Nana shooed the words from Brooke's mouth like they were flies. "I don't want to talk about him. Tell me more about that Daugherty boy."

Brooke climbed out of the car and opened the door to the passenger seat, pulling a pile of clothes and shoes from it and placing them on the ground. "Get in." Nana's long yellow costume had to be stuffed around her legs in order to close the door. "How did you know his middle name?" Brooke asked.

"You first."

"Age before beauty, Nana."

"Well, I am a fresh, unrotten banana, so you have to go first. And I want to know everything. I want *details*. Did you kiss him?" Nana reached her small hand from a hole in the polyfoam fabric and found Brooke's.

"Nana! That's private."

"If there is any person in the world who has heard everything, it is a grandmother. You cannot shock me. You kissed him, didn't you?"

"Yes, but…"

"I knew it! Oh, goodie, goodie gumdrops. Tell me all about it."

"Nana!"

"I promise I will not tell Cornelia."

"If I tell you, will you tell me how you knew his middle name?"

"Yes," Nana said. "But you'd better make it good." Nana leaned back and closed her eyes.

Brooke stared into the darkness as she gathered her thoughts. "We were all on the dock by the swimming hole where they projected *The Martian* onto an old sheet. The two of us had earned that movie for our team because we found one of the hidden ducks."

"Stop right there," Nana said. "You can do better than that. I want to know the details. I want to feel like I was there."

Brooke had no trouble remembering. "The cicadas were just as loud as they are now. The higher the moon rose, the louder they sang. It was sticky, because it was summertime, but I didn't care one bit. I was so nervous, I was afraid to speak. It was like my brain had closed a door and locked my tongue inside with it. Nate didn't say anything either." Just talking about those nerves caused her stomach to burn. "But then he put his arm around me and I let him."

"Tell me you were still in your bathing suit. That's the best part about summertime, waking up in your swimsuit with salty hair and a sunburn." Nana murmured like she, too, was remembering a story about a young version of herself.

"No, that would be Jessa, running around in her purple one-piece, playing games with the teams that didn't win the movie." Nana's hand was cold in hers and Brooke was surprised that she could hardly wait to tell her, in detail, what it was like to have the side of her body cuddled up next to a boy. "It took almost the whole movie for me to get brave enough, but I finally put my head on his shoulder."

Nana's eyes popped open. "And then he kissed you? Tell me all of it."

"He turned his head so that we were cheek to cheek."

She leaned forward. "And you didn't move, right? Let me see." Tilting her head to the left, she put it on Brooke's shoulder. "Now, what'd he do?"

"He moved his head down like this." Brooke demonstrated quickly, her cheek briefly on her grandmother's.

"What a sly little devil he was. Got those lips of his mighty close."

"Yes, ma'am." Brooke giggled awkwardly. "This feels weird, Nana."

Nana pressed down her costume so she could sit up

straight. "Hush with that and tell me more."

"He said, 'I think you're pretty.'" Brooke hesitated. "And, you know what, Nan? That might have been the first time in my whole life that I actually did feel pretty."

Nana patted Brooke's hand in a way that meant *keep going.*

"Well, we both brought our noses together and stopped when there was just an inch between us. I remember it so clearly: his breath was shallow, coming in small puffs. I kept thinking he was kissing me already, that his lips were pressed to mine, but it hadn't happened yet."

Nana's breath was much like Nate's had been. She was barely breathing. "And—"

"When I lifted my eyes, he was looking right at me. I'm pretty sure my heart stopped. I just knew that my life was never going to be the same again."

"This is just like Cary Grant and Deborah Kerr in *An Affair to Remember.* The kiss was off-screen, but I could see it just the same."

Brooke softly giggled. "His lips were soft and warm and a little shaky."

Nana squealed and squeezed Brooke's hand. "What'd you do?"

"I just held still. I didn't know if I was supposed to pucker or not. He pulled away, then kissed me again. That time, I kissed him back."

Nana let go and placed her hands flat on her peel, somewhere near her heart. "Oh, my word. That was better than a romance novel."

"Yeah, and then Gates ruined it all when he yelled, 'Spartans! Prepare for battle!' and came running down the hill, holding a stick like it was a sword. Half of my team jumped into the water, and the others ran toward the woods."

"And what did you and that darling Daugherty boy do?"

"We stayed there. He blocked me with his body and shielded me with his arms. Gates and his team ran around us to the movie screen—which they pulled down and carried up the hill like a trophy. But no one bothered us."

"I declare. That boy sounds just like Caleb."

"Who's Caleb?"

"Forget I said anything. Did he kiss you again?"

"No, Jessa twisted her ankle, and Gates commanded me to take care of her. Which was strange, because back in those camp days, he never spoke to me. Anyway, it was time for lights-out pretty soon after that."

"You certainly are a lucky girl, aren't you, Anna Brooke?" Nana found Brooke's hand again and patted it lightly.

"I'm not so lucky anymore."

"Oh, yes you are. Isn't it curious, though? I have no desire to hear about your kisses with Gates."

"You know what, Nana? I don't feel much like talking about them either."

After almost a full half hour of Nana refusing to tell Brooke who Caleb was or how she knew Nathan's middle name despite the fact that she'd promised, Brooke finally let her out of the car. Then she canceled on Jessa. As always, Jessa didn't seem to mind at all. When Brooke finally slept, she had the most vivid dream. She was kissing Nate underneath the little arched bridge that crossed the dry creek. She was happy—the kind of happy that comes from security, hope, and a bright future. Above her head was a little duck, hidden in a corner of the trestle. It didn't have a number, and it wasn't yellow. It was dirty and white and there was something strange about it. But she'd found it, and it was important.

Nana wasn't at breakfast the next morning. She'd probably stayed up late into the night dancing to big band music and twirling around her cottage. Gates wasn't there either, which was fine with Brooke. She kissed Trig and Cornelia, grabbed a muffin, and hopped into her car. Gates's blacked-out BMW sat in the driveway next to her little white Audi. It felt like a metaphor—he was a sleek designer car. She, too, was a designer car, only she'd had a fender bender and currently housed a used set of towels, twelve unread books, a stack of sweaters, an entire floral bed set, and a toaster that spilled old bread crumbs inside the trunk.

There was no use driving off the island to find a coffee shop, so she went to Fred's gas station and browsed the small space. He had everything from white diatomaceous clay in little baggies from a local woman who sold it as a parasite cleanse, to original artwork, candy bars, fresh fruit, and fine wine. She hugged Fred and bought a small latte and a freshly baked honey bun.

When she arrived at the Saltwater Winery, Jessa had just let out the chickens.

"Hey, Jess."

Jessa jumped and turned as elegantly as an ice skater. "You scared me! I didn't know you were comin' in early." The chickens actively clucked and scratched all around her.

"Do you remember that year in camp when my team won the movie night?"

"I don't know. That was a long time ago." She picked up a white Silkie chicken and petted its soft, feathery head.

"The night you twisted your ankle. It was my first kiss, and we stayed up all night talking."

"Nate Daugherty," Jessa said simply. "Right. What do you think ever happened to him?" Brooke ignored the whistling coming down the road until it was so close that it registered as familiar. "Nana?"

"Coming!" Nana yelled like a schoolgirl, waltzing up the drive by the winery entrance sign. She wore a long black sequined dress and white tennis shoes. She'd drawn on her eyebrows, but her white hair stood straight up like she was trying to be a 1980s punk rocker.

Brooke ran to meet her. "Nan, did you walk the whole way again?"

"The question is, why didn't you walk?" Nana asked, increasing her pace. "Four miles is nothing. I was an athlete, you know. A synchronized swimmer. Still have my swimming cap somewhere if your mother didn't throw it away."

"Why are you here? Don't you have something to do today?"

Nana smirked. "I work here."

"No, Nan. No, you don't."

"I have decided that I do." She kept on walking, right past Brooke.

This was going to be a disaster. Duke Bradley was not going to react well to Brooke's eighty-year-old grandmother taking over the joint.

"Nan, please." Brooke ran after her. "Don't do this to me."

"Anna Brooke, calm your squirrels." She stopped with her hands on her hips, sparkling in her stubbornness. "You will introduce me to our boss, you hear me? You will do it now."

That was it. Brooke's life was officially a glittering disaster.

Chapter Eight

B ROOKE NEVER DID get to introduce Nana to Duke. It was the strangest thing. It was like he was hiding from them. They'd gone straight to Amelia's garden to find him. Brooke knew he'd been there from the freshly turned dirt and the hose still flowing. She'd even called his name but didn't get an answer.

Nana walked around the pink crepe myrtles, through the wide-open rose garden and the shaded wall of hydrangeas to the area where the tomato plants climbed metal towers, all the while calling, "Yoo-hoo, Mr. Braaaaaadley." Brooke followed her to make sure she didn't step on a snake. Soon enough, Salty Dot's food truck rumbled up the road, and Brooke dragged Nana out of the garden in time to see Jessa set up the chalkboard sign by the serving window. The workday was beginning, Duke or not.

Grace "Nana" Sharon Beauregard Warter had indeed gone to work. She ushered guests into the Saltwater Winery in her sequined gown and stuck-up hair, taking it upon herself to occasionally sing "Fly Me to the Moon" or the more popular "Poker Face" from a corner in the gift shop.

To make things worse, Gates arrived just before Brooke's one o'clock lunch break. She was secretly hoping he had already left without saying goodbye. The whole scenario made her question how much she really wanted the winery job. Maybe she should work in a nuclear power plant or someplace where people couldn't just waltz on in.

It was hard to give customers her attention and pretend to be enthusiastic about floral notes and malolactic fermentation while Gates hovered outside of the building. Every now and then he would wander by and look in to see if she was still working before going back to a picnic table and sitting hunched over, staring at his phone.

At least Brooke could be grateful that it was one of Libby's work-from-home days. Jessa flitted around, making sure all the guests were happy and reminding them that the food truck special that day was a meatball sandwich, which paired well with a red blend. She looked especially good today, her light yellow sundress adding a sweet little glow to her already-stunning beauty. It was never hard for Jessa to get a person's attention.

As soon as the customers left, Brooke made her way outside, expecting Gates to jump up and greet her. But he was leaned over, completely engrossed in conversation with Jessa. It occurred to Brooke in that moment that although she'd lived her entire adult life with both Gates and Jessa, she'd rarely seen them in conversation. At least not one that serious. What could they possibly be talking about, aside from her?

"Hey," Brooke said, sitting next to Jessa. They stopped talking as soon as they saw her. "Y'all talking about me?"

Jessa flushed, but Gates came right out with it. "I was asking Jessa for her opinion."

Brooke and Jessa had talked about Gates so many times over the years, she knew exactly what Jessa would say. She smiled at her friend. "Pretty sure Jess just wants me to be happy."

Gates seemed pleased with her answer. Almost too pleased. Jessa piped up quickly, "I told him that he had everything a guy needs to make a girl happy. And if that girl isn't you, there are plenty of others who would be thrilled to date him." Gates watched Jessa carefully as she spoke. "The same goes for you, Brookie. Let's be real—both of you are catches. The best of the best."

"One meatball special for Brooke," Dottie announced, walking up with an overflowing paper plate. "Your nana wanted to take some orders, so I thought I'd deliver it myself." She placed the food in front of her. Judging from the way Dottie's eyes washed over Gates like a scrub brush, Brooke knew the visit wasn't social.

"You remember Gates?" Brooke asked by way of introduction.

"You bet I do." It was like Dottie's eyes were X-ray-enabled, looking past his skin and assessing his innards. "How long do you plan to stay here on Goose Island?" she asked him.

"Well, that depends." He shot a look at Brooke.

Brooke was a little shocked at herself when she realized she was vigorously shaking her head. She almost said *sorry*, then didn't. She'd made her choice and was going to stick with it. Her fresh start, her new sweet personality, it was all going to help her grow and flourish. She didn't need to be Gates Lancaster's chosen one. She needed to choose herself.

She watched Gates, his dark hair newly cut, the muscle in his jaw twitching as he ground his teeth. Dottie peppered him with questions, which Brooke actively tuned out as she stared. Was there such a thing as The One? Or did people simply find a partner—someone they could work with and tolerate? How was a person supposed to know? Gates was a decent guy. They would have beautiful kids. He would be a good dad. She might be making the biggest mistake of her life by cutting him loose—one that could very well mean spending the rest of it alone.

Gates stayed at the winery until the last guest left. He watched Brooke give wine tastings all afternoon while Jessa revolved around the place like a satellite, and Nana performed whatever function crossed her mind for whatever audience would pay her some attention. Jessa gave him a sweet goodbye hug before locking the door and heading to her mother's food truck.

Nana was nowhere to be found.

Brooke called her cell phone, but she didn't answer.

Then she called her mother, inadvertently flipping on Cornelia's panic switch when the woman realized her mother-in-law was not at home and might actually have gone missing. "You stay there and keep looking," Cornelia said, immediately defaulting to what she did best—giving orders. "I will take the Cadillac and see if she's out walking." She hesitated before she added, "Check down by the water."

The last instruction gave Brooke chills.

Gates followed her as she led the way down to the pluff-muddy shore where oysters sat like razors among the cordgrass.

"Nana!" she called. There was no answer.

"Nana!" Brooke heard the fear in her own voice as it carried across the water. Just recently, an elderly woman in Beaufort had been taken in a death roll by an alligator. Nana could be anywhere, doing anything. Ever since Papa died, no one knew what Nana might say or do. She'd become a wild card, a lunatic, and a flight risk.

"Grace!" Gates kept yelling her name from behind Brooke. "I hope she's just walking home."

Brooke nodded. She'd been silently praying the same thing. "Nana!"

They heard tires crunch their way into the parking lot, and jogged up to Cornelia's car. "Did you find her?" Brooke asked, squinting to see if someone was in the passenger seat as her mother rolled down the window. Even in the midst of a crisis, Cornelia had remembered to touch up her lipstick.

The answer was obvious. "No."

"Crap."

"We still have a couple of hours before it gets dark," Gates said. "We should call the sheriff."

"First, I had better call Trigger," Cornelia said. "I was hoping to avoid his involvement, but I can see now that we have got to alert him to the situation."

"Yes, ma'am," Gates agreed.

Brooke racked her brain about where Nana might be as Cornelia explained the situation to Trig. That morning, when Nana showed up, Duke had mysteriously gone missing. Nana had walked the property, calling for him. She'd been determined to inform the man that she was now one of his employees—like it or not.

As soon as she hung up, Brooke asked, "Duke Bradley's house—it's on the property, right?"

"Well, yes, it is on this acreage," Cornelia said. "Of course, I have never been there because, as you know, not one person on the island has ever been invited over. When the Bradleys moved out our way and planted all of the vines, they were not considered friendly."

Everyone on the island had been to each other's homes at some point, but outsiders were not embraced in the same way. Outsiders, meaning they weren't second or third or fifteenth generation natives of Goose Island. The islanders were mad about the winery and probably would be for at least fifty years.

"How do we get there?" Gates asked.

"Well, I am quite sure we take the dirt road off Blue Heron Drive. The one that swings around behind the vines and ends at the Atlantic?" Cornelia must've calmed a bit thanks to the Duke theory, because she went back to phrasing things as questions rather than demands. "My husband once drove by the house and said it is in a different style than most of the homes here on the island. I believe he said it was a Craftsman? Like the tool box? Quite the monstrosity if you ask me."

"I guess we should check there," Brooke said, reluctant to show up without notice to her boss's house.

"Join me in the car," Cornelia said. "I'll drive us."

Just as Gates stepped one foot in, Cornelia received a phone call. It was Trig telling them that Nana had made it home safely. She refused to say one word about where she'd been, but appeared to be happier than a teenager on prom night.

"Good Lord," Cornelia said. "I swear that woman has it out for me. Probably hid in the bushes awaiting my departure so that she could get her son all to herself." Her painted lips thinned. "I declare. She will be the death of me." She took a deep, centering breath. "Now, y'all come on back to the house, and I'll fix us all some supper."

They said their goodbyes and promised to get home soon. Brooke led Gates back down to a table by the water. There was still more to talk about. No relationship was ever over until it had been hashed out six ways to Sunday. Now that she wasn't searching for her grandmother's drowned, half-eaten body, she could concentrate. She sat, but Gates paced like a caged cat.

"What are you doing back on this island, Brooke? You're serving wine?"

"I had to do something."

"So, you did it, huh? You quit your job at the PR agency." He kicked at a small rock, sending it skipping along the ground. "You really weren't planning to come back to Savannah, were you? You left permanently because of one little incident."

"I thought you were fine with this," she said. "You even deleted me off your Instagram."

"I was mad!"

"Wait, stop. It's not about that." She reached for him, and he stopped pacing. "Sit, please."

He did as he was told. She held his hands in hers; all four of their palms were sweaty.

"Do you like who you are when you're with me?" she asked.

"Of course I do. I'm the same person I always am."

"Do you see that as a problem at all? Don't you want someone who makes you better?"

"You do make me better."

"How? By being your plus-one at your work parties? By keeping our house clean and doing the shopping and cooking you dinner?"

"Yes! You make my life better."

"But, Gates, I feel like I have to earn you every day. Like I'm not enough as just me. And let's not forget, I planned a whole party and you did not come home." She didn't mean to raise her voice, but she was definitely getting louder. "And you're saying I make your life better? It doesn't make sense."

"You've been watching too many videos. They're making you selfish." He dropped her hand and stood again. "What about me, huh? We've spent seven years together. I have invested in you." He met her volume and increased it. "I don't like living alone."

"I'm not a bank, Gates. And we shouldn't spend seven more if we're not happy." She tried to calm the conversation, but she couldn't help asking, "Honestly, why did you choose me in the first place?"

"Stop asking me that question. I am so tired of it! People don't have to have a reason. Sometimes things just happen." He stomped up the hill toward the winery building like a child. She followed slowly several yards behind him.

She was nearly to the top when she noticed another car in the parking lot. Gates was standing next to it, smiling and chatting with the driver like he hadn't just had a fight with his ex-girlfriend. She knew immediately who it was: Libby. There was no way she was going to walk over there and join them, so she took a hard right, quietly opened the gate to Amelia's Patch of Happiness, and walked inside. What was stupid Libby Trotter doing here after hours? The place was closed, dammit.

There was a bench underneath an arch covered with jasmine vines, so Brooke checked for snakes, then sat down. The sweet smell helped to calm her. She didn't have to convince Gates. It was enough that she alone knew what needed to be done. Even though it would be easier to stay with him, the fact was, she wasn't satisfied. He wasn't growing, he barely ever smiled. They were both stuck. Just because it was easy and familiar wasn't reason enough to stay. They didn't have kids, they didn't have a mortgage—the only people they'd be letting down was themselves.

She remembered Trig once saying that you had to sell a car before it broke down on the highway. Well, that's what she needed to do with Gates. She had to get out of their deal before they completely broke down in the middle of nowhere. Already, they had too many miles, bald tires, and were leaking radiator fluid.

She'd been sitting there for at least twenty minutes by the time Gates called her name. She wasn't sure she wanted to respond. But the sun was getting lower in the sky, and she couldn't stay in the garden forever, so she answered him and got up to open the gate.

"Why didn't you come say hi to Libby?" he asked as soon as he saw her. He was right back to his earlier mood: highly annoyed with her.

She walked past him toward her car, which was parked

near his. "You coming? Cornelia's probably holding supper for us."

"Libby knew you were hiding from her."

Brooke kept walking. She really didn't care what Libby knew.

"I will never understand you," he said, catching up to her.

"Exactly," Brooke replied.

Chapter Nine

BROOKE WAS GRATEFUL for the weekend. She had survived her first week of work and wasn't scheduled again until Monday. Gates had gone back to Savannah, and Nana offered for Brooke to keep her things in the cottage's tiny office so that her car would no longer be *such an embarrassment.*

The weekend crew was taking over the winery, so Brooke had plans with Jessa to visit the little house she'd bought. That would get both of them out of their mothers' hair for a while.

According to Jessa, it was going to take more years and more money than it was worth to fix up the tiny Lowcountry cottage, but something about it resonated with her. She simply had to buy it.

Built back in the early 1900s, the house needed work on everything. Even Brooke, who knew the island well, was glad that Jessa had picked her up because weeds had grown up over the street sign, making it hard to find. The two-acre plot was like a jungle, but Jessa had cleared enough of it back to appreciate what a cute little bungalow it was. White with black trim and a wrap-around porch—it suited Jessa perfectly. The roof appeared brand-new, but it was clear that the old brick and tabby walls once had Virginia creeper vines holding on so intently with their tendrils and adhesive pads that even though they'd been removed, their remnants still stuck to the house. Somehow, the whole effect was sweet and charming, just like Jessa. Even the black front door had a happy little wreath with large fake white flowers poking out of a circle of magnolia leaves.

"Jess! This is yours? It's gorgeous!"

"It's not much," Jessa said. Every good Southern girl was taught to turn down compliments, so it was gratifying when she added, "But I really like it. It has a history."

Leave it to Jessa to have accomplished more than she let on. The plumbing and roof had all been redone. Most of the inside had been taken down to the studs, but the electrical was to be done next, and it was clear that her home was well on its way to completion. She even had an old couch in the screened-in sleeping porch with a view of the marsh.

Jessa and Brooke lugged in the new outdoor rug and a coffee table from Fred's borrowed pickup truck.

Once the items were placed, they plopped onto the couch, giggling. It was another life transition they were doing together—Jessa creating a new home and Brooke moving back to her old one. There was nothing like spending time with a friend who knew every major event in her life, most of her faults, had witnessed countless mistakes, and loved her anyway.

They were ready to go before lunch. "Is your mama home today?" Brooke had been hoping that Dottie was at home so that she could swing by with Jessa for lunch like she used to as a kid.

"No, she took Tulip and the truck out to Summerville for some kind of festival. Can I treat you to lunch?" Jessa asked. "Maybe we can go into Charleston."

Usually, Brooke didn't like going into Charleston on hot summer days. There wasn't the shade of all of the trees like on the island, and she would swear the concrete both collected the heat and reflected it right back up onto her. But she was so happy to be spending time with her best friend outside of work that she agreed.

Jessa drove Brooke to the Warters' house and waited in the car for her as she ran upstairs to quickly gussy up for the city. Locals would never allow themselves to be seen anywhere near the historic district in grungy shorts and T-shirts. Brooke was almost to the top of the stairs when she overheard Cornelia and Trig having a heated discussion in the kitchen.

"I can't do this anymore," Cornelia cried.

Brooke froze. She shouldn't eavesdrop, but what if her parents were actually breaking up?

"I will not be responsible for a woman I cannot find!" Her voice shook. "We have got to put her somewhere with locks on the doors. I am putting my foot down, Trigger."

"My mother is not leaving," Trig said in his *I'm the boss* voice. "This is what we do in this family. We take care of each other."

"Oh? This is what *we* do?" The sarcasm dripped from her tongue. "You have no idea what *we* do. You have barely been present for twenty years."

"Don't be like that, Cornelia."

"Like what? Like I do everything around here? Like I am the one caring for everyone while you're off in your own world? Is that what we're talking about?"

There was a moment of silence before her mother spoke again. "Trigger Warter, if you're so much as thinking of reminding me that you're the one who pays the mortgage, God help me, I will—" She didn't finish the sentence. "My schoolteacher salary got us both started. And don't you forget it!"

Before Brooke could move, her father stomped past her like she wasn't there and disappeared up the stairs. Cornelia yelled after him, "You either find that woman a place that is not my home, or I will find one for you. Do you understand?"

Brooke turned the corner and made her presence known. "Is Nana missing again?" Ever since that first day at the winery, not only had Nana been *working* with her, she'd been disappearing every afternoon as well.

"She was out until two A.M." Cornelia slapped her hand onto the marble countertop, exasperated. "What does an eighty-year-old woman have to do until two A.M.? I tell you, I am not having this anymore!"

So, Nana was stirring things up as usual. Normally, Brooke wouldn't worry, but this time felt different. Nana might be pushing things too far. Brooke changed quickly and was happy to have Jessa waiting like a getaway driver.

Jessa wanted fried green tomatoes and pimiento cheese, so they found a parking spot on King Street and walked over to Poogan's Porch. By the time they arrived, sweat dripped down their backs and they were more than ready for some strong air-conditioning. Their table for two was in the back of the restaurant—an old home built back in 1891. As always, people in the restaurant watched as they walked in—most eyes were on Jessa, but there were appraising looks for Brooke too. She was grateful that she put on her white silky top with flowy Lilly Pulitzer pants. She felt summery and classy.

They each ordered a mimosa and clinked to Jessa's new home, to their lifelong friendship, and to the fact that they were finally back in the same place again. Brooke was halfway through her drink when she nearly spat orange juice and champagne all over the table. Jessa took her napkin and held it at the ready, but her attention was soon diverted when she noticed Brooke's attention firmly fixed on two people walking into the room. One was a beautiful brunette wearing an elegant white sundress.

The other was Nathan Daugherty.

"Oh my God," Jessa said under her breath. "That's—"

Brooke nodded, unable to speak. Nate was alive. After all of the times she'd tried to find him online, there he was. He was okay. As a matter of fact, he looked great. His shoes alone probably cost more than her entire outfit. And Poogan's Porch wasn't a cheap place for a meal.

Nate and the woman were seated on the opposite side of the room. Brooke turned her back to him as much as possible. "Pretend like we're deep in conversation," she whispered, faking laughter.

Jessa caught on quickly and forced out a giggle.

"Isn't this just hilarious?" Brooke chuckled. "We are so funny. Oh my Lord. That thing you said just a second ago. You are sooooo funny. You always crack me up."

"No, you're the funny one, Brooke." Jessa threw back her head to laugh. "Remember that time you did something that made us both laugh so hard? And that other time when something happened and we just laughed and laughed?"

"Oh, yes. I remember that. I was absolutely dying! It was so funny. So, so funny." Brooke shuddered, every nerve alive and screaming. She leaned in and whispered, "He just noticed us. I saw it out of the corner of my eye." Then as she pulled back, she said louder, "Your mother is going to laugh so hard when we tell her."

Jessa's eyes kept cutting to Nate's table, but she kept up the laughing farce. Then she stopped as quickly as she'd started. Her eyes grew wide. "He's coming."

Brooke couldn't breathe.

"Hi," Nate said to Jessa.

"Hey, Nate! So good to see you!" she replied.

Brooke turned toward him and looked up.

"Hi, Brooke," he said. His hair was shorter, his face mature and angular yet somehow the same. His dark eyes held that sorrowful magnetic depth that still drew her in. The way he looked at her made her pulse quicken—like he saw through the makeup and the outfit and societal expectations and trauma responses and hopes and failures and regrets and long absence and fake laughter to the person she was in her core. A person he liked very much. It was the same way he used to look at her back at camp.

"Hi" was all she could squeak out. There was so much she wanted to say. So many explanations to give. He looked happy. Who was she to assume that he needed or wanted anything from her?

"Do you live in Charleston now?" Jessa asked. Where he lived was the question he would never answer all of those years ago, one of the reasons she could never find him.

Brooke held her breath and he smiled at her before nodding. He lived in Charleston. She felt lightheaded. How long had he been living so close to Goose Island? How many chances to see each other again had they missed? Her eyes went to the girl waiting for him at the table. None of it mattered. It was too late.

"Have you been to the Saltwater Winery over on

Goose?" Jessa asked. "Brooke and I work there now."

Brooke didn't know if she wanted to hug Jessa's neck or kick her under the table—hard.

"Maybe I'll stop by sometime," he said. "You doing okay?" He asked the question directly to Brooke. She could only nod.

"Good. Well, nice seeing you both." As he walked away, his left leg was stiff, causing his stride to be shorter on that side and resulting in a limp. Something about it made Brooke's face heat up and her blood boil. She'd never felt more fiercely like she'd been robbed. Like Libby Trotter had broken into her life and stolen something precious. Nate should have been in her life, somehow, in some capacity, even if they were just friends, for all of those years.

But he'd been taken from her by a lie spat from the mouth of a jealous teenager.

Chapter Ten

J ESSA ATE LIKE she'd never had pimiento cheese before and just discovered that she liked it better than chocolate cake. She followed it up with an enormous salad and two refills of sweet tea. Brooke had barely eaten half of a fried green tomato with bacon jam.

"I hate Libby Trotter," Brooke said. "I'll never understand why people can't just mind their own business. You do you, and I'll do me. I won't hurt you if you don't hurt me. Simple."

"I used to think she was like a vampire, that she smelled her victims," Jessa said. "But she's older now. She's not so bad."

"Hold up. You think she sniffed me out?" Brooke sat straight up, offended. "Why? Why me?"

"It's just that she knew you would never sink to her level, so she could get away with it."

"Well, you wouldn't sink to her level either. So, why didn't she bully you?" Brooke put down her fork with a *thunk*. "Don't say that you smell better. I know the real answer." Gates's words were still very much at the top of her mind. "I'm nice and you're sweet."

"Aren't those the same thing?" Jessa took a large swig of tea.

"Not according to Gates, so I looked it up. Nice is on purpose. It's a choice. But you never know what's hiding underneath it—the meanest person in the world can pretend to be nice. Sweet is just the way a person is. Like, they were born that way. What do people call it?" She felt a surge of envy as the words came out of her mouth. "A sweet disposition." Jessa had to know that Brooke was talking about her. Or, more importantly, that Gates had been talking about her.

"Isn't it the other way around?" Jessa asked. "Nice has an edge, so bullies stay away. Sweet is like a punching bag just hanging out and minding its own business until someone comes along and jabs it." Jessa even argued sweetly.

"No, nice gets punched. Sweet gets left alone because the bully would actually feel like a bully if they hurt her."

"So, you're saying bullies don't want to feel like bullies?" Jessa looked calm and serene even though she clearly disagreed. "I think they absolutely do."

"Some might. But I don't think Libby does. I don't think she has any idea how terrible she is."

"You might be right."

Brooke felt irritable and grouchy, but she had to keep it from her face in case Nate looked over. So, she forced the corners of her mouth to stay tilted up and tried to relax her shoulders as she put a forkful of bleu-cheese-covered lettuce in her mouth. She could be sweeter than molasses if she wanted to. Heck, she could freaking kill Gates Lancaster or Libby Trotter or Nate's beautiful brunette date with sweetness if she chose to.

"Brooke, stop thinking about it," Jessa said.

"How do you know what I'm thinking?"

"Because your face looks weird."

"I hate Libby Trotter," Brooke repeated, doing her best to keep a smile. "I mean, I know I shouldn't hate anyone, so whatever is bigger than the strongest dislike, that's how I feel."

Jessa whispered, "Because you think you would be with Nathan right now if Libby hadn't done what she did?"

Brooke cut her eyes toward the couple in the corner, then leaned in and nodded. "Yes." Then, "Can we go now?"

"You are in no state of mind to go home right now," Jessa said, waving to their server for the bill. "Let's do some shopping."

It only took five minutes for the bill to arrive, but it might as well have been five years with the way Brooke was thrown back into every feeling she'd ever had for Nate Daugherty. She'd always known that he would be the best kind of boyfriend, or husband if that was the case. He was smart, he was a protector, and apparently, he was a provider too. "Do you see a ring on his hand?" She mouthed the words, barely making a sound.

"I can only see his right hand."

Brooke's legs were shaky when they stood and waved goodbye to Nate and his date. When his date waved at them, too, Brooke couldn't help but feel deflated. The woman had that smile on her face—the one that declared they weren't competition at all and never would be.

Brooke was quiet as she walked down the bustling Charleston street with Jessa. It was going to take some effort, but if she was going to use this transition period to become who she always wanted to be, that meant genuinely wishing other women well. Even the pretty ones. Whoever that girl was, she wasn't out to get Brooke—she had simply walked into a restaurant with a guy Brooke happened to have complicated feelings toward. No one had the power to take away from her what she once had at camp with Nate. They had shared innocence together and firsts. That could never be stolen.

"The older I get, the more I understand clichés," Brooke said to Jessa. "Don't dwell on the past. Leave the past in the past. Look to the future." There were more, she just couldn't think of them. "I was Nate's past, and that girl in there is his future." She forced herself to add, "I'm happy for them."

"Me too." Jessa said it easily. She truly was happy for them, and Brooke was just saying the words, hoping that the feeling would follow. That seriously irked her. "Can you ever be mean, Jess? Can you ever just not like someone?"

"You've seen me with Tulip," she said, chuckling.

"Little sisters don't count."

"I should've warned you about this sooner, but don't let her hear you call her Tulip." They took a left onto King Street and kept walking. "It's Tootie now, and if you try to call her Tulip, you will have to suffer through a very long speech about how she is old enough to choose a nickname." They took stock of nearby shopping options. "Clothes, jewelry? What are we looking for?"

"Something cute and cheap," Brooke said. "I'm thinking earrings."

"That one?" Jessa pointed to a boutique across the street, and they simultaneously looked both ways before crossing. "So anyway, Tootie believes that if her father knew that she existed, he never would have allowed his daughter to be named after a flower that hangs its head when it wilts. She's no head hanger." They walked into the air-conditioned store, and Jessa whispered, "Why she'd choose a fart over a flower, I have no idea. But I like it."

"She's still obsessing over her dad?" Brooke swiped through a nearby rack of blouses.

Jessa nodded.

"That's sad."

"Just another epic bad choice by dear old Dottie Boone." Jessa held up a pair of gold hoops from a round table in the center of the store.

"Those are cute." Brooke wondered if Jessa was open to tracking down her own father. Depending on how Jessa was feeling, it could be a touchy subject.

"I love shopping therapy," Jessa said. "Let me buy these for you as a breakup gift."

"Jess. I do not want a breakup gift. This is not worth celebrating."

Jessa frowned. "You don't want them?"

"Thanks, but I already have some gold hoops."

"Then I'll buy them for me."

"They can be your new-house celebration earrings."

Jessa nodded and smiled. "Then that's what they'll be."

Three hours, an oversized beach bag, white shorts, a box of benne wafers, and several miles later, Brooke's feet needed a break. They popped into a little corner Irish pub and ordered two beers. "What a day," she said, putting her feet up on the chair opposite her.

Brooke was happy that she'd taken the seat facing the front window. All day, she'd had one eye on the lookout for Nate. He was in that city somewhere. He *lived* here. They could run into him again at any time. Every male who walked by and was anywhere near his height or with hair the color of brown sugar gave her a start. It was strange to think of Nate as a professional, as a *man*. She wondered what he did for a living. Maybe, despite his horrible childhood, his adulthood was happy and fulfilled.

That's what he would want for her. And that's what she wanted for him too.

The beer was cold and had a nice wheaty flavor. They

ordered loaded potato skins as an appetizer, and soon decided that they should count as dinner too. Brooke ordered another beer, grateful for a full belly and time to relax.

Three beers in, and Brooke and Jessa were roaring about Duke Bradley and his daily disappearing act. "Disappearing Duke," they called him. "Leavin' Leroy. Bye-Bye, Big Guy. Gone Don. Mr. Brad-flee." Brooke hiccupped loudly and laughed even harder. Then something outside caught her eye. She slammed both feet to the floor.

"What is my mother doing in Charleston, and who is that man?"

Jessa practically gave herself whiplash turning around so quickly. "What?" She turned back just as fast. "There has to be an explanation."

A tall man of similar age had his hand on the small of Mrs. Cornelia Warter's back, leading her gracefully into a fancy restaurant.

"Do you think it's their tax man? Maybe your dad is waiting inside."

"Maybe," Brooke said, her eyes glued to the door of the restaurant after it closed behind them. "Let's order something else. I don't want to leave this spot until they come back out."

"Works for me," Jessa said. Then she reached across the table for Brooke's hand. "I'm sorry, honey."

"It's fine," Brooke said. "I'm sure it's fine."

Chapter Eleven

N ANA MADE HERSELF a nametag. She was not on the payroll or the schedule, but it appeared as if no one was going to inform her that she did not actually work at the Saltwater Winery. Grace, it said, Miss South Carolina, 1959.

"Nana!" Brooke said. "You were Miss South Carolina? How did I not know that?"

"Don't be silly," Nana said. "I would never."

"But your tag!"

"I am simply being interesting, my dear. It was either this or Nobel Prize winner, but I didn't want to deal with all of the questions."

Brooke laughed. "Nana, you are interesting enough without pretending."

Nana's eyes wrinkled into puffy creases with her smile. "Why, thank you, darling. That is just the sweetest thing to say."

Sweet. The word felt hopeful.

All day Brooke wondered if Nate would show up at the winery. He knew where she worked now. Maybe he wanted to catch up as much as she did. They had things to talk about. Well, at least one main thing: why she never reached out to him all those years ago.

Each hour ticked by slowly, carrying with it so much hope and anticipation that she could barely communicate with her customers. She kept forgetting words like *mouthfeel* and *astringent*. She even called their King Tide blend dry when it was definitely sweet and fruit-forward. Her cash tips would suffer for sure.

By closing time, Nana had disappeared and Libby had popped in three times looking smug and snooty with a phony smile and a pencil skirt that hugged her thighs and perky behind so tightly she had to take baby steps to get across the room. Allie was head down in her office all day, Jessa flitted around like Tinker Bell sprinkling happy, magical pixie dust on everyone, and Nathan Daugherty never showed up.

Brooke drove home feeling dejected, which was ridiculous because she was the one who had ghosted him all those years ago. She was the one who dated and eventually moved in with Gates Lancaster. She was the one who barely said a word to Nate at the restaurant. What did she expect? That he was going to throw himself at her? That he was going to show up at the place of employment of a girl who kissed him back in high school? People didn't do those kinds of things in real life.

Cornelia was setting the table as Brooke drove up to her imposing family home. Through the large front window, she watched her mother placing dessert forks on the left side of her good dishes. Cornelia was wearing heels, as she always did, putting them on before the meal and taking them off afterward. The woman was deeply committed to the show. Yet she'd been out to dinner just two days prior with some other man. Brooke and Jessa had waited until she came out of the restaurant. They watched the two embrace on the sidewalk—with Brooke holding her breath for every second of their minutes-long hug—and saw clearly that when they pulled apart, Cornelia was crying. The man looked down at her with the tenderness of a lover. He put a hand to her cheek and asked her a question.

That was when Mrs. Cornelia Warter, wife of Trigger Warter, tilted her head back, lifted her chin up, and kissed another man.

Brooke wanted to turn the car around and instead go straight to Dottie's. Her head was still spinning; her mother felt as unknown to her as outer space. She put the car in Park and walked inside. This was how life would be for a while. Complicated and unfulfilling, like she was living her parents' lives instead of her own. Only now there was the added anxiety of a high probability that her parents' lives were also about to change. Her soft place to fall was about to explode like a match in a gas can. Especially if she told Trig what she saw.

"I'm home!" she called, leaving her shoes at the front door and jogging up the stairs.

"Dinner in thirty minutes," Cornelia answered.

From her room, she watched Nana leave her cottage and head toward the main house. It looked like she would be having dinner with them after all. In her hand was a large bucket.

Brooke unlatched her window and threw it open. "Hey, Nana!"

Nana stopped and shielded her eyes from the setting sun. "Hello, love."

"Whatcha got in the bucket?"

"My share of the shrimp."

"What shrimp?"

"From my night shrimping."

"You went night shrimping? Out on the water?"

Nana ignored the question and walked forward, swinging the bucket like it was perfectly normal for an eighty-year-old to randomly go shrimping in the dark of night.

"Nana!"

"What?" Now she was annoyed.

"Who'd you go with?"

"Wouldn't you like to know?" she said, making her way up the back porch steps and out of Brooke's line of vision.

"It was Duke, wasn't it?!"

"I'm not telling!" Nana let the door slam shut behind her.

That was as good as a yes for Brooke. *What in the heck?* Nana and the old man who tended to his dead wife's garden?

The strange boss who hid from everyone?

Ever since she'd gotten back to Goose Island, it'd been one thing after another. Her mother had a boyfriend in Charleston. Her grandmother had a boyfriend on Goose Island. And Brooke was completely alone. It was time to focus extra hard on saving her money. She needed to go someplace else. Anywhere else.

The ruckus of Nana entering the kitchen where Cornelia was preparing the meal could probably be heard by the fishermen all the way out on the marsh.

"Trigger!" Cornelia used her outdoor voice. "Come here this instant!"

"What?" he answered from his dark-paneled office on the other side of the house.

"Why does your mother have a bucket full of shrimp?"

Nana's voice was just as elevated. "Just cook them, Cornelia! All you've got to do is throw them in some boiling water."

"I have already prepared a meal for us this evening, and I will not be starting over."

"Then put them in the gall-danged freezer!" Nana yelled.

"Grace! You will not tell me what to do. Do you hear me?" Cornelia said. "I have had enough of you and your antics. Your disappearing. Your stupid banana costume. I cannot be expected to tolerate your treatment of me another instant. It is too much for one woman to bear."

"Well, you're sure on edge, little miss priss," Nana said.

From her bedroom, Brooke heard Trig's footsteps on his way to the kitchen. Finally, his deep voice cut through the chaos. "Come on now, you two."

"Don't you talk down to me, Trigger Warter," Cornelia said. "I have had it!"

Wisely, he aimed his next statement at Nana. "Mama, I need you to treat my wife with respect."

"Her? *I* am supposed to respect *her*?" Brooke imagined Nana sneering and pointing an arthritic finger at Cornelia.

Cornelia gasped, and in that one little noise, Brooke heard exasperation, anger, surprise, and a very real chance that she might storm out the front door and never return.

Trigger jumped to her defense. "Cornelia works hard for this family, Mother. She feeds you, she drives you to your appointments, she puts up with your"—he paused—"eccentricities. She deserves your gratitude."

"And you're so grateful?" Nana bit back. "I don't see you telling her how great she is all the time. Maybe I'm just following your lead. Huh? Did you ever think about that?"

"Mama, I love my wife."

"Mm-hmm. Does she know that?"

"Of course she does," he said.

"Do you?" Nana asked Cornelia.

Brooke couldn't hear her mother's response.

"Cornelia," Trig said, clearly surprised. "You know you're the best thing that ever happened to me."

"It's about time you grew a sack of balls," Nana said.

"How long were you going to let me treat her like a mule before you said something?"

Brooke moved to stand in her doorway, listening through the sound tunnel of the stairs. As much as she was furious with her mother for what she'd seen in Charleston, maybe it wasn't unpredictable. Nana clearly saw it too. Trig needed a good talking to, but not about the other man.

Chapter Twelve

"GRACIOUS, IT HAS been a week," Brooke said. Some customers had posted viral content about a rustic little winery way out on an island called Goose, and when viewers saw folks hanging out with chickens, cats, and goats in the shade of drippy old oaks sipping wine, crowds flocked to the establishment. It was Friday, and the popular jazz band Notes of the Marsh was scheduled to play, so both tourists and locals jammed their cars into the gravel parking lot and all the way down the tree-lined street like it was the Fourth of July parade. Both Brooke and Jessa said in quick passing that they wished they hadn't volunteered to work that night.

Old Mother Nature must've been in her giggles, because she saw them all coming and decided to turn up the thermostat, successfully ensuring that everyone was red-faced and sweaty as they danced and sipped libations. The air-conditioning in the tasting room could barely keep up with the door opening and closing so much, so Brooke sweated along with them. Nana, who seemed impervious to the heat in her red cotton top and hula skirt, stationed herself by the front door, handing out wet paper towels she'd placed inside a bag of ice. Tips were graciously accepted, of course. Cornelia would be horrified.

The good news was that the tasting room was about to close. Everything on concert night took place outside, and the temperature would soon drop a few degrees. Dottie locked her truck up tight after she ran out of pulled pork and coleslaw. She'd had lines no fewer than ten people long all day. Jessa managed to talk her mom into helping out instead of heading home, so Dottie was on the grounds making sure there was toilet paper in the bathrooms, empty trash cans, and no broken glass in the dirt. She was grumpier than the goats, Skip and June, who had apparently banded together to knock some poor soul off a bench from behind. But she soon discovered that if she put her bottled waters and Cokes in a half wine barrel filled with ice, she could charge five dollars a drink and people would willingly pay it. Dottie-the-entrepreneur was unstoppable.

Finally, the night was orangish-black and the moon won the fight for the sky. The band struck opening chords and the guests settled into their spots. The ones who planned ahead sat on blankets with baskets of charcuterie and drank from real wineglasses—the women with their legs tucked under their long skirts and the men in polo shirts and shorts leaning back into their beach chairs. The rest of them sat on hammocks, Adirondack chairs, tree roots, picnic benches, and patches of grass.

Brooke sat at a table near the main building, where she sold small plastic glasses of wine from a cooler. The white scuppernong wine would be especially quenching on this particular night, she told people, and it sold quickly.

Once the doors were locked, Nana took her pocketbook full of cash tips and attempted to disappear. Only this time, Brooke watched as her grandmother walked with purpose, grass skirt swaying, to Amelia's Patch of Happiness. She opened the gate and vanished like a ghost into the garden. She was definitely headed through the vineyard to Duke's place. She had to be.

As much as Brooke was trying to ignore her, Libby was there too. And she'd brought along her fiancé. He wasn't as good-looking as Gates Lancaster, but he surely never had trouble getting dates. What did he see in Libby Trotter? And why had he given her a ring twice the size of Asia? Didn't he know that she would find fault in it? She found something wrong with everything and everyone.

Brooke tried not to watch them but couldn't help herself. Libby, of course, was one of the prepared guests. Not only was she not working the event, she wore a puffy-sleeved white dress and set up her picnic on a short portable wooden table complete with a vase of fresh flowers in the center. She and James sat on fluffy cream-colored pillows and picked at their spread of olives, soft cheese, honey, crackers, salami, and grapes, to be followed by a silver tray of miniature cupcakes. The pillows, napkins, and tablecloth were monogrammed, of course.

I'm happy for them, Brooke tried to convince herself. But it didn't work. Not at all. She wasn't happy for them, and saying it in her head wasn't going to change that. So, she changed her tack. *Their happiness does not affect my life in any way. They have no power over me.* Those thoughts helped a little, but as soon as she watched Libby take a sip of rosé with her ostentatious, self-righteous, bratty little pinky held upright like royalty, Brooke wished fervently that Skip and June would prance over there and headbutt her into oblivi-on. *People who steal happiness from others do not deserve to have it for themselves.* Libby was a happiness stealer. So why did she have absolutely everything? Brooke poured herself a cup of scuppernong wine and chugged the whole thing. Shouldn't karma be having its way with Libby Trotter? Hurry up, already.

Brooke had to tear her eyes away. It would be nice if Nate showed up in that very moment. They could confront Libby together, her fiancé would finally see her for what she was, and her wedding would be canceled. Libby Trotter would be left curled into a little ball on her fancy pillows, crying her eyes out because her life was ruined. And Brooke would not help her. As a matter of fact, Brooke would laugh. Yep. Just like Libby had done to her. And then she'd say something like, *You get what you deserve*, or *Karma sucks, doesn't it?*

Brooke caught herself smiling widely. *Shoot.* She hadn't

meant to let cattiness take over like that. She had to stop those kinds of thoughts. They were mean, and she was not a mean person. She was supposed to be sweet. She would never stoop as low as Libby. But the feeling of retribution, of *justice*, even though only imagined, still warmed her from the inside.

Revenge really did feel good.

"I saw that." Dottie sauntered over, her nonalcoholic drink station only a few yards away. "You living in your head these days?"

"Just processing." The band played a menacing riff that highlighted her point nicely.

"What you put out into the universe comes back to you, you know."

"I know. You caught me having a moment."

Dottie's eyes cut toward Libby and James. "Generations of hatefulness. That's what she comes from." Dottie made no bones about staring right at them. "Ooh, Lordy. She's a piece of work. I tell you what, I can see plain as Bermuda hay that she comes from a long line of selfish assholes."

"Day," Brooke mumbled. "Plain as day." There was no use correcting Dottie. Anyway, Brooke was done thinking about and talking about Libby. Libby was responsible for her actions, long line of assholes or not.

"Just remember that the folks who judge you got a whole lot to be judged for themselves."

Brooke nodded. "I just wish I knew why she decided to

hate me. There are millions of people in the world, and she chose me." Dottie appeared to have her attention diverted toward her daughter, who was laughing it up with a group of folks seated around a picnic table covered with food, candles, and flowers. Brooke joined Dottie in the vision of Jessa acting as the human version of sunshine. "How did you teach her to be so sweet?"

Dottie was no longer listening. "Something's coming for you." It was like the words came from the inside of Dottie's skull instead of her mouth. It was creepy.

"Is it good?" *Oh, please let whatever was coming be good.*

Dottie moved her eyes to Brooke and sucked in her upper lip, exposing the hole where her bottom tooth should be. Her eyes were shut tight, light brown eyelashes sticking straight out, shaded by the edge of her blue knit cap. "There's more. I mean, I can't see it all. There's goodness in it. Yes, plenty of good. But also risk. Big risk." Her eyes popped open. "Oh, honey child. There is a storm swirling all around the edges of your life, ain't there?"

Brooke shuddered. There sure was.

THE NEXT MORNING, the vortex of Brooke's storm was swirling inside Trig and Cornelia's house. If she had to clock the winds, she'd say 72 mph—hurricane force. Cornelia was fired up, and all of her anger was aimed at Trigger, who looked shell-shocked in his plaid bathrobe and slippers at the breakfast table.

"All I asked for was the ketchup," he said. "You know I like ketchup on my eggs."

"Then get it yourself." Cornelia took the hot pan from the stove and threw it with a loud crash onto the tile. Bits of scrambled eggs flew all over the lower kitchen cabinets and floor.

"Cornelia!" Trig shouted. "What is up with you?"

Brooke hadn't said anything to anyone about what she'd seen in Charleston. And she had no intention of telling her dad, but she sensed that the other man and Cornelia's current behavior were linked.

"I am tired of this! I am tired of doing for everyone else all the time. None of you people care. None of y'all even know that I'm here unless I'm serving something up for your bellies."

"Don't be ridiculous," Trig attempted.

"Now you're calling me ridiculous? If you want to see ridiculous, I will show you ridiculous!" Cornelia's finger shook as she pointed it straight at her husband's forehead. Her face was bright red.

Brooke sat frozen at the table. Her parents rarely fought in front of her. In the Warter home, voices were not allowed to be raised. If a person was angry, they were to go to their room until they calmed down.

"I'll hire a cook," Trig said, trying to fix things but missing entirely what his wife was actually saying.

Brooke's heart pounded. She should stay out of it. But her dad needed to learn, and for the first time, she had clarity about her mother. The thought came out of her mouth before her brain could run interference. "You don't get any appreciation around here, do you, Mother?" It had been years since she'd called her anything but Cornelia.

Cornelia's frenetic movements slowed as her eyes shifted to her daughter.

Brooke continued. "You work hard at a job no one notices, for no paycheck and only the rare thank-you."

"I share my bank account—" Trigger began.

Brooke shot him a look. "This is about Mother. And let's not even talk about the fact that you just called the bank account that you own with your wife of thirty years *yours*."

Her father paled and shut up.

"You've created a beautiful home for us, Mother. You make things nice. You raised me, you feed and clean up after us, you handle every little detail of this household, including Nana."

Cornelia leaned against the kitchen island, her face no longer red.

"I noticed the new hand towels in the guest bath," Trigger said sheepishly. "They're real pretty."

Cornelia shot fire at him with her eyes.

Brooke asked softly, "Do you feel like you're the only one here concerned with other people's well-being? Like you're solely responsible for your family's health and happiness?" The words came out in a torrent, and Brooke found herself saying things that she'd known but never actually took the time to think about. Despite the fact that Cornelia was a control freak, she did have the best intentions. "I see that you do all you can to keep things running smoothly around here, that you have a million responsibilities."

Cornelia nodded.

"But, a person can only do it for so long, right? It isn't just you, Trig. None of us pays attention to how much she does—to how much thought and effort goes into it."

Cornelia came over and sat at the table next to Brooke. She looked exhausted.

"I'll clean up the eggs," Brooke said.

"No, I made the mess, I'll—"

"No, Mother. I'm cleaning them."

"Thank you." She slumped into her seat.

"Cornelia?" Trig asked.

Cornelia acknowledged him, but her face turned dark.

"May I take you out for a nice dinner tonight?"

Cornelia thought for a moment. "No, thank you."

Trig stiffened and frowned. "Well then, I'll just take my coffee to the den." He accidentally spilled coffee onto the table as he stood. He noticed the mess, ignored it, and walked out of the room.

Brooke had better talk to her mother privately about the other man. The sooner the better. Her parents' marriage might depend on it. But not now. Sharing the fact that she saw her kiss another man while Cornelia was in an emotional stew might very well send her mother running.

As Brooke picked the gooey eggs off the painted wood cabinets, she considered why Cornelia insisted on treating her like a guest. Brooke was another family member to have to serve and worry about and try to control. When it came to Cornelia's particular personality type, one more person was simply too much. It had nothing to do with how much she wanted her daughter there. The fact was, Cornelia Warter loved her daughter, and her daughter had been misjudging her since the day she was born.

Chapter Thirteen

F OR THE REST of that Saturday, Brooke looked for places to live. She had enough savings to make a small down payment on an apartment. It would be tight, but if she got a studio, she could probably pay rent and still be able to eat. She could make a commute work, so she might even look for a place in Charleston. And, no, she told herself, it had nothing to do with the fact that Nate lived there.

Brooke was feeling good. The morning drama actually added to it. She felt like she'd done something right, like she was meant to be there in that moment to help her mother. It was proof that a shift had taken place—she was not just their kid, she was also an adult. And what she'd done had been genuinely sweet, not pretend nice. It was empathetic and straight from her heart. She curled her hair into soft waves and put on crisp white shorts. She was going to wear a black short-sleeve button-down until she found a Carolina blue blouse left in the chest of drawers. It reminded her of the grungy little boy she met at camp. What he had in the Walmart bag was his only other outfit and a toothbrush. That outfit was a Carolina blue T-shirt and a pair of jean shorts. He wore that T-shirt every day.

So, light blue it was.

There were three apartments she wanted to look at that day. One in Charleston and two in Mount Pleasant. She decided to start in Charleston and swing by Lewis Barbecue on her way out of town. Allie and Sam had invited her and Jessa to dinner that night and she'd insisted on bringing a side dish. There were plenty to choose from at Lewis.

The Kensington was almost as tall as St. Matthew's Lutheran Church. Of course, in Charleston, nothing was allowed to be taller, which was more than three stories. It was an old mansion slightly north of Broad Street with a garden out back and rooms for rent. Each had been retrofitted with an en suite bathroom, and most were studios with a small kitchenette. The one available was in the front of the house, which would be noisier but still within walking distance of all of her favorite restaurants and shops. She'd made an appointment to meet with the leasing agent at noon.

What was immediately noticeable about the location was that parking would be an issue. Street parking was at a minimum and the nearest paid parking was three blocks away. The sky was quickly darkening and it looked like rain on the horizon. Brooke almost turned around when she realized that not having a nearby space would totally suck on rainy days, not to mention the expense and safety issues. But she wasn't the sort to purposefully miss an appointment. She found a spot a block away and fast-walked to get to the house on time. When she opened the Charleston black front door, there was a beautiful brunette in smart casual slacks and a thin silk blouse waiting in the foyer. Brooke nearly turned right back around and left. It was Nate's girlfriend or wife or lunch date or mother of his twelve adopted children and twenty-seven rescued dogs. The girl was walking toward her with her hand outstretched.

"Nice to meet you," she said. "I'm Noelle."

"Brooke," she said, suddenly feeling hot and sweaty despite the air-conditioning. Surely, her Carolina blue shirt was screaming her secret: *Nate wore this color at camp! He kissed me! We liked each other!*

Brooke followed Noelle up the narrow wooden stairs and down the hallway. The apartment smelled like all of the old Charleston houses: like sea breezes and long unopened attics. It was a nice space, about the same size as her room back home. But her eyes felt glazed over, her body on high alert for Nate.

Noelle sweetly explained the lease structure and timeline, fees, and rules. She asked whether Brooke planned to have a roommate, and informed her that pets were not allowed. But it all sounded like gibberish. Brooke's brain was filled with questions about Nate. Things that needed to be said, mysteries that needed to be solved. Starting with, where was he, and who was Noelle to him?

Clearly, Noelle did not remember her from the restaurant. Brooke could bring it up. It could be her entry into asking questions about Nate. But would it look like she was a stalker? Like she'd somehow turned FBI agent and tracked down Nate's girlfriend's place of employment? Her mind spun. She didn't want to lose the opportunity. Coincidences like this didn't happen often. She might never run into either of them again for the rest of her life. She had to seize the moment. She had to say something.

Noelle had finished talking and was looking at Brooke like she was a frozen chicken cutlet and there were two thousand different ways she could cut her up and cook her. Brooke finally answered, "It's nice," even though she didn't know the question.

"Here's my card." Noelle handed her a thick white rectangular business card. "Call or text me if you want to move forward."

"Thank you." Brooke took the card and followed her back down the stairs.

When they reached the bottom, Noelle swung around. "Poogan's Porch! I thought you looked familiar!"

Brooke took a step backward, then met her enthusiasm. "Yes! I was wondering the same thing!"

"Nathan said he knew y'all from his old summer camp days."

Brooke nodded. "That's right." She had to ask the questions, and fast. "Does he work here too?"

Noelle laughed. "He'll say he does, but no. Hardly ever

makes it in anymore."

How could she ask without being too obvious? "So, you work together?"

She laughed again. "He'd say we do, but no. I work for him. He owns the place."

So, they were coworkers. And still probably dating. "He owns this?"

"Yeah, he went to school for biology, so he likes to say that he went to school to learn how to keep things alive and ended up reviving dead buildings instead. Isn't that how things work in life? Like, I was sure I was going to be a teacher, but here I am leasing out rooms. My husband is stationed here with the navy."

Husband! Navy! The words pierced her ears first and her heart second. Her entire body went from stiff as concrete to soft and safe with those two little words.

Brooke sang in the car as she drove toward the BBQ restaurant. She still wasn't sure if Nate was single, but it sure seemed that way. She was practically bouncing as she waited in line to buy a pint of Cowboy Pinto Beans and three singles of Green Chile Corn Pudding. She was excited to get to know her coworker Allie better, and Sam sure seemed great. Even though he hadn't started medical school yet, the fact that he was an EMT was enough for the islanders to make him their resident healthcare specialist.

She had to dodge the people running inside as she went to leave. Rain was aggressively pouring from the darkened sky. It'd been ages since she'd checked her weather app. Surely, it was just a normal summertime afternoon thunder shower. She did her best to keep the brown paper bag holding her beans and corn pudding dry as she ran to the car. Water dripped from the ends of her hair as she opened the door and climbed inside. The deluge was so strong, it flowed like a river down her windshield. The wipers couldn't create a dry spot long enough to see. She pulled up the radar app on her phone. A large swath of red was approaching and it was clearly going to last a long time. Band after band of stormy weather followed in shades of yellow and orange with an enormous dark red center. There was no choice. She needed to head back to Goose Island now, or risk getting caught up in flooding.

She could barely see as she pulled onto the road. Every car nearby was driving under twenty miles per hour. They were probably thinking the same thing. *Just get home. Immediately.* Brooke's phone dinged with a text message from Allie.

"*This storm is a monster! Sam's been called into work. The ambulances are about to be crazy busy. Let's reschedule our dinner for another time.*"

Brooke responded when she stopped at the first red light. "*Sounds good!*" At least she had food if she got stranded, and at best, Cornelia would be happy to have the side dishes.

She couldn't help but look at every car and wonder if Nathan was inside. She had Noelle's business card now.

Maybe if she got stranded in Charleston, she would call her. And maybe Noelle would tell Nate that his old friend from camp needed help. And maybe Nate would come to her rescue. And maybe…

Brooke shook her head to dislodge the thoughts. *Stop fantasizing about Nate. He's just a dream from years ago. You don't even know him anymore.*

It was strange how one person could have such a strong pull on another. Strange how she'd felt a connection to him the minute she saw him years ago, and strange how, at least for her, that connection was still there. There was a part of her that, despite all of her other life choices and dreams for her future, had never let go of him. He still felt rare and special. And her instincts or God or the universe seemed to be whispering in her ear that she and Nate had been chosen. Chosen for what? To be friends? Chosen to be in love? Chosen to save old buildings? She had no idea. But they were chosen for something.

Yes, definitely something.

Chapter Fourteen

THE STORM SYSTEM was still blowing the next morning. It kept the crowds away from the winery, so after inching her way to work and running through puddles to get inside, Brooke decided it was a good time to organize the gift shop and deep clean the tasting area. Nana hadn't shown up for a ride to work that morning, which was not unexpected considering she'd claimed to be allergic to rainwater for as long as Brooke had known her. The woman snuggled in on rainy days like her house was a protective bubble and her oven was the secret to survival. Brooke would stop by after work and see what sort of goodies she had baked.

Large droplets beat against the tin-roofed building so loudly that it sounded like someone had set an old TV to static at the highest volume possible. Rainwater pooled all over the grounds. Certainly, no one would be making the trek to the end of the island that day. Some of the roads were completely flooded out. Even Dottie had kept the truck at home, and Dottie never missed a chance to make money.

Jessa was doing paperwork in her back office, Allie was in the lab, and Libby was probably using the company computer to browse wedding ideas. Brooke worked alone, finding things to keep herself busy. If she was getting paid to be there, she would find something useful to do. It was nice to have a day to detail clean and organize. It gave her time to listen to her thoughts rather than stuffing them into the part of her brain that was supposed to act as a lockbox but instead leaked like a broken faucet.

Gates. His face would always be engraved on her heart. His old attempts at a sense of humor made her smile. He wasn't funny, but he tried to be. She used to feel special walking into a room on his arm, noticing the women leaning over to whisper about him. Like Jessa, people couldn't keep it to themselves when someone as good-looking as Gates showed up. Some people went so far as to point at him. He pretended to be oblivious to it, but he definitely noticed. She knew by the subtle changes in the way he stood taller and tried to hold a little smolder on his face—his eyebrows slightly lifted and his cheeks sucked in. That part always made her laugh, even though he didn't think it was funny.

She would always care about him, and yes, she missed him. But that didn't make him the person she should invest her life in. She sprayed Windex onto a glass display table and wiped it off in circles. She hoped he was okay. How could he not be? He was better off without her too. He had a great life in Savannah, plenty of friends, a good job in finance, and their little apartment that she'd painted and wallpapered and made into a home. She hoped he'd been watering the fiddle-leaf fig in the kitchen.

Then a thought hit her. Was her father like Gates for her mother? Had Cornelia settled? Was Trigger never right for her to begin with? And, what did a person do when they'd been married to someone for thirty years and didn't like them anymore? Her hands stopped circling the surface, even though there was still a wet spot of glass cleaner. Had they tried working on their relationship? Did they talk about their wants and needs with each other? How long had her mother been feeling unseen?

Brooke finished the table and began setting the cork-lined trays, coffee table books, and decoupaged oyster shells back where they'd been. It wasn't like her mother could fill her car with everything she owned and take off to stay with her parents. Despite Brooke's anger about the man in Charleston, she felt a rush of empathy. Which was quickly followed up with a sickening worry for her father. How would he survive alone? He was used to people taking care of him, to coming home to women full of life and chatter and activity. He would be lonely and miserable.

Her whole family was drowning.

She moved to the raw-edge wooden tasting counter and sprayed a special wood cleaner all over it. She'd just started wiping it down when she remembered something Nana had once said. *I might be old, but I am not inclined to put myself on mute. No, ma'am. I am turning up the volume.* At the time, Brooke thought it was funny because it was Nana, but she hadn't stopped to think about what it meant.

Not only was her mother unseen in her own home, but the older she got, the more invisible she was in society. People no longer listened to her opinions—they called them old-fashioned. They didn't notice her beauty—it had faded. They couldn't see her value. With each passing day Cornelia became more and more powerless and irrelevant. *How scary. And unfair.* Yet, Brooke was just as much a part of the problem as the rest of the world. Everyone seemed to forget that they were growing old too.

Heck, Nana is a freaking genius. At least the kooky lady gets noticed.

She realized she'd been wiping the same spot on the counter for the past few minutes, so she set down the cleaner and the rag and sat on a barstool. For the first time, Brooke thought about what it must have been like for her mother when she was twenty-three. The world was different, she'd had fewer choices. Did she like how her life turned out? Did she like who she was?

One day Brooke would be in her midfifties, maybe married, hopefully settled somewhere, and on the downhill side of her life. What would she want?

The answer was easy. She would want family. Both the one she already had, plus a solid, loving, supportive family that she created herself. She wanted to be friends with the future version of herself—to like her, respect her, and be proud of her choices.

A loud clap of thunder made her jump, causing a spurt of adrenaline, a healthy pinch of fear, and a sharp reminder of how alone she was, even though there were other people somewhere in the same building.

The bells on the front door jingled, and Brooke assumed it had blown open with the wind, so she jumped again when she saw a person standing there.

"I heard this place has the best scuppernong wine this side of the Mississippi," the man said. He turned to hang his black rain slicker on a wall hook. He had light brown hair, broad shoulders, and an athletic physique. When he turned around, she immediately felt lightheaded.

"Nate. What are you doing here?"

"Seemed like a perfect day for wine tasting."

Brooke laughed. Something about him standing in front of her, just the two of them in a room with a storm raging outside, made her giddy. He was taller than she'd realized while sitting down at the restaurant—at least as tall as Gates, and maybe taller. His jaw had sharpened with age, and he even had a shadow of a beard. But his eyes still crinkled in the corners like he approved of her, like she brought him joy. She laughed much harder than his comment deserved. She laughed until she had to cover her mouth with her hand, and her stomach spasmed with guffaws. Tears ran down her face. She was intensely aware that she looked like a lunatic, but could do nothing about it.

"I'm sorry." She ran behind the counter to grab a napkin

and dabbed at her face while her outburst finally, mercifully, began to subside. "I'm so sorry," she said again, trying hard to squelch the unwanted display of emotion.

He took a seat on the barstool in front of her. "You okay?"

The hysteria was mostly tamped down, but tears still emptied onto her cheeks. She tried to breathe normally, but each breath was choppy. "I don't"—she took two rough breaths in—"know"—she wiped her eyes and nose, trying to pull herself together—"why I can't stop laughing."

"Did I scare you?" he asked.

She nodded her head even though it wasn't fear. Not at all. Maybe it was the fact that he looked like a better version of the teenager she'd spent so many years dreaming about? Or that he had made such a big effort to get to her? She didn't think so. No. That wasn't it. She looked into his face, sitting so handsomely across from her. There was no anger in the set of his mouth, just concern in the squint of his eyes, and maybe a little amusement. She knew exactly what had brought on her flash flood of extreme emotion.

It was hope.

Chapter Fifteen

NATE SAT ACROSS from Brooke as she worked to pull herself together. In a way, she wished the tasting bar wasn't between them so she could give in to the strong urge to hug him. In another way, though, the impediment seemed like an appropriate metaphor. There was more than a bar between them. There was a world of explaining. She'd never called him. It was so long ago, and they were different people now. But he'd given her his phone number that terrible day at camp, left her with a way to reach out, and she was the one who never did.

The feeling she'd had back when she was fifteen years old grabbed her stomach and twisted it like a fist. It was the same nauseating sickness that shook her when she realized she may never see or talk to Nate again. That old Camp Dogwood day may very well qualify as the worst day of her life. "Stay where you are," she said. "I'm going to fix my face. I'll be right back."

She scurried off to the safety of the bathroom, her mind fully engulfed in teenage flames, in days gone by, and the dog days of summer before camp came to an end. She and

Nate had found another duck hidden in the stack of kayaks. It was number two, which meant a dance party. It was a small miracle that the same people had found two of the three ducks—probably a camp record. They'd been standing by the jumping rock—a flat one that jutted out over the water, and Brooke was so happy she was pretty sure she could do a triple flip with a twist into the cool depths.

"I can't do this to you," Nate had said.

"What? Do what?" She couldn't hold still. She danced and spun across the rock.

"What's already happening."

"What are you talking about?" As far as she was concerned, she'd just experienced the best twenty-four hours of her life. Plus, her first kiss—a great one. A bonding one. He had to have felt it too. She spun past him with a grin.

"They've targeted us, Brooke, and I'm not going to let you suffer because of me."

"Who?" Brooke stopped dancing.

"Someone stole my stuff last night. Everything. My suit and my toothbrush."

"Let's go tell a counselor. They'll find them."

Nate shook his head. "I'll handle it. But for now, you need to stay away from me."

"I'm not afraid, Nate. I don't need to stay away from you."

"You know how it works here. As soon as someone is a target, the whole pack joins in. You're safe with Jessa. Stay with her. But we shouldn't be seen together."

The freedom and light she'd felt just seconds ago turned as dark and heavy as tar. "Look, if you don't like me, then just say so."

Nathan took her hand. "I like you, Brooke. I've liked you since the first day of camp when you smiled at me. I saved all year for this fancy camp, and I promise you, it's not for the campfire songs."

She didn't hear much past the part about looking forward to coming to camp because of her. "I like you too," she'd said. "So, we don't need to change anything."

"What kind of man would I be if I didn't protect you?"

Man? He was a boy. "I'm not afraid of whoever is behind this."

"I'm just saying we need to be careful, and winning another prize is going to make things worse."

The duck in her hand had a large number two written in black sharpie. "Then I don't want this stupid duck."

"Maybe we should hide it for now," he'd said. "We'll turn it in when things calm down. There's only a week left of camp. Let's be smart."

She'd handed him the duck, and he tucked it into his shorts pocket. "But we're not changing anything, right?" She remembered feeling vulnerable asking the question, but her feelings for him were big and powerful, and just thinking about ending things made tears sting and threaten.

Nate's eyes met hers like they had the night before. The

green flecks and dark lashes were familiar now. So was the feeling that he could actually see her—past her looks, past her wealthy parents, past her lack of confidence, and straight into the core of who she was. He'd leaned over and kissed her. That time she was prepared. She kissed him back, applying more pressure to send him the message that she really, really liked him. His breath was choppy again and he met her passion, his hands touching her hair, then her cheeks, then wrapping around her waist and pulling her so tight that her entire torso was pressed against his. That was what making out felt like. Like heat and force and closeness. Like the breathless excitement of first kisses and first loves.

"Brooke!" Her name was screamed in a high, panicky pitch. "Brooke! Are you okay?" Standing by the bridge was Libby and one of her followers.

How long had they been there? How much had they seen? Libby had her hand over her mouth, her eyes wide. "Get away from her!" she'd screamed at Nate, before turning her head toward the heart of camp and yelling louder than a fire alarm, "Help! Someone help!"

Nate jumped off the rock and calmly walked toward her. "What are you trying to do, Libby?"

"Oh my God!" she'd screamed. "Don't touch me! Help! Brooke, run!"

He wasn't even within touching distance, and nothing about his affect implied that he was about to touch her.

Brooke calmly joined him. The girl standing next to

Libby appeared to be both scared and invigorated but said nothing.

"Stop yelling, Libby. There's nothing going on here." Brooke did her best to sound authoritative, but what she truly felt was horror and confusion.

"I know you," Libby said, an excited gleam in her eye. "You would never break the rules like this. I know he was attacking you."

What rules? The no-fraternizing rule? Everyone broke that one. Or, at least, everyone had wanted to. "Libby. Stop. You're being ridiculous."

"We just want to make sure you're okay. Right, Karen Anne?"

The girl beside her nodded.

"Let's go," Nathan said.

Libby chuckled as they walked past. "Help!" she yelled again. "He's getting away!"

"You're awful." Brooke no longer tried to modulate her voice or keep her face passive. "How can you live with yourself?" She'd never hated anyone as much as she hated Libby Trotter. How could a person be so evil?

Libby had responded by switching her tune to sweet and innocent. "This is how you treat someone who's trying to help you?"

Karen Anne jutted out a hip and waited for an answer on Libby's behalf.

"You're not helping me and you know it." Brooke wanted to punch her in the mouth.

Three counselors came running.

"Libby is lying," Brooke had said as soon as they were within earshot. "Nathan didn't do anything."

"I can't breathe," Libby huffed, her hand on her heart like she was having palpitations. "I saw it. Zippy attacked her." It was like she knew that using the cruel nickname would intensify her accusation.

"He didn't attack me!" Brooke screamed. "Libby's making this up!"

The tall male counselor turned to Karen Anne. "Did you see what happened?"

The girl nodded, and Brooke saw Libby kick Karen Anne's ankle with her toe. "He attacked her," she confirmed, without looking them in the eye.

"You're lying," Brooke said with force, directly at her. "Tell them the truth."

Karen Anne kept her eyes on the ground and shrugged. One of the female counselors put a hand on Libby's back and guided her gently toward camp. "It's okay, honey," Brooke heard the counselor say. "It can be traumatizing to see something like that. You did the right thing." Brooke wanted to throw a rock at them.

Libby walked up the hill with the counselor, pretending like she was crying. The remaining counselor, a female who was more often seen doing paperwork than interacting with campers, had stayed behind with Brooke. "We're gonna need to call your folks."

That was it. Brooke's mother was informed that her daughter had been the victim of an inappropriate boy, and although Brooke had insisted that it was consensual, they had two witnesses giving a different story. It was assumed that Brooke would stay at camp, but Nathan was being sent home.

Brooke was angry. And, she was glad he'd taken the duck with him. No one would get the dance now, and as far as she was concerned, the whole camp didn't deserve it.

She'd spent the rest of the day like a zombie, doing her best not to interact with anyone aside from Jessa. Just before lights-out, an announcement came over the intercom. The duck hunt was over, and every team was invited to a dance party the following night. It was a slap in the face. They must've found the duck in his pocket. She pulled the musty covers over her head. He'd been so terribly misunderstood, and there was nothing she could do about it. The injustice of it burned her innards like hot embers and every intense emotion she felt was aimed directly at Libby Trotter.

Nathan Daugherty was not a thief, he wasn't a sex offender, or a liar, or a player, or a bully—he was simply the best guy she'd ever met. One who'd perpetually been looked down on because he was different. Libby Trotter was pure evil.

Brooke was immersed in her reverie as she wiped the mascara from under her eyes and applied a fresh coat of lipstick in the Saltwater Winery's employee bathroom. It wasn't until she washed her hands and the cold water hit that she was pulled back to the present. But she didn't want to be there yet. It felt too good to remember. The man Libby had taken from her was currently sitting on a barstool in the tasting room and he might very well tell her that he's married or terminally ill. He was the same man who'd risked more trouble in order to sneak back to camp the very night he was sent home. He was the same man who'd waited in the underbrush and flagged her down from the edge of the woods after dinner.

"Can we talk?" he'd asked. The pines were so thick, she could hardly see his face. It was a strange feeling. Despite being raised on one of the wildest, most uninhabited of the South Carolina sea islands, she was afraid of whatever else might be out there. They ran deeper into the darkness and stood facing each other, her back against a tree. Even with Nate as a defense, she still jumped at every little rustle and knock.

"My uncle came to get me," he'd said. "He took my cell phone as punishment. Then as soon as we got around the corner, he kicked me out of the truck—said it wasn't part of our deal for me to come home yet."

Brooke could barely see him, but she touched him on the chest, trying to express to him that it was okay.

"It's no big deal. I'm fine out here alone. But I didn't want to leave you that way."

He was planning to live in the woods until camp was over?

"The camp won't let me come back." Under his breath, he'd added, "They finally found their excuse to boot me out."

"I'm so sorry," she breathed.

"Don't be. None of this is your fault." She'd dropped her hand, but he found it again and put it back on his chest. "You are the one who—" He stopped. "It was your smile. It's always been about your smile."

She'd brought her face close to his so that he could see her better in the dark, but he didn't kiss her. He seemed to be taking in the moment, committing her to memory. "What do we do now?" she asked.

"Well, I'm not going to get you into any more trouble." From his shorts pocket, he pulled out something. "But I have something for you."

In his hand was a little yellow duck with a large number two written on its back. There was just enough light to see dark writing on the bright yellow surface. It was smooth and almost felt alive as he placed it on her palm.

"They didn't take the duck!" She'd been surprisingly thrilled to see it.

"Turn it over."

She saw more black writing on the bottom. "What does it say?"

"It's my phone number. I don't want to lose you,

Brooke."

"I don't want to lose you either." She'd never been more sincere in her life.

He leaned in and kissed her on the forehead. She lifted her chin and found his lips.

"I'll walk you to the edge of the woods," he said. "Get to your cabin before someone gets suspicious."

She really just wanted to stay there with him—even if it meant spiderwebs and glowing-eyed night creatures. But he was right. She had to go back. "I'll come find you tomorrow."

"Don't come looking for me," he'd said. "I'm gonna have to be far enough away to not get caught. Just call me when you get back home. You have my number now. I'll come see you. We'll figure it out."

"Nate?" she'd asked. "Is your uncle going to come back and get you?"

His voice dropped. "I'll catch a ride with somebody."

"Where do you live? Maybe my parents can take you. We can pick you up down the street from camp." In a matter of seconds, she saw it play out in her head. "I can make up a story. Your mama's car broke down."

She sensed he was shaking his head. "Probably not a good idea."

"As soon as we get our cell phones back from camp lock-up, I'll text you. That way you'll have my number and you can call me if you need a ride." She'd spontaneously leaned in and kissed him again. "I want to make sure you're okay."

"Don't worry about me," he chuckled in his nothing-can-bother-me way. "I'll be fine."

She had trusted that he would be. He was like what she imagined pioneers or adventurers would be like. He could handle anything. Nothing scared him.

She hid the duck in the front pocket of her backpack as soon as she got back to her cabin. It was strange how well she slept that night. It was as if Nate was her guardian in the woods, everywhere all at once, her shield against the evil of the world.

When she woke up the next morning, the tell-tale lump in the front of her pink backpack was flat. She tore through the bag, feeling sick to her stomach. The duck wasn't there. Someone had stolen it. Which meant Nate's phone number, her lifeline, was gone.

Chapter Sixteen

B ROOKE BLEW HER nose, took one last look in the Saltwater Winery mirror, fluffed her hair, and walked back into the tasting room. Nate sat straight and tall at the bar, waiting. "How bad is it out there?" she asked, trying to make her voice sound normal.

"I had to go around some downed trees, and water is still accumulating on the roads. I wouldn't expect many guests today."

"Does it seem like it's getting worse?"

"It'll be pounding this area all day."

The real question was, why did he choose to visit on a day like this? She almost asked him, but instead said, "I should text Jessa." She found her phone by the register and sent a quick note.

"Noelle told me you came by the mansion," he said. "You're looking for an apartment?"

Was he here on business? Was he desperate to rent that room? Brooke nodded. "You remember at camp how they used to tell us not to yuck someone else's yum? Well, my folks are yucking my yum. If I stay with them much longer I will lose my mind."

He watched her thoughtfully. She felt uncomfortably seen. "How long have you been living with your folks?" he asked.

"A couple of weeks." It seemed hardly long enough to be exasperated, unless your parents were Trig and Cornelia.

The interior door swung open and Jessa walked in. "It's getting bad out there—" She stopped. "Nate?"

"Hey, Jessa," he said. Like a gentleman, he stood and walked over to her, his hand extended.

"I am not shaking your hand, Nathan Daugherty," she said, moving in for a tight hug. "I can't believe you're here! Picked quite the day, didn't you?"

Jessa did a double-take when she saw Brooke. Her nose red, her mascara gone. "Brookie! Are you okay?"

"Yep." She nodded. "I'm just a weirdo."

Jessa looked back and forth between the two of them. "Is there anything I can help y'all with?"

Nate smiled warmly.

"Can you inhabit my body for a while?" Brooke said. "Help me pretend to be a normal person?"

Jessa chuckled. "He always did bring out the cheesecake in you."

Cheesecake? Brooke frowned at her.

"Something about him has always turned you sweet and mushy." She smiled knowingly at her friend.

Sweet. Brooke perked up at the word. There was something about Nate that made Brooke feel like the best, most authentic version of herself.

"That might be the nicest thing anyone has ever said about me," Nate said.

Just how pleased was he? Brooke couldn't tell. But it didn't seem to be the *I have something over you* or the *I know I have the powe*r, or *I'm going to use this to my advantage* kind of pleased. It wasn't the kind of pleased she was used to. "Mushy sounds like an overripe banana."

"But cheesecake is much more romantic," Jessa said. "Okay, y'all. I just came in here to tell Brooke that I'm closing up shop. No reason for us to be here today. I'll put a notice on the website, and you put the sign on the door. 'Kay?"

If only Brooke had a key, she and Nate could stay here together after Jessa left. Jessa pulled a ring of keys from her pocket and handed them to her like she'd just read her best friend's mind. "Turn out the lights and lock the doors up tight." She grinned. "I'll tend to the chickens and the goats. Don't let any of the cats inside. They've got shelter out back. Now, y'all take some time to catch up." She moved toward the door she'd just come from. "Hope to see you again soon, Nate!"

Somehow, the steady thrumming of the rain made the silence feel louder after Jessa left.

Brooke hoped Nate would speak first, but instead, he seemed perfectly comfortable in the awkwardness. It was almost like he was in some sort of dream state—calm, with the tiniest hint of a smile on his face. It had been an odd sort of déjà vu having all three of them alone in a room after so many years apart. "Can I pour you some wine?" Brooke asked.

"I'd like that."

"Since you came for the scuppernong, we'll start there." She had a bottle of Ocean Harvest Reserve chilling in the mini fridge. "I don't usually drink on the job, but since we're closed now, I figure it's okay." The cork came out easily. She set out two wineglasses and poured, then slid one in front of him, lifting hers for a toast. "Cheers."

"To—" he began. "To getting caught up."

Maybe he really was here for her instead of looking for a renter. "To getting caught up," she repeated, lightly clinking his glass and taking a small sip. He still didn't try to make conversation.

"I can't believe you're in Charleston now," she said.

He nodded, fixed on her like everything she said was amusing. Like it didn't matter what came out of her mouth, as long as it was directed at him.

"And you're back home," he said. "With a new hair-style."

"The real me." She attempted a giggle but was afraid that he hated her brown hair. Weren't men supposed to prefer blondes?

"I like it," he said. "You're more beautiful than ever."

The relief made her feel physically lighter. He had to have noticed that she was thinner now, her breasts filled out, her nose sharper. Apparently, he approved. "I don't know how much you know," she began. She had to tell him, there was no way around it. "But I dated Gates Lancaster for a while."

"I know," he said, sucking a healthy dose of wine into his mouth.

How? "We just broke up. That's why I'm looking for a place to live."

Finally, he took his eyes off her. They wandered around the room like he was seeing it for the first time. She wanted to ask him if he was dating anyone, but she didn't want to appear forward. Knowing full well that she was drinking it too fast, she took a large swig of the cold wine. It was calming her nerves, so she didn't care.

A flash of white cracked through the room, and the interior lights flickered and cut off with a thunderous clap. It had become so gray and ominous outside that there was little light coming through the window. Brooke audibly gasped.

"It's okay," Nate said in his always-calm voice. "The power will come back on."

"I'm coming over to sit with you," she said, feeling her way around the bar. He was only a silhouette now, but when she moved toward him, the smell was familiar. Not musky, not outdoorsy, just warm and somehow deeply known to her.

Yet she didn't know him. She used to know the kid version of him. Just like she'd changed, he surely had too. She found the chair next to him and sat. He moved his whole body toward her, his knee making contact with her thigh.

"Can I tell you something?" she blurted out. It was easier to talk to him in the dark, even though she was starting to be able to see him better now that her eyes were adjusting. "Someone stole the duck. The one with your phone number."

His spine straightened, and she felt his thigh stiffen.

"You never told me where you lived," she spoke fast, finally stating what she'd been dying to say for years. "And I couldn't find you on social media. I tried so many times." No matter what happened next, at least now she wasn't forced to live her whole life wondering if Nate thought she'd ghosted him. "When the duck was gone, I went out searching for you. I thought I was gonna die in those woods and got in a little trouble for it too." She chuckled. "I was a full-on missing person for almost twenty-four hours." The trouble that had felt life-ending at the time was nothing now.

Her eyes had adjusted to the dark enough to see him clearly. When his eyes met hers again, they were red-rimmed. "You couldn't find me." His deep voice echoed in the room. "I was afraid of that."

They sat in silence, the world outside blustering and blowing against their little bubble.

"Was it real, Nate?" she asked, heart pounding as fast as

the rain. "Or were we just stupid teenagers?"

"It was real," he said with grave seriousness. "Very, very real."

Brooke needed Nate to know that not a day went by that she wasn't thinking of some other way to find him. "I only had your name. I didn't have anything else to go on."

"It's my fault," he said.

She could barely see him, but she felt every movement, sensed every shift.

"I figured you'd be better off without me. My life was a mess." He breathed in sharply. "Camp was an escape from reality for me. I forgot for a while who I was, and then when I was kicked out, I remembered."

"Who you were? The Nate I knew was the kindest, bravest—"

"No, Brooke. He was a broken little kid. He's still broken." She could see the shimmer of his teeth—a sad smile in the darkness. "My people were unsafe."

"You mean your family?"

"I didn't have a family. Not really. Unless you count my uncle. All he did was give me a roof over my head— sometimes—and a world of hurt."

"I knew it had to be bad. But you never said anything."

"He's dead now. Overdose."

"Oh." She let that sink in. She'd wondered about his childhood since the first day she saw him. "What happened to your parents?"

"Are you sure you want to hear this now?"

"Please," she said.

He took a deep breath. "I don't like talking about it."

She reached over and gently took his hand.

"I was nine. My dad had just gotten his private pilot's license. He took my mama for a ride in a seaplane for their fifteenth wedding anniversary. They were headed to our property—the one that's now Camp Dogwood. He'd even hired a chef to come out and cook them dinner." With a flash and a whir, the lights began to flicker back on. Neither of them acknowledged it.

Brooke's heart stopped. He hadn't been lying. His family really had owned Camp Dogwood.

"The power company had just strung some electrical lines on the island across the way. I'm told that when he went to land, he flew straight into them. They crashed into the water. No one knows if they were electrocuted or if they drowned." His face was now brightly lit, and it felt rude, like his deepest pain was suddenly under a spotlight. Brooke wished she could snap her fingers and turn the lights back off.

"I wish you had told me. We were right there where it happened the whole time."

"I learned not to talk about it."

"Is that why you went to camp?"

He nodded. "At first. I wanted to be as close to them as possible."

She hesitated to ask but needed to know. "Are they still in the lake?"

"No, they were recovered. Granddad was still around then, and we had a funeral. They're buried out in the Summerville cemetery."

"Is that where you grew up?" She'd asked the question so many times, and he'd never answered.

"Nearby" was all he gave her.

She decided not to press. "So, how did you end up with your uncle?"

"I was placed with my mom's side of the family since Granddad was so old and my dad's folks lived in a retirement place in Florida. My uncle was the only sibling, and everybody thought I'd be better off staying in a familiar environment." Nate spoke with no emotion, like he was telling a story about someone else. He stood and reached for the bottle of wine. "He used to be a decent guy. But enough about that. It's depressing." He poured some of the golden liquid into her empty glass and then filled his own.

"I'm so happy to know more about you," Brooke said, her heart both dismayed for him and somehow gratified. "I want to know it all."

The wineglass stopped at his lips, and he set it down before taking a sip. "The truth is, I probably shouldn't be here," he whispered.

"Why?" The conversation was beginning to feel like the storm outside, turbulent and unpredictable. She braced herself to hear that he was married or had a girlfriend.

"I'm moving," he said. "I started a new business venture, and I just bought a place out in Atlanta."

"When?" She felt like everything hung on his answer. How much time did they have left together?

"Next week."

Even though the lights were back on, her world just went dark. But that was presumptuous of her. It's not like they could pick up where they left off all those years ago. They were different people now. They'd been kids back then. And all of these years later, she'd just gotten out of a relationship, and he—well, she didn't know anything about his love life. But she'd just found him, and now he was leaving.

"I think we both had to give up on each other years ago," he said. "But today, I knew it wouldn't be crowded here, and I knew you were out looking for a place to live alone, and I just figured—I mean, I just really wanted to talk to you."

She wanted to say that she never gave up on him. But that wasn't the truth. If she'd thought she could find him, she may not have stayed with Gates so long.

"Did you find someone else?" she asked. "Are you happy?" Maybe there was a woman in Atlanta.

"I tried." He pressed his lips together, then said, "None of them stuck."

The emotions from when she first saw him welled up again. She wanted to laugh or cry or both. But she forced it all down, holding her breath. She didn't dare speak.

"I figured you were happy with Gates," he said.

"How did you know about him?" she squeaked.

"It wasn't hard to find you both online." He paused. "He seemed good to you. He was a better choice."

"You're on social media?"

"With a fake name. First to make sure you were okay and then to keep up with my Florida grandparents. I never post. I like to consider myself a consumer rather than a purveyor of information." He chuckled.

"You mean a stalker." She laughed. All those years, and he was just a fake name away. "What's your online name?"

"Duck Hunter."

"I am so stupid," she said.

"You're the furthest thing from it." He paused. "You know, I overheard people yelling your name that day after I left camp. I knew you'd gone to look for me. I waited for you under the creek bridge."

"The bridge? I thought you went off in the other direction. When we said goodbye, you turned that way."

At the same time, they both said, "I should've known."

Brooke remembered everything with stark clarity. "So all that time I was moving as fast as I could into the woods, I was actually running away from you." The air in the room was still and humid. The rain had stopped, like one band of storms had passed, and another would soon be coming up behind it. The calm would be brief, and then the full strength would hit again. "It was all the details," she said.

"The tiniest things could have kept us together, but instead, the tiniest things kept us apart."

He looked like he wanted to say something but held himself back.

"What?" she asked.

The sky opened again and the rain pounded the roof with renewed fury, the wind blowing harder against the windows and doors. Nate Daugherty, now in his midtwenties, looked her dead in the eyes. He shook his head sadly, and the lights went dark once again. She couldn't see it, but she felt his hand on her arm, and as it moved to her back, she leaned into him. He pulled her into a hug like he was protecting her from the outside world, like he'd missed her, and like high school Nate was still alive and well inside of adult Nate. Brooke wanted to savor every sensation, every bit of closeness, and commit it to memory forever.

Chapter Seventeen

I F THE WIND outside was 50 mph, then the old feelings were coming back at two hundred. The chill bumps, the fluttery tummy, his name swimming around in her head. She snuggled into him, and he rested his chin on the top of her head. Hopefully, the lights wouldn't come back on. She kept flashing back to his face at camp, and it strengthened the connection between the boy she once knew and the man here now. This time, she knew more about life and how rare it was to find passion and connection, especially with someone with whom she shared a history.

"Oh my dear holy God," a voice bellowed from inside the room as the wide beam of a flashlight hit them.

Brooke jumped away from the safe embrace of Nate's arms. She hadn't even heard the door open.

"Y'all know this place is closed, right?" It was spoken in the most judgmental and salacious tone, but the excited look on Libby Trotter's face was pure joy. "Do I need to call Duke on y'all?"

"I work here, Libby," Brooke said, once again wishing her monogrammed tormentor would spontaneously combust. "And I have the keys to lock up."

"You call this working? You and Zippy, breaking the rules, just like old times," she sneered.

Nate stood and physically put himself between the two women, shielding Brooke against her. "Nice to see you again, Libby," he said. "We can take things from here." He forced her to back up just by kindly moving toward her.

Libby aimed the flashlight directly in his face. "I believe it is my duty to inform Mr. Bradley of these goings-on."

"Don't be stupid, Libby," Brooke said, wanting nothing more than to throw the half-full bottle of wine directly at her head. "We haven't done anything wrong."

Libby pulled out her cell phone, brazenly held it up, and snapped a blinding picture of the two of them.

"You do not have our permission to take a picture!"

"Don't need it. Now I have proof of your fraternization. And I should probably send it to your boyfriend, Gates. Do you think he'd be interested?" Her voice was as sweet and saccharin as fake sugar.

"You do realize that we're not in high school anymore, right?" Brooke said, feeling the adult in her gain strength over the bullied teenager still living in her bones. "You can stop this now."

"I am not the one caught grubbin' all over Zippy when I'm supposed to be working."

"Like you said, the winery is closed."

"Yeah, well, your legs should be too."

"That's it," Nate said. He walked confidently past Libby and opened the interior door. "Goodbye, Libby. You're leaving. We'll lock up."

Thankfully, she walked through the door with nothing more than a huff. Nate closed and locked it behind her.

"It's okay," he said, rushing back to Brooke. He took her in his arms again, his strength and the steady beat of his heart working to calm her. "Let's get out of here."

"I hate her," Brooke said, so angry that she was shaking. She held up the ring of keys. "Let's go."

Her car was the closest to the building, so after locking the exterior door to the tasting room, they ran through the rain and jumped in.

Despite the downpour beating against the vehicle and rushing down the windows in sheets, it was still somewhat warm outside. A flash of white in the distance caught Brooke's eye. "Did you see that?"

Nate leaned forward, straining to see through the water on the windshield. Brooke turned on the car and the windshield wipers so they could both get a better look.

"There!" she called. "Someone's in Amelia's garden." Inside the short picket fence between the crepe myrtles and tall flowering shrubs, a white-haired head bobbed around. "I think it's my nana."

Brooke put the car in Drive and pulled as close to the garden as she could, shining her headlights into the foliage. Sure enough, Nana appeared to be miles from home, in someone else's garden, dancing and spinning in the rain. Her hair wasn't in her signature black-ribboned ponytail but instead hung straight down to her shoulders, as thoroughly soaked as the bright floral muumuu that clung to her bony frame. "I need to go get her."

"Give her a second," Nate said. "She looks happy."

They both watched as Nana ignored the headlights and danced to whatever music played in her head. Brooke squinted when another person came into view. "Who is that?" It was Duke Bradley in a soaked white shirt. He had a black ribbon tied around his neck like Colonel Sanders. Nana's black ribbon. He twirled her and laughed as the rain dripped from his face. They were elderly children playing in the rain.

"We should be like that someday," Nate said.

She didn't know if he meant individually or together. But she agreed either way. As much as Nana was a little eccentric, she was also utterly dazzling.

Brooke put the car in Reverse and backed up slowly. She didn't want to ruin the moment for either of them. So...Nana and Duke. Was it romance? Weren't they too old?

"None of this was what I thought would happen when I came out here today," Nate said.

"What did you expect?" Brooke drove slowly out of the winery parking lot, leaving Nate's car behind.

"I guess I've learned not to have expectations," he said. "I just wanted to see you again before I left. After you remembered me at lunch, I guess I had hope."

The road had puddles but wasn't flooded out, so she kept driving down the length of Goose Island. Wind gusts shimmied the car, but her main worry was a tree falling. She drove carefully to avoid scattered limbs but felt compelled to keep going.

Nate never once asked where they were headed, but as they crossed one bridge and the next, it became obvious that she was heading to Camp Dogwood. "There's no electricity, of course," Brooke said, "but the side door is open. One of the cabins is unlocked too. I stayed there a couple of weeks ago."

"By yourself?"

She nodded. "After the breakup, I needed some time alone. So I went to the only place I could think of."

Nate didn't seem bothered at all. As a matter of fact, he acted like it was perfectly normal for a girl to head alone to a dilapidated ghost camp for some thinking time. Just like going there now in the middle of a severe thunderstorm had been a forgone conclusion.

"There's a Piggly Wiggly coming up," he said. "Food, wine, and indoor camping sound okay?"

"Hot dogs and s'mores?"

"Perfect."

Half an hour later, they pulled into the overgrown and abandoned grounds of the former Camp Dogwood.

She pulled up next to the old clubhouse building and the carved wooden sign still hung over the double doors: THE DOGHOUSE. Brooke put the car in Park.

The place felt like it belonged to them.

They sat in the car taking in the scene. It was eerie and gray. Trees swayed with the rain, their branches low and darkly wet, and the old brown structures appeared less sound, like the wind was causing them strain. In all the years Brooke had come to camp, they'd had many pop-up thunderstorms but rarely a day that was consistently as dark and ominous as this one. She and Nate were quiet, consumed with memories and mesmerized by the metronome-like intervals of the windshield wipers swiping back and forth, back and forth. They both stared off into the distance, down the hill to the half-sunk floating dock in the old swimmin' hole.

"Do you remember your parents well?" she asked.

"Sometimes I wish I didn't." The wipers whooshed across the windshield two more times, and she turned them off when the rain momentarily stopped. "I was happy with them."

Brooke didn't know what to say. She desperately wanted to help, to make him feel like the world was good and there were people who cared.

He had to know that she was listening intently, that she wanted to know more, but he chose to say, "Let's eat," instead. "While there's a break in the rain."

They carried two thin plastic bags of groceries, a small pack of firewood, and a gallon of water into the building as the sky reflected bright red onto the fast-moving clouds. Inside, The Doghouse was dirty and spider-infested, but overall uncannily familiar. The old cafeteria tables were still there with their attached circular seats and laminate tops. Even the corkboard with old photos and a printed list of teams remained on the entry wall. Whoever tried to sell the place must have had trouble, considering the island was a preserve and the property was limited as to what it could be used for. It was deserted now, stuck in a time gone by.

Cell phone coverage was spotty, which was probably good considering they drove out of range just as she texted her mother that she wouldn't be home for dinner that night and not to worry. She didn't say where she'd be, so there were sure to be follow-up questions. It felt like a benevolent act of God when a text from Duke came through informing her that they were hiring a cleanup service to deal with the aftermath of the storm and the winery would be closed for the next two days. Maybe, just maybe, she and Nate would stay there together.

Nate was unloading the groceries onto the kitchen counter when she held up her phone for him to read the message. He smiled like he, too, was privately thanking God for the extra time.

"What's your schedule?" she asked.

"I set my own hours." He held up the package of hot

dogs. "Hungry?"

"Starved." She hadn't eaten since breakfast. And, if anything in the world should make sense, it would be that intense emotions burned the equivalent of a feast's worth of calories. She deserved at least two hot dogs.

"I have a better idea," he said. "Are you willing to risk getting wet?"

"As long as I can dry off."

He put the items back into the bags and hung both over one arm. Then he grabbed the jug of water and said, "Follow me."

They fast-walked down the slope ending at the water, then turned left toward the bridge and the jumping rock. Water flowed quickly down what was usually a summertime-dry creek bed. Nate led her along the wooded path, and she knew they'd come out on the other side of the island—the beach side, by the lighthouse. She couldn't think of any shelter out there, any overhangs or structures where they might have a chance of getting a fire started in the rain. Even though the rain was just a sprinkle at the moment, her hair was saturated from water trickling off the pine needles overhead. Wetness flowed from her head, inside her shirt, and all the way down to her muddy tennis shoes. Every now and then, a wind gust blew a chunk of slick hair onto her face, where it stuck until she pulled it off. Nate had promised she'd be able to dry off, and she trusted him.

The way the woods opened up to the beach with the

lighthouse had always been her favorite. The tall concrete and brick structure stood staunchly at the end of the peninsula like the lifeguard of the sea. Even though the light had never shone all the years she'd lived nearby, it still felt like a beacon of hope and safety.

The sand was packed and wet with rain, making it easy to walk on. When they reached the lighthouse, Nate went straight to the thick gray metal door in the middle of the concrete platform. The door handle looked like a steering wheel, or the entry to some sort of jewelry safe or submarine. Rainwater dripped off the front of his hair, and he shook his head like a dog before spinning the wheel to the right three times, stopping it carefully, then once to the left, to the right again twice, and finally settling a quarter turn to the left. Then he pulled, and the door popped open with a metal-on-metal creak. Brooke audibly gasped.

He grinned proudly. "You remember when I said I would live alone until the end of camp?" he said. "I was here."

"What?"

"My granddad bought this way back when it was decommissioned. This was our vacation home."

"There's a house in there?"

"It's a mess," he said. "The windows have been broken out and nothing's been kept up." They stepped up into a large square room. "My granddad sold this place to Camp Dogwood after my folks died. He couldn't stomach being here anymore. The new owners didn't care much about the old lighthouse. There's a lot of damage, and not much left inside. But the little woodstove is still on the second floor where the light keeper used to live."

It all felt like such an adventure. She followed Nate around the brick room where plaster fell off the walls in chunks. "This was the bunk room." He pointed out two sets of old metal bunk beds with black-and-white-striped mattresses. In the middle of the room was a twisty black cast-iron staircase. "There are 114 steps that lead to the top."

She held on tight to the handrail and followed him up to a round wooden-floored bedroom. A small kitchen was separated only by the white hexagonal tile floor. "The bathroom is there," he said, pointing to a wooden door. "Next floor is the service room, which used to be where the Coast Guard would keep the light running, but later it was where Granddad put the electrical and water treatment units. Above that is the beacon and the widow's walk." He was already kneeling in front of the small cast-iron stove, putting the firewood they'd bought at the Piggly Wiggly inside. He struck a match, and in an instant, the place felt downright homey. It was nice to have the extra light instead of relying on their cell phones. It didn't matter that there was no furniture.

Brooke opened a bottle of wine and poured it into two plastic cups. They punctured their hot dogs with skewers and held them over the flames until they sizzled and glistened.

After stuffing them into a bun and adding ketchup for Brooke and mustard for Nate, they both took a bite. "I wish I'd known about this a couple of weeks ago."

"How long were you here alone?" he asked.

"I made it a full week. And I'm surprised I lasted that long. I thought about you living in the woods, and figured if you could do it, I could do it." She laughed. "Little did I know."

"Were you scared?"

"A little." The truth was, she'd been terrified. "Full disclosure? I slept in my car. And I went to Walmart and got bear spray and window coverings. But at least I knew enough to use buckets of water to flush the toilet."

"You'd be surprised at how many people don't know that little trick." She loved how straight and white his teeth were when he smiled.

She pointed at herself. "Southern girl right here."

The only reason she knew anything about survival, and broken toilets, was thanks to Dottie. If it had been left up to her parents, she still wouldn't know how to do laundry.

"As friends, Brooke. And I mean that. No pressure. No ulterior motives." His voice sank deeper than she'd ever heard it before. "Would you stay here with me tonight?"

She wasn't sure she wanted to just be friends. She wanted to languish in his arms, snuggle into his chest whether it was in the car or on a moldy mattress in an old lighthouse. She wanted to kiss him at least one more time in her life.

"I don't want either of us to get hurt," he said.

She knew exactly what he meant. "Because you're leaving."

"Yes."

He was right in some ways, but wrong in others. If they stayed together, her heart would open up to him. It didn't matter if they talked all night or jumped into the sack like honeymooners. Her heart was already softening, remembering, wanting.

"Let's stay," she said. Three weeks ago when she fled to Camp Dogwood, she thought she was saying goodbye to it for good—that it would eventually be torn down and all of the memories she'd made with Nate would be lost.

Yet there they were, making more.

Chapter Eighteen

B ROOKE HAD FORGOTTEN how good hot dogs were. Their clothes and hair were beginning to dry as they held the second round of skewered meat over the fire. "Do you know what I miss most about camp?" Brooke asked.

"Chiggers?"

She laughed and shook her head.

"Oh, I know. Spaghetti nights."

"I swear they used roadkill to make the meat sauce."

"That was the rumor. And the cook had no idea that Italian seasoning was a thing."

"Or salt." She laughed. "The noodles were mushy and tasted like water."

The hot dogs actively sizzled. She handed him her skewer and set two buns on a paper towel.

"I give up," he said. "What do you miss the most?"

"The duck hunt."

"That was my favorite too."

They used the buns to pull the meat from the stick and added their condiments.

"I didn't go back my senior year," she said. "None of us

did. Not Jessa or Gates or Libby."

"I know," he said, taking a bite.

She chewed and swallowed, afraid of what he was going to say before he said it. "You do?"

"I was finally allowed back."

"No." She set her food down. "No, no, no."

He nodded sadly.

"Why did everything go wrong for us? Why did we keep missing each other?"

"Timing."

She was lost in what he'd just said—in the fact that they could have had a summer together without Gates or Jessa or Libby. Her whole life would have been different. "Where did you go afterward? What have you been doing all of these years?"

"I've been trying to right some wrongs."

"Well, that's vague," she laughed.

He stuffed the rest of the hot dog in his mouth and smiled slyly. Then he held up a finger and went down the spiral stairs at astonishing speed. He came back up seconds later dragging one of the old black-and-white-striped mattresses. He placed it on the floor in front of the fire, and she crawled over to sit on it. He put his legs on either side of her. "I'll be your chair," he said, sitting firmly so she could lean her back against his chest. She finished eating, her tummy and her heart perfectly content.

Spatters of rain blew in through the broken windows,

but it wasn't enough wetness to bother them. If the wind changed direction, it could become a problem, but it felt like the storm would soon blow over. Thankfully, like so many Southern summer storms, it was still warm, and despite the humidity, the encroaching night didn't portend too much misery. "I grew up south of Broad," he began. "The first nine years of my life were perfect. My dad was a lawyer, so he had everything in order. When they passed, I should've been taken care of. I should've been able to go to college and have enough inheritance for a good start in life." He spoke softly and matter-of-factly.

"But then, your uncle."

"Then my uncle."

"You've been in Charleston this whole time?"

"He sold that house the first year my folks were gone. Put the money into property not far from Goose Island. Had dreams of building himself a big house and raising horses, and at that time I had no idea that he was using my money to do it. We lived in a trailer on the property. No neighbors, no friends, just him and me all the time." He wrapped his arms tightly around her.

She wanted to thread her fingers into his but placed her hands on top of his instead. "How bad was it?"

"You know, the usual stuff that happens when someone gets a bunch of money they don't know how to handle. Gambling, drugs, and the next thing you know, he's lost everything but that terrible trailer, and he hates me like I was the one who did it to him."

She picked up his hand and kissed it.

"Back then, I thought maybe some of my old Charleston friends might be going to camp, and it was like a switch flipped inside of me. I had to figure out a way to get here. I have never felt so much determination in my life. It was like Camp Dogwood was my grandparents and my parents all mixed together. I thought it would somehow save me. Which is ridiculous, of course."

Brooke wanted to cry for him—for the little boy who showed up to camp with nothing but a bad suit and an almost-empty plastic bag.

"How'd you do it? Did you get a scholarship?"

"Not that first year. I made a deal with my eighth-grade teacher. I had an idea, and she said she would be my first investor. She drove me to Walmart and paid for three boxes of those Otter Pops—the ones that come liquid in the plastic—and a little red cooler. My uncle had a deep freeze outside the trailer where he kept his deer meat, and I put the popsicles in there. I took that little red cooler to school every day and filled it with ice from the machine in the teacher's lounge. Then I sold the popsicles for a dollar each at the end of the day." He laughed. "That first day, I made twenty-seven bucks."

"Really? That's incredible!"

"I tried to give it all to that teacher, to pay her back, but she refused to take it. Then every week, she'd show up with more Otter Pops for me."

"I love that woman. Don't know who she is, but she deserves an award."

She felt his body soften and the hard edge left his voice. "She does. She deserves everything good in the world."

"What's her name?"

He waited a beat before he said, "Mrs. Warter. Cornelia Warter."

Brooke jerked away so she could face him straight on. "No. That can't be. My mother?"

He nodded.

"You went to Whitehill Middle School?" All of those years he'd been right down the road at the only other nearby school? And he knew her mother? Cornelia helped him? *Cornelia?* It seemed so out of character. Brooke's brain whirled. "When did you know it was me? I mean, when did you know that my mother was that teacher?"

"I didn't put it together right away. I mean, I knew Mrs. Warter had a daughter named Anna Brooke, because she talked about you all the time. But I didn't know it was you until years later. Then I just figured I should've known. You were the best girl in all of camp, so of course your mother was Mrs. Warter."

Brooke was floored. Her mother knew Nate, and Nate actually liked Cornelia. "Did you say my mother talked about me all the time?"

"Always. Every day. You were the same age as us, so she

would use you as an example—what shows you were watching, what games you were playing, what homework you were assigned, and things like when you went to New York City for Christmas and got lost in Times Square, and when you finally got up on water skis after trying for years. She told us about the time you tried to make them boxed macaroni and cheese for dinner and you somehow burned the noodles, so you served them Cheerios with the packet of cheese dust sprinkled on top. I thought you were the smartest, happiest, luckiest girl."

"You remember all that?" There was no way he could have known those things unless her mother truly did talk about her. Yet when she looked back on her childhood, she felt like she was always in the way or causing them problems. Was it possible that she wasn't? So much had changed with her perception of her mother in the past week that she didn't know what to think anymore. But what did it matter if her mother said nice things about her? It was probably just like keeping the drapes open at suppertime—all for show.

"I lived for those stories about you," he said. "You had everything that I was missing."

Her phone buzzed, but she ignored it. It'd been steadily buzzing since the second hot dog when her phone seemed to suddenly connect with a network. She probably should check in case her mother was freaking out. What would Cornelia think if Brooke told her she was at an abandoned lighthouse with Nathan Daugherty? She grabbed the phone off the floor.

"*I'm almost there.*"

It was the final text from a long thread beginning with Gates saying that no one knew where she was, her mother was worried, he'd tracked her to Camp Dogwood.

Now he was on his way.

Her perfect night was about to be ruined. She dreaded saying the words, "Nate, we have to go." She handed him her phone and watched his face fall as he read it.

"He's not your boyfriend anymore."

"It's not just him."

"Yeah, but you can call your mother so she won't keep worrying."

"I want to stay here with you. I promise, I do. But Gates and I just broke up. And we're still friends. He's been driving for more than two hours now. I can't just send him away because I'm with another guy."

"I will do whatever you ask of me," Nate said calmly. "But if it was an ex-girlfriend of mine, I would kindly ask her to leave."

Brooke had an idea. "*I'm fine,*" she texted. "*Please don't come here.*" "Maybe this will work."

Her phone rang immediately. "Hi, Gates," she said, apologizing to Nate with her eyes.

"Your mother is completely freaking out. Not only have you been missing for I don't even know how many hours, but your grandmother is missing too. Your mama is about to call the sheriff."

"I told her I wouldn't be there."

"Well, she didn't hear you."

"Hold up." Brooke checked the text she sent her mother and saw that it had never been delivered. "Shoot."

"Why are you at the old camp? This place is out in the boonies!"

"Gates, I'm safe. I'm good. You can stay in the guest room at my parents' house. I'll see you tomorrow."

"What are you up to, Brooke?"

"Nothing. And Nana isn't missing—she's with Duke."

"Not true. Duke hasn't seen her either."

"What?" Now Brooke was alarmed.

"Listen, your whole family is going crazy. You have got to come back."

"Okay." She shot another look of sad apology at Nate before saying, "Turn around and go back to Goose Island. I'll meet you there." She threw her phone into her purse.

"You're leaving," Nate said.

"I have to. Nana's missing." She began cleaning the remnants of their meal. "I'll take you back to your car."

He was silent as he worked beside her, throwing trash into the thin plastic bag and finishing his wine in one large gulp.

"Are you mad?" she asked.

"Of course not."

They were soaked again as they trekked back to her car.

On the beach, rain beat sideways into them, stinging their faces. It seemed worse somehow to be out in the weather without something to look forward to. Just like always, leaving Camp Dogwood meant going back to the real world, and the real world wasn't always the best place to be.

When they pulled into the Saltwater Winery, they were shocked to see so many cars in the parking lot. They counted seven, including Trig and Cornelia's maroon Cadillac. Fred's falling-apart pickup truck was there, Dottie's food truck, as well as Jessa's old Acura, Gates's black BMW, and a shiny gold car Brooke had recently learned to recognize as Libby's. Sam and Allie were both in bright orange raincoats walking up from the beach with Buttercup in the lead, tugging on them to move faster.

"Is this a surprise party?" Strangely, in an alternate universe, it did feel like everyone should be celebrating Nate's return with her. He was definitely worth a party. "Nana must be here." She parked and pulled her phone from her purse. There were text messages from everybody, including Dottie and Jessa. They'd all been out looking for Nana and ended up at the winery. "Will you come inside with me?" she asked Nate. Since both Gates and Libby were there, it seemed like he should have a choice.

"If you want me to."

She hadn't really thought it through when she asked. Bringing Nate into a room with Libby was probably okay— he could help manage her. But waltzing him in knowing full well that Gates was there was stupid. She'd have to introduce Nate to her parents too. One of whom he already had a relationship with. So, that was probably going to be a big deal. All of this ran through her head as they splashed their way through weedy, gravelly puddles to the front door.

There were raincoats and umbrellas and muddy foot-prints all over the tasting room and gift shop. Everyone was inside, including Nana and Duke. Libby sat on a stool in the middle of the bar with Nana's arm around her shoulders. She was crying.

What in the crazy mixed-up outrageous world was going on? Wasn't Nana supposed to be the one in distress? Instead, Jessa was in full compassion mode patting Libby's back. Noting that Nana was safe, Brooke scanned the room for her parents. Cornelia was holding a marble cheese board, showing the price tag to Trig. They'd barely noticed that their daughter had just stepped into the room with a man. God forbid she should interrupt their shopping.

Gates noticed Brooke and Nathan first. He had the same look on his face that he had when he finally came back to their apartment after missing his surprise party—like he was shocked at her betrayal.

"What is going on?" Brooke asked no one in particular.

By now, Cornelia had diverted her attention. "If you would check your messages, you would know that we have found your grandmother." Her voice changed from repri-manding parent to devastatingly disappointed when she said,

"And now we have found you too." Brooke was surprised she didn't add *with a man*. Her parents had long ago made it clear that they wanted Gates as a son-in-law.

"Mother, this is Nathan Daugherty."

Cornelia might have popped something internally with the way her face went slack with shock. She squinted up at him. "My Nathan?" As soon as she said it, the stiffness she always held in her joints relaxed, and a smile lit her face. "Oh my word. You're a grown man. Are you okay now? Are you good?"

If Brooke's feelings for Nate weren't already hovering in the no-oxygen part of the atmosphere, they skyrocketed past the moon the minute Nate took her mother into the sweetest, most reverent hug. "Hi, Mrs. Warter," he said.

"Who is that?" Nana yelled over the table of books and knickknacks for sale.

"I have been wondering about you for years," Cornelia said as they pulled apart. "Let me get a good look at you." She gazed lovingly at his face, taking it all in. Then she turned to Brooke. "If I'd had my way, this young man would have been your adopted brother."

"This is him?" Trig asked from his protective spot behind his wife.

Cornelia nodded. "This is him."

Chapter Nineteen

SOMETHING ABOUT THE word *brother* must have made Gates back off. He stood behind the bar across from Dottie, Jessa, and Libby. He looked either sad or thoughtful, Brooke couldn't tell which, but he was clearly watching Cornelia hold on to Nate's arm like he was the relative she'd been pining to see for years. He had to know. He had to know that Brooke had feelings for Nate. He might even know that she'd always had those feelings. Gates had been there for everything.

Trig and Cornelia asked questions and gushed over Nathan, while Brooke's attention was turned to the drama at hand: Libby.

Jessa and Dottie were firmly on Libby duty and could barely even wave hello. Nana, however, easily abandoned the sobbing girl. She was never one to follow social cues anyway.

"What's wrong with her?" Brooke asked.

"Oh, first it was the barn venue for her wedding—the thing came down in the storm like it was made of toothpicks," Nana said. "Then something about her fiancé suggesting that they postpone the wedding got her all pissy and she ran off."

"So, she came here?" Things were starting to make a little more sense now.

"Well, yes, and anyhow, I decided to come into work and I found her," Nana said.

"You came into work?" Brooke asked, as if Nana had any work to do while the winery was closed. Or even when it was open. "So you were never lost." That meant Brooke could've stayed at the lighthouse with Nate. Why did all of the details keep working against them?

"Oh, heavens, no. I wasn't lost. Duke said he was thinking of adding some baked goods for sale at the gift shop, and I thought it best to come into the store for inspiration."

"I never said that," Duke grumbled.

Nana smiled sweetly at him. "But you agreed with me."

He nodded, unable to keep the hint of a smile from his face.

"As I was saying," Nana addressed the larger audience of Trig, Cornelia, Fred, Duke, and Brooke—everyone except the group hovering around Libby, "Duke is considering adding some baked goods to the gift shop. Now, everyone knows that drying a muscadine is sticky business, but I believe I can substitute muscadine raisins for the Medjools in my date bar recipe, and I promise you that people would kill their own mothers for a bite of one."

Cornelia flinched.

"I meant it as a surprise," Nana said in a tone designed to

leave every human in the room feeling guilty. "Leave it to y'all to converge on me and spoil everything."

"If you would take your cell phone with you, then we wouldn't have to worry the way we do," Trig pointed out. "Please stop leaving it in your cottage."

"Now, look here," Nana said. "If I am trying to get away from you people for some free time, it makes no sense at all to bring with me the one thing that handcuffs me to everybody. I will decide when I will and will not bring along that hateful thing."

"Brooke," Dottie called. "Come on over here, darlin. We need a word."

Brooke took a long breath and walked to the bar. Dottie reached for her hand and pulled her closer. "Libby needs our help," she began, one hand holding tight to Brooke and the other rubbing circles on Libby's arched back. Libby's head was down, her face covered with a handful of small drink napkins. "Tell her, Jessa."

Brooke could tell Jessa was trying to choose her words carefully. She looked for affirmation from Gates, who stood behind the counter like a bartender, before she began. "So, not only is Libby's wedding venue now gone, but most of her bridesmaids have had other things come up." She quirked her eyebrows at Brooke in a *do you understand what I mean?* sort of way. "I think that's bound to happen when you hold a wedding on a holiday like the Fourth of July." Jessa made it sound like people dropping out of a wedding at the last minute was perfectly normal. "People have other plans."

Libby lifted her head long enough to say, "They don't have other plans."

"Well, I'm sure they have a good reason," Jessa said.

Brooke could tell from the look on Dottie's face that she was trying to hold her tongue. That didn't last long. "Nope. Nope. We are not doing a little cha-cha dance around this." Dottie swung her pointer finger back and forth. "It ain't helpful. Let's deal with the truth of it. Libby, did your bridesmaids ditch you because you started acting like an entitled bride? Like you were the queen and everyone else was there to please you?"

Libby nodded without lifting her head.

"You got too big for your britches, and now everything's exploding in your face like a shook-up can of Pepsi-Cola."

Libby nodded again.

"And how much did their dresses cost?"

"Three hundred and fifty dollars," Libby said quietly through her tear-soaked napkins.

"Uh-huh." Dottie shook her head. "And I bet you expected them to have parties for you too."

Libby nodded again into her palms.

What kind of masterful manipulation was Libby trying to pull off? Brooke had never seen the girl cry before, and now she's sitting here weeping in front of a crowd? It wasn't right.

But it did seem like she was telling the truth. For once.

"I guess there's no way to have the wedding here at the winery," Jessa said. "The band is booked, and we're almost sold out of tickets for the Independence Day party."

Brooke didn't realize that Nate was directly behind her until he spoke. "You might be able to have it at Camp Dogwood," he said. "We've got a month to get it ready."

We? The word made her simultaneously excited and pissed-off. She would work on anything with Nate, even if it was for Libby. But she wasn't sure why he was being nice to *her*.

"Yes, and this group is very creative," Dottie said to Libby. "We could make it a real nice wedding in a month."

Libby lifted her head.

"And Jessa and Brooke will be your bridesmaids," Dottie added.

If Brooke had access to eyeball laser beams, she would have shot them directly into Dottie's head.

"Oh, how lovely," Cornelia stepped in. "When I was in my twenties, I was a bridesmaid every wedding season for years and years."

Dottie shot Cornelia a look of disgust.

Brooke spun around. Her mother, Trig, Duke, and Nana were all watching the scene unfold. The best course of action at the moment was to stay silent. She didn't have to refuse to be in the wedding right then and there. She could refuse later when no one was around to try to convince her otherwise. But one thing she knew for sure was that there was no way she would put on an ugly dress, especially a $350 one, and stand up in front of a bunch of people pretending to be happy for a girl she couldn't stand.

"My granddaughter will not be in your wedding," Nana announced like she was reading Brooke's mind.

"Nan!" Brooke said, shooting her a *shut up* look.

"There is certainly no need to play games," Nana reprimanded her.

Of all people, Brooke wanted to say. Nana was the number one game player, attention seeker, time waster. "I can handle this, Nana."

"Trigger? Why is my granddaughter turning on me?"

"I'm not turning on you!" Brooke just didn't want to face off with Libby under these conditions.

"Radar's showing we're at the tail end of the storm," Trig said, looking up from the app on his cell phone. "Cornelia," he said. "Shall we?"

Yes, Brooke thought. *Please leave.* She noticed how Dottie watched her parents carefully—did Dottie wish she had a husband to monitor the radar app too? Dottie sucked in her lower lip, hiding the missing tooth, before placing her hand on Libby's back again. "Now, Libby, you need to go on home and set things right with your man. We've done enough fixin' here to get your wedding back on track."

Libby had since lifted her head and glanced around the room, but not once did she lay eyes on Brooke. It was like Brooke wasn't there.

"Nana, you're coming with us," Cornelia said. "Anna Brooke, you and Gates will follow us home, and Nathan—"

"The hell I am," Nana interrupted. She had put on her oversized yellow slicker with the hood pulled up over her wild white hair. She grabbed hold of Duke's hand. "I have baking to do."

Duke didn't appear indifferent anymore. He looked— what was it? Guilty? Sort of. But also surprised. And as his eyes moved back up from confirming that her small hand was indeed holding tight to his, he appeared downright pleased.

Fred stood in a corner, chuckling and taking it all in. The lawyer turned island gas station owner had clearly moved back for times just like this.

"Do not come looking for me," Nana said. "I mean it."

Trig looked perturbed, but it was Cornelia who said, "Let her."

"I'm so sorry, Nan. I don't know what got into me," Brooke said. She was mad at Libby, and she'd taken it out on her eighty-year-old grandmother. "Truly. I didn't mean it."

"Oh, just do whatever it is your mother says," Nana said. "I'll try to behave myself."

"Thank you." Brooke gave Nana a quick hug. "I'll be home soon."

"Yes, I expect you will," Cornelia replied as if her expectations were direct orders. "With Gates. I will not have him driving back to Savannah in this weather."

Gates shrugged, and Brooke could tell he was uncomfortable. No one knew how to properly handle the current situation.

"And Nathan?" Cornelia asked. "Where are you living now?"

"Charleston," he answered.

"Oh, bless," she said. "You are nearby. Please come visit us. Either tonight or tomorrow, or any time at all. I must know everything that has happened in your life since I last saw you."

What would Cornelia think if she knew that at that very moment, Brooke's feelings for Nate were growing inside of her like a kudzu vine—at the rate of one foot per day.

"Yes, ma'am," Nate said, leaning down to hug her again. "I would love to."

"Bye," Dottie said with a thicker accent than usual. "Y'all take care now. Fred, you are free to go too." She pointed to Gates, Jessa, Nate, and Brooke. "Don't y'all four move." Then she took Libby by the arm and walked her to the door that Trig still held open. "Drive safe now, Libby. And let Jessa know when you get it all worked out."

Libby agreed, and actually followed the group tiptoeing over the soaked ground and covering their hair from the sprinkling rain out to her car without arguing, blaming, or trying to make herself look like something other than a distressed bridezilla who'd just been hit hard over the head by karma.

"Well, now," Dottie began after closing the door behind her. "I have been waiting for this moment."

"Mama, it's going on nine o'clock. I think we'd all like to go home now," Jessa said.

"This won't take but a second. I have been dying to get the four of y'all in a room together for years. Let me have my moment.

"There's something powerful about that camp," she began. "Something I can't put my finger on. But y'all went there and it got all spirally and out of whack. First off, my nose was right. Libby is hiding something. I felt it in my forehead this time."

That meant it was scary and must be taken seriously.

"Then why are you having us be in her wedding, Mama?" Jessa asked.

"Because it will help. What happened here today is already helping."

"Helping what?" Gates asked.

"Helping Libby. Why do you think she acts the way she does?"

Brooke knew the answer to that question. "Because she's spoiled and entitled and judgmental and hateful and—"

Dottie was shaking her head. "That's all a cover. Don't ask what's wrong with somebody, ask what happened to them."

"Not everybody has some deep dark trauma that makes them horrible, Mama," Jessa said. "I think Libby likes being that way."

Dottie had zoned out. It was like there were irises on the

backside of her eyeballs looking inside her own head. "She's two," she said. "There are two sides of her. One side that likes being on top—it's the side that tries hard to forget about the other one. The second is the side that's been held down. Held down hard. That side struggles to be seen."

"But she's getting married," Brooke said. "James must see her. Isn't that enough?"

"No one sees everything," Dottie said. "Especially the things we hide."

"Well, then, she needs to stop hiding whatever it is," Gates said, always the one to avoid gray areas. "Seems like that would solve the problem."

Nate muttered, more to himself than to anyone else, "I wonder who hurt her." If anyone in the world could understand what it was like to be perceived as one thing, when inside you were another, it would be Nate.

"Exactly," Dottie said. "I'm telling you. She might be bitchy, but she's not evil."

Jessa and Brooke caught eyes, and Brooke knew that in all her sweet goodness, Jessa would not only be a bridesmaid, but she would do it with a genuine smile and the most helpful, celebratory attitude. It was exactly the way Brooke was trying to be. If she behaved as if she was as sweet as Jessa, maybe the feelings would follow. Maybe she could actually learn to be happy for Libby. She would be doing it for herself, for her own growth, not for Libby's appeasement.

"Fine," Brooke said. "I'll be in the wedding."

Chapter Twenty

THE GREEN WOODED island smelled clean and fresh, like rainwater and pine. Nate and Gates both opted to drive home after the unplanned winery get-together, so the fresh morning meant relief rather than tension. It was the embodiment of a brand-new day: sunny and recovering from the previous day's disturbance. By midmorning the sun would dry up most of the puddles and the humidity would be higher than the fluffy white clouds. Brooke and Cornelia sat at the kitchen table. Cornelia had prepared two footed glass dessert bowls filled with Greek yogurt, honey, and fresh berries. Duke confirmed via text that Nana would not be joining them that morning.

"Did you know that some of the highest STD rates are found in retirement homes?" Brooke asked, collecting a spoonful of blueberries.

"Now, why would you tell me such a thing?" Cornelia giggled despite the horrified look on her face. "I suppose she might as well have some fun while she still can."

"It's not hurting anyone, right?"

Cornelia smiled at her daughter and popped a raspberry

into her mouth. "Might actually be helping someone."

Brooke covered her face. "I don't want to think about it." They shared a rare moment of laughter together, then lapsed into silence. "Hey, Mother?"

Cornelia looked up from her quest to find another berry she could pinch without getting honey or yogurt on her fingers.

Brooke had to say it. It was too big a secret to keep bottled up. "I saw you the other day in Charleston."

Cornelia froze but took only a second to recover. "I thought we were going to talk about Nathan Daugherty. Don't you have questions? We haven't had a chance to talk about him yet."

"Yes, but Mother, did you hear what I just said?"

"Nathan was a special boy. He was in my eighth-grade class."

"Really? You're not going to acknowledge it? I saw you in Charleston with a man."

Cornelia calmly sipped her coffee. "His parents died in a plane crash, and I was just beside myself with worry for that boy. Your father and I talked about him at the supper table every night for weeks and weeks. I even made some inquiries into guardianship."

"Trig agreed to that?"

"Well, of course. He's always wanted a boy."

The words felt like a punch in the stomach, even though Brooke had always suspected it was the case.

"We didn't get very far," Cornelia said. "Nathan had a guardian, and we didn't have any claim to him. You know how those things go."

Brooke had no idea how those things went. "Well, that's too bad. He could've used some help." Nate getting help from her family meant they would have grown up together like brother and sister. Sort of. In a nonbiological kind of way. What would that have been like, living in the house with Nathan? Having him sleep in a room next to her? Christmas mornings. Sicknesses. Family vacations. Crawfishing in the creeks. Swimming all day in the surf. Going to the same high school. Eating the same packed lunches. She suddenly felt like she'd missed so much. She wanted to do all of that with Nate, and more.

"He seemed good yesterday. He was so tall and handsome. Well-dressed too," Cornelia said. "I had forgotten about his cerebral palsy. The limp suits him, though, doesn't it?"

So, that was why he had a limp. Brooke had never even thought to ask.

Cornelia was wistful. "All that worrying I did over him was for nothing, I guess."

"He's good now," Brooke pointed out. "But he wasn't then."

"I declare. All this time and we never put it together that you two were friends at camp."

"No, we never did." Maybe if she and Cornelia had a

relationship like Jessa and Dottie, they would have shared pieces of their lives and figured out that they were both worrying about the same boy. But Cornelia's lips were sealed tighter than a home-canned mason jar—one with botulism swelling the lid and threatening to explode.

"Can we talk about what I saw now?" Brooke pressed.

Cornelia stood with her coffee cup and moved to deposit it in the sink. She paused before she clinked it onto the porcelain bottom and filled it with water. "I assure you, things are not as they may have appeared."

"It looked pretty clear to me. Who was that guy?"

"Anna Brooke, there are things about my life that you have not been privy to. Do you understand? You are my daughter, not my best friend."

"Don't you think it's time we became friends? Isn't that what happens once your kid leaves and starts a life on her own?"

Cornelia pursed her lips.

"I am only staying here temporarily," Brooke added. "And who knows where I'll end up this time."

"And you want to be my friend?" Cornelia put her perfectly manicured dusty rose-fingernailed hand over her heart.

"Cut it out, Mother. Of course I do."

"Well, then, as my friend, I expect you to keep this in the strictest confidence."

"I'm not planning to tell Trig, if that's what you're worried about."

"Trigger already knows."

Brooke was not expecting that. "About that other man?"

"Andrew is his name. And yes."

Oh, Lord. She was about to be told that her parents were divorcing. "Andrew? Are you in love with him?"

"I have always been in love with Andrew."

Here it comes. She braced herself.

"But he hasn't been my boyfriend since 1986."

"You used to date him?"

"Way back when. He was my first love."

"I thought Trig was your first love."

"Now, why would you think that?"

"I don't know. You never talked about anybody else."

"Are you going to talk about Gates once you're married to someone else?"

"Probably not."

"Exactly. And Trig does not like to hear about my old boyfriends."

"But Mother, you kissed him."

"Yes, I did. And I do not regret it. I would do it again."

It didn't seem like Cornelia to be so brazen. She'd loved someone else? She would kiss him again?

"Did you tell Trig that you kissed him?"

"You can wipe that look off your face, young lady. Andrew is dying. He has pancreatic cancer. He was in town to tie up some loose ends, and I was one of them." Cornelia looked away, pretending to look for something in the upper cabinets. But Brooke knew she was pulling herself together.

In her mind's eye, Brooke could still see the kiss clearly—the tall man looking directly into her mother's eyes, so serious, before pulling her tightly into a deep kiss. A goodbye kiss? She'd seen passion between them for sure. Had it been raw emotion rather than sexual chemistry? If Nate, or even Gates, were dying, she might do the same thing. She'd once loved both of them. And if she had to say goodbye, it would probably look just like what she'd witnessed between Cornelia and Andrew. She let out a long breath. "I'm so sorry, Mother. I guess I didn't know what I was seeing."

"Do you know what we do, Anna Brooke? All of us. We take bits and pieces of things we think we know, and we fit them together into something that makes sense. We might be missing half the facts, because we don't know what we don't know, right? As a matter of fact, I think we are usually missing a good portion of the information. But we just plow on ahead, thinking that the puzzle is complete when it was actually us who filled in the empty spaces with our own imaginings. Then we have the audacity to walk around declaring that the puzzle is complete and that we have the definitive answer, when many of the pieces are fiction, pure conjecture."

Cornelia was right. Brooke had made a judgment about what she saw and decided the worst was true when the fact was, she had none of the details. Her mind immediately went to Libby. "I'm probably missing half of Libby's puzzle and filling in the missing pieces with my guesses. I don't really know much about her."

"You know I have no patience for girls like her. And I don't give a flip what she's been through, missing pieces or not. She's still responsible for how she treats others."

"Yeah." Brooke thought for a second. "I mean, Nate had a terrible childhood, but he doesn't go around bullying people."

"Right. Some girls have no excuse. They just decide to be terrible."

"Well, either way, now I'm stuck in her wedding."

"And you'd better not try to outshine her. Dim your light, baby girl. That's the only way to survive it."

"Do you think she was acting? You know, with all of the crying yesterday. Was it fake?"

"I wouldn't put it past her."

It was the strong smell of Chanel No. 5 that made both women turn toward the back entrance to the kitchen. How long had Nana been leaning against the doorframe looking taller than normal? She had a peaceful little smile on her face that matched her soft pink boudoir set. Her French-twisted white hair matched her white feathered slippers, and the effect was that of a 1940s movie star.

"Grace!" Cornelia said. "I didn't think we'd see you this morning."

"Nana, you're beautiful," Brooke said.

"I am, aren't I?" Nana helped herself to the dregs of the

coffee decanter. "I am a woman in love."

"With Duke?" Brooke asked.

"What other single man past his glory years do you know on this island?"

"Love?" Cornelia questioned.

"Yes, love. That's what I said, isn't it?" The sassy edge to Nana's voice was in full force. "When you get to be my age, love doesn't come softly or take its sweet time or ease its way into your heart. No, you purposefully grab it by the small hairs and scream *yes* straight into its face."

"I'm not sure the tone of this conversation is appropriate for your granddaughter—" Cornelia began.

"Mother," Brooke said. "I lived with a man. I know about small hairs."

Cornelia put her hands over her ears and Nana snickered. "Are we offending your sweet sensibilities, Cornelia?" Then she turned to Brooke. "I have an idea."

"Oh, no," Cornelia muttered.

"Hush," Nana said. "My man Duke is overseeing the cleanup today, and I do not intend to be bored out there in my cottage on this sunshine-y day. I am far too happy to sit around, and I no longer feel like baking. So, my dear granddaughter, you, your mother, and I are going to have ourselves an adventure."

"I can't have an adventure today," Cornelia said. "The Women's Club has me in charge of organizing a meal train for Maddie Smalling. She just had a baby boy, and I heard tell that he's a fussy one. Got that colic going on."

"Don't be silly," Nana said. "You have the time."

"Tell that to the club who voted me in as secretary. They rely on me for this sort of thing."

"No one is relying on you, Cornelia. You are just trying to fill up your time, and today, I have got something else for us to do." Nana winked at Brooke. "It's high time the Warter women venture out for a little fun."

"I don't think I can, Nan," Brooke said. "I'm supposed to drive over to Camp Dogwood with Jessa and Libby to see if it's an option for her wedding."

Nana sipped her coffee through wrinkly pink-painted lips. "That will do just fine."

"What?" Cornelia said. "That old camp?"

"Yes."

"It's going to be muddy, Nan. And there isn't any electricity or running water. Maybe you and Cornelia should go into Charleston and get some lunch or shop or something."

"Cornelia, are you afraid of a little mud?" Clearly, Nana had no intention of giving up.

"I don't think I own a pair of galoshes anymore," Cornelia said, "and I don't have any shoes I am willing to ruin."

"Why are we talking about shoes right now?" Nana put her coffee mug down with a clunk. "Do you think any of the great adventurers cared about shoes? I'm certain Amelia Earhart did not care. Or Davy Crockett. Or Sacagawea."

"I'm pretty sure Amelia Earhart and Davy Crockett cared

about their shoes. And Sacagawea had moccasins."

"But they still went out and got them muddy, now didn't they?"

"One would presume. But I am certain they were not happy about it. They couldn't just order a new pair online if theirs were ruined."

"But you can." Nana smiled wickedly. Game, set, match. "Anna Brooke, we will be joining you and your friends today. At what time are we leaving?"

"In about an hour."

With a flourish of pink and a few stray feathers floating behind, Nana left the building.

"Well, Mother, it looks like you're coming with me," Brooke said, surprised that she wasn't more excited. Going to Camp Dogwood with Cornelia and Nana felt like a violation. It was hers, like a secret she didn't want to share. Was there anything in her life that was her own anymore? Aside from the remnants of her apartment with Gates sitting in a pile inside Nana's cottage, everything felt like it belonged to someone else.

Chapter Twenty-One

N ANA IN A bathing suit was a sight to see. She was fearless, standing on the half-sunk dock like she was sixteen, gorgeous, and invincible. Cornelia sat beside her in a pair of shorts and her grungiest blue-and-white-striped puff-sleeved blouse, which wasn't grungy at all. They looked like friends instead of in-laws. Brooke couldn't hear what they were saying from the top of the hill near The Doghouse, but it appeared as if Nana was performing a comedy act given the way Cornelia had her head thrown back with laughter.

The place was a mess. Brooke, Jessa, and Libby moved from rotting buildings, over downed limbs, and across rain-soaked ground covered with layers of pine needles thicker than a shag carpet. They were all trying to stay positive when the fact was, not only did a month seem 365 days too short to pull off a wedding in a disaster area, but they had no idea from whom to get permission. Did the former proprietors of Camp Dogwood still own it, or did it now belong to a bank?

Brooke checked her phone for a text from Nate. There'd been a good-morning text at six A.M. but nothing since. She barely had service out here, so that was probably why. She stuffed her phone into the pocket of her sundress and forced her brain back to imagining Libby's wedding. Libby had just as much claim to Camp Dogwood as Brooke did. So why she felt like she didn't want to share it made no sense. How could she feel so possessive about something that wasn't hers? Something that had never been hers? Like Nate. He'd never been hers either, yet she felt like she alone had dibs on him. Every potentially interested person in all seven continents, and heck, in all of the infinite universes, had better back off.

To her surprise, Libby hadn't made one passive-aggressive comment for the entire hour they'd been together. Not only was she strangely quiet, she was downright nice. The chances that her tears from the day before had actually been genuine were increasing.

"So, if we can get permission, we'll have to figure out electricity. Can you imagine twinkle lights all around the woods leading the swimmin' hole?" Jessa asked, much more enthusiastic about planning a wedding than Brooke would have ever guessed she would be.

"And if we can get the dock fixed, you could walk down the hill from The Doghouse," Brooke said. "Maybe have an arch of flowers at the end by the water? It would be so pretty. Or, if it rains, we could always do up the inside of The Doghouse. Remember the dance?" The last part gave her a pang of regret. The dance that happened right after Nate left. The one where Gates spun her around and claimed her as his own. His classic good looks—tall and dark with perfectly straight white teeth, and dark-lashed eyes that held both blind entitlement and a crinkly sort of appreciation always surprised her. She should have had shivers all over her body. She should have been dizzy with excitement. But as a fifteen-year-old girl dancing with the Prince Charming of Camp Dogwood, she'd felt nothing. She remembered his arms heavy on her shoulders as he swayed to the music. "Hey, can you do something for me?" he'd asked, leaning down and speaking directly into her ear.

Brooke stayed silent.

"Say *whisper*."

It was a strange thing to ask. "Did you say *whisper*?"

As soon as her lips were in the "R" shape, Gates abruptly kissed her. She was so caught off guard that she just held still and let him. So he kissed her again. That time, she partially kissed him back, mostly as a reflex. He would never need to know that her heart had plummeted to her feet and her neck became hot with embarrassment because everyone in the room had seen them. Her first kiss with Nate had been just two days earlier and already she was kissing someone else. Every eye watched them pressed together in a slow dance, and she hid her face in his chest. She hated herself. Yes, the hottest guy at camp had chosen her, and that should feel good, but she didn't want the attention, and she didn't want him. There was no victory for a two-timing, weak, selfish, tramp. She wished to God that Gates was Nate.

Details. Timing. So many things had to go right in order

for a couple to get together. And even more for them to stay together. Nate was the right person at the wrong time back then. But who was he now? The right person at the right time? Could she possibly be so lucky?

Brooke tried hard to stay focused on wedding ideas, but the truth was, it was impossible to be anywhere near Camp Dogwood without thinking about Nate. It was hard to think about where to set up the cake table when all she wanted to do was run to the lighthouse and sit on its concrete platform, alone with her hopes and fantasies. Alone with her what-ifs and could-bes.

Cornelia let out a yelp, and all three girls turned to look as Nana managed to both tread water and yank Cornelia by the ankle.

"No, Grace! I am not coming in the water! I'm not wearing a swimmin' suit!"

The girls walked closer to the scene as Nana yanked harder and Cornelia began to lose precious dock space for her behind. Nana's cackle reverberated off the trees, soon joined by the piercing sound of Cornelia's scream and a subsequent splash. When Cornelia came up for air, she sputtered, "Grace Warter, Trig is going to think I look like a drowned rat."

"Good," Nana said. "He's probably sick and tired of you always looking like you just came off the floor of a wax museum anyhow."

Cornelia ducked under the water to slick the hair back

from her face. "Lord, it's been a long time since I've been swimming."

"You're welcome," Nana said.

"It's freezing." Cornelia breast-stroked her way toward shore.

"Not if you stay in longer!"

"Did you bring a towel?" Cornelia shouted back.

"I'll get it," Brooke called out, jogging back toward Jessa's car. She hadn't failed to notice that Nana had brought a beach bag the size of a large cooler. She checked her phone again along the way. Nothing from Nate. But why would there be? He was surely in Charleston, back at work, and very busy. Anyway, he'd texted good morning and she replied by wishing him a nice day. She hadn't asked a question. He wasn't leaving her hanging. How much more did she want?

She grabbed the bag, which felt like it weighed as much as a medium-sized pig. No wonder Nana left it in the car. She hauled it down to the dock and plunked it on a freshly sun-dried wooden picnic table and pulled a towel out from the top. "Here you go, Mother," Brooke said.

Cornelia, sopping wet, her bra visible beneath her now see-through blouse, reached for it. Nana stayed in the water, happily doing the backstroke like she was a teenager instead of an eighty-year-old grandmother.

"What's in here, Nan?"

Nana flipped over and breast-stroked closer. "One call to

Fred last night and we have ourselves a traditional lunch today."

Traditional lunch? It was only eleven, not quite time to eat. But Brooke hadn't intended to spend the whole day here, or even half of the day. What if Nate wanted to see her? "Is anybody hungry? Should we eat now?"

Nana was already exiting the lake. Brooke couldn't remember the last time she'd seen Nana without her painted-on eyebrows. She was really quite pretty. Her body was a testament to the effects of age and gravity, but also to a lifetime of active living. Cornelia handed her the towel, and Nana bent easily to dry her feet, wiping her way up to her head, where she carefully patted her face, even though her eyebrows had long since washed off.

"Now," she began, "back when we'd come here in the summers, we would always pack egg salad. Your granddaddy would be so disappointed if we didn't have the egg salad. Sometimes I think they were just trying to be difficult what with asking for mayonnaise-type sandwiches in the summertime. Back then it wasn't as easy to keep things cold. Anyhow, I'd always add a side of those little sweet pickles. They were his favorite." She dug through the bag. "Fred said he had some." A minute later, she victoriously pulled out a jar of sweet gherkins. "We've got the fried chicken, and the—"

"Nana, did you just say you used to vacation here?" Brooke was stunned. Was it just another made-up story?

"Oh, yes. Our friends owned this place. We spent weekends swimming all day and sleeping in the lighthouse. Isn't that just the end-all be-all?"

"Nana, are you talking about Nate's grandfather?"

Nana waved the conversation away like a bothersome fly. "His son and daughter-in-law died in a plane crash, so the topic was not to be discussed."

"Those were Nate's parents."

A flash of compassion came over her face, and she looked like she was trying to remember. "What were their names? David and Stella? Yes, David and Stella Daugherty." Brooke watched as Nana's face darkened, her emotions stuffed back down where they'd been before. "And why does it matter?"

"Because of Nate, Nana! You knew his family!"

"And the next time I see him, I will tell him that I once knew his family. I'm sure there are hundreds of other folks who also knew them."

Nana acted like it was no big deal. But for Brooke, it was a clear sign that Nate was supposed to be in their lives. At least in *hers*. Their families were connected in ways that should mean something. Brooke looked around for Libby and saw that she was heavy in conversation with Jessa, far enough away that she wouldn't hear.

"Is it a coincidence that he has come back into my life, that Mother had him in her eighth-grade class, and that you knew his grandparents? Doesn't that seem unlikely?"

"Oh." Nana chuckled with a wicked smile. "I see where

you're going with all of this. You're talking about the fishing line—those invisible strings that reel us in."

"Right. We're attached somehow. I knew it from the first time I saw him."

"You did not have this same sort of attachment with Gates?"

"No, Nan. I questioned it all the time. There was nothing wrong with him, but I kept wondering if he was right for me and if I was right for him. I was never comfortable. Does that make sense?"

"Darlin', if you're wondering if it's right, then it's probably wrong."

"I need to talk to Dottie about the fishing lines," Brooke said. "They're reeling us all in. I can feel it."

"If you talk to that woman," Nana said, "I want the full story."

Brooke appreciated Nana's interest, considering Cornelia thought Dottie was full of hot air.

Nana's eyes twinkled, and she flashed a knowing smile. "So, you're in love with this boy."

"I never said that. It's too soon. But I've always felt love for him."

"And you met him here."

"Yes, years ago. And we were just at the lighthouse yesterday."

"He knew how to work the door?" she asked, with a clear appreciation for the magnitude of the spinning and pulling required.

"He did." Brooke wanted to go back there with him, have him open the door again.

"That lighthouse was once my favorite place in the world," Nana said. "You know I have never been a morning person, but I'd get up early just to watch the sunrise from up top near the beacon." She shook her head at the memory, like it was hard to believe it actually happened. "Oh, dear. What a time we had. It was just a couple of summers that we had here. Our kids had gone off into the world and our little group was having a renaissance. It was like we were young again. Your granddaddy and Caleb Daugherty were good friends. I was fond of his wife as well, but she died early on."

So that was the Caleb she'd mentioned a while back. Nate's grandfather. Brooke felt closer to her grandmother in that moment than she had in a long time.

"What are y'all talking about?" Cornelia sat on the bench near them, her hair towel-dried and recently fluffed.

"Just this place," Nana said. "How magical it is."

"I do like it here," Cornelia said. "It's a mess, but there is quite a bit of potential."

"It only takes about fifteen minutes to get over to Goose Island on Duke's boat," Nana said. "But you might as well drive to New York City for the time it takes to drive a car over here."

"It's only forty-five minutes," Cornelia said.

"Only." Nana smirked. "That's like half the time I have left on this earth."

"Oh, stop it, Grace. You've got a long time left."

"Speaking of time," Nana said, digging through her bag again. "I believe it is time to have us some lunch. I see that Fred added in some of his homemade Moon Pies, bless that man's sweet soul."

Brooke brushed dirt and pine needles from the table with a napkin, then helped set out the food. She hadn't planned to stay long enough to need a meal but thank goodness Nana had. Something about Camp Dogwood made her want to slow down and stay as long as possible.

Libby and Jessa joined them at the table. Jessa chowed like a grown man with a bodybuilder's metabolism, and Libby pulled the crispy skin from a chicken leg and ate only the meat before claiming she was full. Nobody questioned her. In one month, she would need to fit into a bridal gown.

Nana and Cornelia went off to check the creek for watercress. There was nothing like the delicate pepperiness it added to salads, and it was hard to find in the grocery stores. Brooke left Jessa and Libby to brainstorm wedding ideas and took a hike to the lighthouse. She wanted to see it again, and was also hoping to find some cell reception. She sat on the weathered concrete steps and texted Nate. *"You're not going to believe this. My nana and your grandfather knew each other. She used to come here and stay in the lighthouse!"*

She waited for a response, but none came. The sound of the waves lapping the shore and her full belly made her tired, so she climbed up onto the gray square platform of the lighthouse and stretched out in a particularly shady spot. It was crazy how just the day before there had been a ferocious storm, and today the sun shone sweet and hot like it'd been napping and was happy to be refreshed and awake again.

Brooke didn't know how long she'd been asleep when her phone rang. She answered it while still lying down. It was Cornelia asking where she was; the group was ready to go. The sun had moved, beaming heat onto Brooke's spot. For the first time, she looked up, and noticed a small white canvas bag hanging from a hook underneath the rounded edge of the second level. She stood on her tiptoes to get a better look. Could it be a wasp's nest? No, the strings were evident. It was definitely a bag of some sort. Maybe it held pennies to keep the flies away? But those were usually hung in plastic bags filled with water. It made no sense.

She would need a small ladder to reach it. She tried jumping. If someone was around to give her a boost, she could get it. As it was, she kept missing by about a foot. There was nothing she could use to step on. And, truth be told, she didn't want to share her find with her mother or Nana, and certainly not Libby. Jessa was with all of them, so the best bet would be to leave the bag here and come back for it another time. It looked grungy, like it'd been weathered for years. Hopefully, no one else would find it between now and when she had a chance to return.

It would be a great excuse to bring Nate. If he would ever text her back.

Chapter Twenty-Two

B ROOKE, JESSA, AND Libby sat on Jessa's sleeping porch, each on their phones trying to figure out who to contact about permission to hold a wedding at Camp Dogwood. As far as they could tell, it had gone into bankruptcy and was now owned by a bank. That didn't look good. Plus, it was after five, so the bank was closed.

Brooke was in a rotten mood. Nate hadn't texted her back. How could he not respond to her text about their grandparents knowing each other? That was big news! She didn't know whether to be worried, mad, or disappointed, so she was all three. The last thing she wanted to do was be part of the current discussion about who would be doing what kind of work to make Libby Trotter's wedding perfect. Raking up pine needles? Fixing the floats on an old dock? All for Libby? She'd rather cut off her arms with a butter knife.

They all leaned forward on the couch looking at everything Libby had chosen for the wedding—light pink roses and ranunculus, white anemones, clematis, and sprays in snowy whites and creams. It was all too pretty and pleasant for someone like Libby. She deserved black roses with sharp thorns and blackberry bramble for her bouquet.

Before the barn collapsed in the storm, Libby was going to have mason jars filled with lights hanging in the windows and from the rafters. They could do the same with the pine trees, Jessa said. They could have hundreds of them, *hundreds*, leading down to the water. Brooke could only imagine that she would be the one assigned to climb the ladder and hang the darn things. She was already a terrible bridesmaid, and didn't have one more fake smile left in her. She was plum out of words like *Wow, I love it, perfect, yes,* and *gorgeous.*

It was time to leave.

"All right, y'all, I'm gonna head out now. Call me if you need anything."

"Wait," Libby said. "I need for y'all to get some things on your calendar." She pulled up her Notes app to a list that would take ten minutes to scroll through. "I've got the bridal shower coming up, of course. I'm gonna need one of y'all to plan the bachelorette party. Mama's doing the bridesmaids' tea, there will be the rehearsal dinner, and of course, if I'm having my wedding out at The Dog, we're gonna have to plan for several days of cleanup."

"Text it to me," Brooke said, unable to tolerate being here one more second. She walked out of Jessa's front door wondering why on earth she was torturing herself. Was she being weak, or a compassionate person? Was staying and putting up with Libby's demands the definition of sweet?

She wasn't sure. It felt more like the definition of a pushover.

Brooke drove straight to Dottie's house where Tulip answered the door holding a fistful of green-dyed wool and a large needle. "Hey, Tootie," Brooke said, remembering Tulip's new nickname. "Is your mama home?" She needed her advice. There were too many otherworldly things happening.

"She's with Uncle Fred. They're deep-frying turkeys for next week's menu."

"Out at Fred's place?"

"Yep." She stabbed the needle into the wool several times in quick succession.

"What are you working on?"

"It's called felting," she said. "I'm making an alligator."

Tootie had a new obsession every time she saw her. "You okay here alone?"

"I'm fifteen now, you know." She shot her an annoyed look and kept stabbing at the fuzzy pile of green wool.

Her quirky bowl haircut made her look like she was twelve. The rainbow sweatpants didn't help. "Oh, right. Okay, I won't keep you, then."

"Cool. Hey, when you're there, can you tell Uncle Fred to order me some more of those circle hooks for shark fishing?"

"Sure." Back in the car, Brooke checked her phone again. Still no text from Nate. She couldn't text him again, could she? Would it be stalker-ish to ask if he was okay? She wished she knew who his friends were so she could ask them. She did have a business card with Noelle's number on it. But if she reached out to her, that might be stalkery too. She had no choice but to sit tight and hope he contacted her soon.

Dottie and Fred stood in the middle of a clearing behind the old gas station. It was easy to tell they were related. Their smiles were exact replicas, except for the fact that Fred had all of his teeth. They even had the same haircut: short and brown. Fred's long beard was perilously close to the boiling vat of oil as he pulled up a toasty dark brown turkey and walked it toward a metal pan to cool. Brooke waited until the bird was set down before she said hello.

"Well, hey there, sweetness," Dottie said. "You got here just in time. We finished the birds, and are boutta crack open some beers."

Fred's big brown dog came up to sniff her. She reached down and scratched his soft head. "Hey, Whiskey. Stay away from that hot oil, 'kay?" Fred had disappeared through the back door of the station with the cooked turkey. "Thanks, Dottie. I can't stay. I was just hoping you could help me with something."

"Whatcha need?" Dottie moved closer. "Wait, don't tell me. Let me guess." She took a deep breath like she was pulling magical air into her lungs and then placed her hands firmly on top of Brooke's head. "You can't stand that girl Libby, and you've got a massive crush on a guy with a limp."

Brooke physically recoiled. How could Dottie be so spot

on?

Dottie laughed. "My Carolina Jessamine has been tellin' me everything."

"Oh." Brooke laughed with her. Of course Jessa had been spilling the tea. "Okay, seriously, though. Do you have a second?"

Fred reappeared and walked right past them without saying hello to Brooke. He climbed the step ladder into his houseboat, which had been on blocks behind the station for so long that tall grass had grown around the concretec. Then, like he suddenly remembered they were there, he said, "Y'all want to come in for a beer?"

"Wait for me," Dottie said. "Now, then." She turned back to Brooke. "You got off track years ago. Is that what you wanted to hear?"

"What do you mean?"

"You have always had a strong tie to that camp. It's a connection that is not of this world but the flow of positive energy was interrupted long ago."

"How?"

"I can't tell you specifics. But you left with something you weren't supposed to have." Her brow furrowed. "No, no. That's not right. You left something behind? No, that ain't right neither." She squeezed her eyes shut. "It's the interruption that I feel."

"What interruption?"

"Don't ask me questions I can't answer."

Brooke was used to Dottie's gruffness. "Can you tell me if I should be in Libby's wedding?"

"I already told you!" Dottie sighed, then stared at the brick wall of the gas station for a full minute. "It's not going to take anything from you." She stared some more. "And it will make a difference for someone else."

"I don't want to be nice to her," Brooke said. "After all she's done to me, she doesn't deserve it."

"It's not like you're being forced. I don't see you getting duct-taped into a bridesmaid's dress. You get to decide." She bent down and fiddled with Whiskey's ear before saying, "Are you going to live in the small square of your own little life, or are you going to open up wide and give yourself freely?"

"But what if I give too much of myself away?"

"Maybe the wedding is not for Libby."

"How is me being a bridesmaid going to help anyone other than her?"

"Anna Brooke, you are starting to annoy me. You know I can't answer that." Dottie began walking toward the houseboat. "And anyway, what if it is meant to help her? What's so awful about that?"

"Wait, Dottie. I have one more question."

"Ask it quick."

"Should I call Nate?"

"For heaven's sake, girl." Dottie didn't stop walking. "Use your own intuition. You've got it too, you know." She climbed the step stool onto the white marine plastic stern where Fred sat on a lawn chair sipping a beer. "You can join us if you want."

"No thanks," Brooke said.

"Grab yourself a cookie before you go," Fred called out. "Hot plate's still warm and the back door's open."

There was no way Brooke would leave without a cookie. "Thank you!" she called before ducking into the store. There were few places she loved more than the gas station. It might look abandoned from the outside, but the inside was immaculate and stocked with every necessity that anyone on the island might need—and plenty of fun extras too. It was the heart and soul of Goose Island. And Dottie's food truck was the outreach.

Brooke hadn't gotten the definitive answers she'd hoped for, but she should've known better. Dottie almost always left people to decide for themselves. She checked her phone for the millionth time. Still no text from Nate. It was going on six o'clock. If she hurried home, she might get there in time for dinner.

Shoot. She forgot to tell Fred to order those circle hooks for Tulip. She hopped back out of her car and jogged to the houseboat. As she approached, she overheard Dottie and Fred. "I see a duck with Brooke," Dottie was saying. "But I don't know what it means."

"Don't look at me," Fred said. "I'm just gonna tell you you're nuts." There was frenetic shuffling, scratching, and chittering, then, "Roscoe! I don't have nuts for you. Get off me."

"That's what you get for keeping a squirrel as a friend," Dottie said. "Git! Roscoe! I don't have 'em either!" The scratching and chattering quieted down after a minute. "Back to the duck. It's not a real one, I don't think. So, it means good luck, maybe?"

"Why are you always asking me about this stuff?" Fred said. "I don't know what a danged fake duck is supposed to mean."

"I hate symbols," Dottie said. "They are impossible to interpret. She might just be about to travel somewhere."

Brooke hid near the step stool and heard Fred say, "Now, I'm not saying I know anything, but if I have to give you a meaning to get you to shut up, then I'm gonna say the duck you're seeing is love. And maybe stability."

"I don't know how you get all that from a little ol' duck." Dottie slurped her beer. "All I know is that girl has been tied down harder than a cruise ship at port. And once Brooke gets back on track, maybe Carolina Jessamine can get there too."

Held down? By Gates? By her parents? Brooke heard Whiskey wandering around, and she didn't want to be caught eavesdropping, so she quickly snuck away and drove home. Tootie could ask her uncle for the circle hooks herself. How had Jessa been off track? She was the same Jessa she'd always been. Plus, she had a good job and her own house.

She didn't want a man, so she wasn't missing anything there.

Was it Libby? Was Libby interrupting Jessa's energy flow? But if that was the case, wouldn't Dottie be doing something about it? The whole thing was making her tired.

Brooke pulled in front of her parents' house and saw them all sitting at the dinner table, an empty spot set for her. From what she could see, Nana had on a normal button-down shirt, so maybe it would be a drama-free meal. She ran up the front stairs. "Sorry I'm late!"

"Fix yourself a plate," Cornelia answered. "We're just getting started."

Brooke loaded herself up with chicken and rice and a side of green beans. Despite the cookie she'd just devoured, she was still starving. When she walked into the dining room, she almost dropped her plate. Neither Cornelia nor Nana had bothered to fix themselves up for the meal. They wore dried ocean water in their hair, and their cheeks were makeup free and red from the sun. Trig was actually smiling, and so were the two women. It was like walking into another dimension. Brooke took her seat at the table, wide-eyed.

"And I'd have thought it was an alligator grabbing hold of my ankle if it weren't for the white hair sticking out of the water." Cornelia laughed, continuing a story that Brooke had missed.

"Lordy," Nana agreed. "It was fun."

The banter continued through the whole meal, and afterward, Nana didn't run off to her cottage but took a seat on the couch to watch *Family Feud* while Trig sat in his recliner sipping his evening whiskey. Cornelia went to the kitchen to do the dishes.

"Sit, Mother. I'll take care of this," Brooke said.

"You will?" She put down the casserole dish she held in her hands.

"Go watch TV with Trig and Nana."

"Cornelia!" Trig's voice bellowed from the den. "Put those dishes down and come sit with us."

"Someone has to clean them," she yelled back, her face holding questions as she shrugged at her daughter.

"I'll do it in the morning," he said.

Cornelia grabbed hold of the counter like she might fall over. "Did he just say he would do the dishes?"

Brooke met her astonishment. "I think he did."

"Miracles do happen." She winked. "Leave them in the sink."

It felt strange leaving the dishes for Trig to do. Never had that ever happened before. She felt a buzz from her back pocket and pulled out her phone, heart pounding.

"*Sorry.*" It was finally Nate! "*I had to take care of some business in Atlanta. I can't believe our grandparents knew each other. What a small world.*"

She pulled out a chair at the breakfast nook and plopped onto it. He was okay. And in Atlanta. Now, how to respond. She wanted to know when he would be back, but was it too forward to ask? She read his message again. Was the tone a bit cold? It was awfully short and to the point. But maybe he was just a dry texter. She stared at the phone, hoping he would text again, add a little more, answer the questions she didn't want to ask. But after several minutes, nothing else appeared.

"*Hope all is well in Atlanta,*" she decided to write. "*Let me know when you're back in town.*" She tried to match his tone the best she could—not too interested but still nice. It felt awful.

She left the dirty kitchen and went to her room with plans to stare at the phone until he responded. Or, rather, if he responded.

Chapter Twenty-Three

B ROOKE WAS CUDDLED up into her blankets, thankful for the sixty-eight degree air-conditioning set point that Trig insisted on. It made her bed feel that much more snuggly. She'd stayed up too late waiting for a text from Nate that never came and wasn't ready to fully wake up yet, but her phone rang. Jessa didn't even start with hello. "The bank said someone put an offer in on Camp Dogwood. They won't divulge who it is."

"Jess," Brooke whined. "It's early. I'm still asleep."

"Well, our plan for Libby's wedding might not work, and I'm afraid to tell her. We have got to come up with something else." Jessa was talking so fast that Brooke was forced to merely listen. "You don't think Nate could be trying to buy it, do you?"

"I—"

Jessa cut her off. "I mean, he does own that house in Charleston, and he has people working for him in some sort of real-estate-type thing, and he ate at Poogan's Porch, which isn't exactly cheap."

"Well, we ate there, too, and we hardly have any money.

You don't really think he's rich, do you?"

"Naw, that kind of stuff only happens in the movies."

Despite his nice clothes and real estate investments, Nate still seemed like the poor boy who tried hard. He had too much to overcome. Surely, he was just overextended and overworked with whatever he had going on. "Unless he inherited it, it would be practically impossible to have that much money at our age. And I'm pretty sure he wasn't left with anything."

"Call him and see if he made an offer," Jessa said. "That might solve all of our problems."

"Maybe Libby can just get married at the Goose Island Baptist Church and have her reception at home like everybody else."

"She's not even from here, Brooke."

"Okay, then her hometown church. Even better."

"Are you going to call Nate or not? Because if you're not, I'm going to need to start researching other venues."

"I don't get it, Jess. Why are you so invested? It's like you were replacing me with Libby, and then I moved back and got in the way of you and your new best friend."

"Brookie." Her voice sounded like a pout. "Come on. Never."

"Then what is going on? Libby should be finding her own wedding venue. It's not your problem, and it's certainly not mine." She knew it didn't sound sweet. But heck, it was the truth.

"Can't I do something nice for someone without all this?"

"All this? Really, Jess? You do remember who Libby is, don't you? You remember what she did to me at camp?" Just mentioning Libby and camp made Brooke want to throw the phone. "You know what? I hope that Nate is buying Camp Dogwood, because I will tell him to ban Libby Trotter from the premises. If she gets anywhere near it, she will be arrested. You just go ahead and find that other venue, because I'm done with this. And so is Nate."

She hung up. Brooke normally didn't lose her cool, but once she hit threshold, all of the emotions that had been brewing exploded like the fireworks Libby had planned for her *selfish, steal the spotlight from America on the country's Independence Day, make everyone dress up when they should be in shorts drinking beer on the beach, force people to be brides-maids, expect a million parties, treat people like crap* wedding. It didn't matter if Libby was two people or wounded or whatever it was that Dottie said. She was awful. Not to mention Brooke was sitting in her stupid childhood bed-room that felt like a hotel room, doing a job that amounted to a big demotion, alone after leaving a decent guy only to come home to family dysfunction and her childhood bully.

And now her best friend was turning on her and the man she'd dreamed about for almost ten years was ghosting her. Perfect. Just perfect. No, she would not be calling Nathan freaking Daugherty to see if he bought Camp Dogwood. She pulled the covers over her head and tried to go back to sleep, but her heart and mind kept racing. Finally, she gave up and went downstairs for coffee.

There, in Cornelia's white granite and painted wood kitchen, sat Nana with Duke and Trig. Cornelia was at the island putting together egg, bacon, and biscuit sandwiches. Brooke stopped at the entrance and stared. The folks at the table were all taking turns looking at pages from a stack of papers. Brooke stepped into the room, deciding to say hello first to her boss. "Hello, Mr. Bradley. Good morning, Nana, Trig, Cornelia." She helped herself to a mug of coffee.

"Oh, honey, come sit by me," Nana exclaimed. "You will not believe what I have done."

Brooke knew immediately what the papers meant. She slid in beside her grandmother. "You bought Camp Dogwood."

"Why yes, I most certainly did!" Her face was alight with glee. "And we will begin our new endeavor by hosting that bratty girl's wedding. What do you think about that?"

Brooke didn't have the words to answer.

"Don't look shocked. It's not about her. It's about all of the folks who will see the potential of that old place."

"It's just that she doesn't deserve it, is all."

Nana squeezed the skin above Brooke's knee too hard. "Don't let the bride test your pride."

Cornelia stepped in. "Nana had forgotten how much she loved that place. And it is a direct boat ride from the grounds of the Saltwater Winery. Correct, Mr. Bradley?"

Duke nodded, his face somehow different—softer, less fierce.

"Oh, this is going to be a fun adventure!" Nana said.

"You're going to run a camp, Nana?" Brooke asked.

"Well, not a little kindergarten camp or that teenybopper camp you went to. I am far past that nonsense. No, it will be a nice resort."

"And people will have a place to stay just a short boat ride from the winery," Cornelia added.

"Mr. Bradley and I are entering into a symbiotic relationship," Nana said with a voice that sounded so Marilyn Monroe sexy that it made Trig visibly cringe. She switched back to bossy just as quickly. "And, in answer to your question, young lady, no, I will not be running it. You will."

"What?" Brooke definitely did not see that coming.

"So, we'll begin with cleanup, of course, and fix up the lighthouse for you to live in." Nana was talking a hundred miles an hour. "Then, on to renovating the building at the top of the hill, I believe it is called The Doghouse. We'll fix it up and add some more cabins—the new ones will be the high price suites. We'll have a separate café that will serve local coffees in the morning and Saltwater Wines at night, and we're gonna fill the stables with horses. Honey, we're about to provide so many jobs for this area that ol' Fred's place might even start turning a profit."

Brooke's head was spinning. She was going to be in

charge of all that? And did Nana say *lighthouse*? "I can't believe it" was all she could say. She should be elated. She should be absolutely beside herself with happiness. Not only had Nana found a place to put her money, but this amounted to Brooke's greatest dream. To rebuild, market, and run a place she loved so much? It was the greatest gift. So, why did she feel disappointed? Why was she trying to fight back tears? She stuffed the feelings and held up her coffee mug for a toast. "Ba," Brooke said.

"Nana!" said Trig and Cornelia, holding up their mugs.

Duke looked confused, but Grace "Nana" Sharon Beauregard Warter had never appeared more in her right mind than at that moment.

No one moved from the kitchen table for the next three hours. The family was awash with ideas and dreams and excitement. Brooke forgot all about her fight with Jessa and Nate's suspicious absence. She was filled once again with the hope of Camp Dogwood.

When lunchtime came, Brooke went outside to pick tomatoes and Cornelia turned them into soup. They paired it with grilled cheese, and Trig cleaned up the dishes. Little old Duke stayed seated in their kitchen looking more content than a sugar ant on a half-licked lollipop. There was nothing scary about that man, especially when Nana was near. When lunch was over, he dug into one of his pants pockets, pulled out a hard caramel candy, and slid it across the table to Nana. She looked at him like he was King Louis giving her the Hope Diamond and kissed him sweetly on the cheek before opening it and popping it into her mouth.

Those two felt like proof that it was never too late for love.

"If you'll excuse me," Brooke said. "I have to make a phone call."

Jessa answered before Brooke heard it ring. "I could never replace you, Brooke. You know that. You've been my best friend my whole life, and you always will be."

"I know," Brooke said. "I'm sorry. Everything piled up on me, and I took it out on you."

"Good," Jessa said. "So, we're over it?"

"Yes." Brooke always marveled at how easy it was to get along with Jessa. "And I have good news."

"Oh, please, tell me it's about a venue. At this point, Libby's going to have to make some new friends to help her. Unless she wants to have it in my weedy backyard, we're running out of options."

"Nana is buying Camp Dogwood." Saying the words felt too good to be true. "I mean, it's not hers yet, but she has made an offer and requested a short escrow."

Jessa sucked so much air through the phone that it hurt Brooke's ear. She repeated the words slowly. "Your nana's buying Camp Dogwood." She gasped again. "I think I'm having a heart attack."

"Can you believe it? And if it all goes through, I might need to put in my resignation soon, because she said she wants me to run it."

"Oh my word, Brooke! That is such good news. I mean, not for the winery but for you!"

"But I'll still be working with you, because we're planning to tie the two places together by boat."

"By boat?" Jessa asked.

"Yes. And with Nana and Duke's *symbiotic relationship*." Brooke mocked her grandmother's sexy voice.

"That is the coolest thing I've ever heard. Both things, I mean. The boats and the old folks getting together. I'm so happy for them. Duke has been needing someone like Nana in the worst way."

Brooke's phone buzzed in her hand. "Nate's calling."

"Answer it. But first, Libby's wedding?"

"I think we can do it."

"Whoop!" Jessa yelled. "Okay, answer that man!"

Brooke switched lines. "Hello?" She didn't have time to get nervous.

"Hey." She was still getting used to the fact that his voice was so much deeper than years ago when she'd fallen for him. "Are you busy tonight?"

"No." She attempted to match the tone of his voice and tried to subdue herself as she added, "Are you back in town?"

"Just got here. It's been crazy. I owe you an explanation." He sounded trepidatious, like he'd done something wrong. "Will you let me take you to dinner?"

"Sure." Her nerve endings felt raw. He was acting far too

serious. "I think I can do that." The fact was, nothing could stop her from going to dinner with Nate Daugherty. She wanted to hear everything...*anything*...he had to say.

Chapter Twenty-Four

I F EVER THERE was a time to dress to impress, it was for her date with Nate. Brooke was settling for the same plain dress she'd worn to Gates's graduation when Cornelia knocked on her door. "Honey?" she asked. "How's the gussying coming along?"

"Not very well." Brooke opened the door and gave a halfhearted spin in her cap-sleeved black dress.

"Hmmm," Cornelia said. "When was the last time we went shopping?"

"A few years ago," Brooke said carefully, trying not to make her mother feel like she'd done something wrong. It was true, though. As soon as Brooke left the house, Cornelia acted like her job as a mother had come to an end.

"I have an ivory silk blouse I think would be just perfect with that gray thing you have—the one that looks like a miniskirt in the front and shorts in the back?"

"My skort?"

"Yes, that's the thing. And you could pull the top half of your hair back to show your beautiful face. I'll even let you borrow my diamond earrings."

"Really, Mama?" Brooke had only called her mother Mama twice in her life—once when she had her wisdom teeth out and was still high on whatever it was they administered to her, and in that moment where it just somehow felt right.

"You know you can look in my closet any time you like."

That was astonishing considering it had always been off-limits. "Are you sure?"

"Of course I'm sure. They're just clothes, and you're my favorite daughter."

"I'm your only daughter." Brooke chuckled. It'd been a long time since Cornelia was in such a good mood. She wanted to savor every moment.

"Is Nathan coming to pick you up?"

"Yes." Brooke grabbed her phone from the dresser to check the time. Her hand shook as she held it. "He's supposed to be here in ten minutes."

"Plenty of time," Cornelia soothed as she went to fetch the promised items. "Your reservation is for six thirty?"

"That's what he said." Brooke happily unzipped the old black dress. It was far too funeral-like for a date. Then again, maybe it was perfect. Judging from the sound of Nate's voice over the phone, the date might not be a happy occasion.

Brooke waited in the kitchen so she could see him pull up. She'd wait for him to come to the door, of course. Every young man was required to shake her father's hand before she was allowed to leave with him. It didn't matter how old she was or if her father already knew the guy. It was an inflexible rule. She was so antsy, she kept hitting her wiggling ankle on the table leg. Finally, she got up to help her mother with the *setting of the dining room table* performance. Waiting patiently was not working. She'd just set out the water glasses when she heard a high-pitched quacking sound. It sounded like a duck screaming in distress.

"Cornelia, do you hear that?"

"Trigger!" Cornelia yelled, looking out the window. "Something's caught up in my vegetable net!"

Brooke was already running toward the front door. Cornelia's vegetable garden was in a raised bed off to the right of the house. It had posts holding up green netting to keep the pests out. As soon as Brooke made it down the front steps, she saw what was causing the ruckus. There was a mallard twisted into the net and hanging by his bright orange webbed foot. He was all feathers and wings in a full flapping panic. Brooke was afraid to get near him. A few minutes later, Trig appeared with his rifle.

"No!" Brooke blocked his path. "No. Please. You can't kill it."

"That duck has probably got a broken leg by now," he said, checking to see if there was a bullet in the chamber. "I have to put it out of its misery."

"Daddy, please. I'll get him out. I'll get the clippers and cut around the net. Please put the gun away."

"It's just a duck, Anna Brooke. People hunt them all the

time."

"Please. I'll handle this, okay? I'll take care of it. You can go inside."

"I will not leave my daughter out here alone to wrestle with an injured duck." He walked past her, and Brooke knew she'd lost. There was no arguing with Trig once he made up his mind.

As if on cue, Nate turned into their driveway. "Nate's here! He'll help me." If it hadn't been for her determination to save the duck, Brooke might've been nervous seeing Nate's car heading toward her. But now, not only could this date be the end of her fantasy that Nate was her soul mate, but she had implicated him in the rescue of a terrified duck. Not to mention, he was about to shake her father's hand while he held a loaded rifle.

Through the front windshield, their eyes locked. Nate's expression gave nothing away. "Y'all need some help?" he asked as he opened his car door.

Trig placed the rifle barrel down next to his leg and held out his hand. "I was just about to handle this." The two men shook. Nate glanced over at Brooke and must've seen the distress in her face.

"If you don't mind, Mr. Warter, I'd be happy to release him."

"Yes!" Brooke grabbed him by the hand, and they jogged together toward the duck. "We've got this, Daddy!" she called to him behind her. She swore she could hear Trig chuckle. She hadn't called him Daddy since she was a child.

"All right. Y'all call for me when you realize he's too far gone to save," Trig said as he took his rifle back up the steps and into the house.

Nate and Brooke, dressed for a nice dinner and not for a dirty duck rescue, exchanged glances. "Should I get a towel?" she asked. "Maybe throw it over him? One of us can hold him while the other one gets his leg out. I'll get some clippers, too, in case we need to cut the net."

Brooke sprinted inside. When she came back out, Nate was holding the duck calmly in his arms, soothing it. The skinny orange foot was still stuck in the net, but the duck's wings were tucked, his little body held tight. Brooke snuck around behind them and carefully snipped the net to free him.

"There you go, little buddy," Nate said, placing him gently on the ground. The duck quacked and walked in a circle with an obvious limp.

"Poor baby. He's hurt," Brooke said.

"Maybe there's a wildlife place we can call?"

Nate and Brooke sat on the edge of the raised garden bed and searched wildlife rescues online. There were only two and both were closed. The duck sat in front of them, unmoving. "Don't worry, little guy," Nate said. "We'll figure something out."

"I'll call Fred," Brooke said. "He's got a squirrel. Maybe he'll take a duck too."

Less than half an hour later, Brooke and Nate had missed their dinner reservation and instead had a quacking duck sitting in the back seat of Nate's car. In a strange way, Brooke couldn't help but feel protective of it the whole way to the gas station. The duck felt like it belonged to them, like their adopted child.

Fred was out back. Nothing alarmed him. He was just as slow and languid as ever as he closed the fiberglass door of his houseboat, telling Whiskey to stay inside. He took his time climbing off the boat, while Nate and Brooke stood by their opened car door. When he finally sauntered up, he chuckled when he saw what was in the back seat.

"Welp," Fred said, pulling on his long beard. "Looks like we got us a plain ol' mallard. Green head, bright orange feet." He reached in and easily picked up the duck, looking him over carefully before tucking him under his arm. "I've got some seed in the store he might like."

"We can take him to the wildlife rescue in the morning," Brooke said. "He just needs a safe place for the night."

"I'll make him a nest inside Whiskey's crate. He'll be safe." Fred walked away like he'd rescued ducks a million times before.

"Thanks, Fred." Brooke was hesitant to leave. The duck kept staring at her and quacking from Fred's arms like he didn't want to be separated from her. It tugged at her heart.

"You don't think Whiskey will try to eat him, do you?" she yelled.

"I'll keep Whiskey away."

"Do you think his leg is broken?"

Fred stopped walking and turned. "Doesn't look like it. Probably just wrenched it."

"So you think he'll be okay?"

"I do. We'll let him rest here for the night and if he's doing all of the proper duck things in the morning, we'll release him." The top part of his beard stuck straight out as he bit his bottom lip to appraise her. "Do you need more time with him?"

Brooke looked over at Nate, and he nodded. "I think I do."

"Come on up," Fred said. "Y'all want a beer?"

"Yes, please," Brooke said. A beer for dinner was better than nothing. She and Nate followed Fred up the step ladder and helped themselves from an open cooler filled with ice and beer. "Did we interrupt anything?" Brooke asked, suddenly realizing that Fred had a life outside of being everybody's go-to guy.

"Naw. Just said goodbye to my sister. Have a seat." He pointed to several empty lawn chairs spread around the boat deck. Brooke and Nate sat next to each other. "Now, don't go telling Dottie about any of this duck business. I hate it when she's right." Whiskey's metal crate was by the door underneath the helm. Nate jumped up and opened the latch so Fred could deposit the duck inside.

"What was Dottie right about?" Brooke asked, not wanting to admit that she'd overheard his conversation with Dottie.

"She said there would be a duck in your life, but she saw a fake one. I guess that makes her only half right."

Brooke shot a look at Nate.

"Do you know if there were any numbers on the fake duck?" Nate asked.

"She didn't say."

The twinkle in Nate's eye was back for a second. "I think this little guy's a good omen."

"I'll go get that seed," Fred said, leaving them alone briefly.

"He's a lucky duck." Brooke giggled.

Nate reached over and touched her arm. She instantly turned nervous. "We need to talk," he said.

She nodded. "Do you still want to try to get some dinner once Fred returns?"

"Yes," Nate answered.

The duck wasn't happy in the cage and kept trying to chew on the wires, his bill clunking against them. "Do you think he's okay?"

"He'll calm down. He'll like it better once Fred gets him some food and water."

"I hope so." She couldn't hold in her curiosity any longer. "Whatever it is that you have to tell me—is it bad?"

He shook his head. "I wouldn't call it bad."

She couldn't bring herself to meet his eyes. "Okay."

Fred came back out with a bowl full of bird seed and two wrapped sandwiches. "Y'all hungry? Looks like you missed some dinner plans."

"Thanks," they both said, each taking a sandwich.

Fred put the dish in the crate, and as soon as he locked the latch, the duck ate like he'd just been served the finest seed in all of Goose Island. Fred chuckled and went inside the houseboat to get a bowl of water.

"We'll go out for dessert," Nate said, opening up the paper to see a meat-filled Cubano sandwich inside.

"I make a pretty good banana pudding if you want to come to my house," Brooke said. Back in their camp days, Nate used to give Brooke his cookies, but he never shared when they had banana pudding.

He tilted his head at her. "You remember."

"I do." She paused for courage. "I have to tell you something," she began, "but I feel weird about it."

"Your nana put an offer in on Camp Dogwood."

She sat straight up. "How'd you know?"

"Because I contacted the bank this morning. I was going to see about making an offer too."

"Oh, no! Are you going to bid against her? Do you want me to talk to her?" Nate could afford to buy Camp Dogwood?

"No." He took her hand. "My relationship with that place is complicated. Your nana buying it is perfect."

Brooke relaxed. "She's been to the lighthouse with your

grandparents."

Nate nodded knowingly. "I remember."

"You do?"

"I didn't put it together until you said she knew my granddad. I saw her there once. She was just Miss Grace to me. Our grandfathers used to smoke cigars and get into all kinds of trouble."

"Is he still alive?"

"My granddad? No. Between my grandmother and my parents, I think he died of a broken heart. It didn't take long."

"You had to go through all of those deaths alone. So did my nana. My granddaddy died around that time too."

Nate nodded solemnly. "I guess we have that in common too."

"You and my family were grieving for many of the same people. Nana went a little crazy, and you became strong and resilient." As soon as she said it, she felt horrible. "I take that back. Nana's not crazy. She's just whoever and whatever she wants to be." She thought for a second. "Maybe that's because she's strong and resilient too. She knows life is short and unfair, and that sometimes societal rules are outdated and hold us back."

Nate looked peaceful, genuinely happy that Camp Dogwood was about to be owned by Brooke's family.

"I'll introduce you to her," Brooke said. "Again."

"Tell you what," Fred said, appearing in his narrow

doorway with a strange fatherly look on his face. "I'll make sure this duck is safe, okay? But y'all have got to git. There's something going on with you two. I don't know what it is, but what I do know is that y'all certainly don't need me here watching."

Nate stood, holding his sandwich in one hand, and offering Fred his other. "Thanks, man." They shook like old friends.

"Thanks so much, Fred," Brooke said, hugging him tightly. She'd always been grateful for Jessa's uncle Fred.

"I'll see y'all in the morning and we'll decide together if the little guy can be released," Fred said. He looked Nate straight in the eye. "You take good care of my girl now."

"I promise," Nate said.

Brooke knew in her soul that Nate meant it.

Chapter Twenty-Five

NATE AND BROOKE drove right back to the Warter mansion where they started. The broken net on Cornelia's vegetable garden was already tied together with twine. One night wide open on the island would surely mean no more heirloom tomatoes in the morning. If the raccoons didn't get them, the deer certainly would. The sun hadn't finished setting and the moon was already rising full, so there was enough light for a brief walk. They didn't have to say anything, they both just headed in the opposite direction of the front door into the yard where the mermaid-hair moss hung in tendrils from the old oaks, toward the round iron bench that hugged the middle-most tree.

"I told you I don't have a girlfriend," Nate began with a whisper, "but that wasn't the whole truth."

Brooke's heart sank, and she nearly tripped. He grabbed her by the arm and led her along. "So, you were with her in Atlanta?"

"Yes." He said it like he didn't want the trees to hear.

Why could they never get the timing right? Was her whole life going to be a series of missed opportunities? She swallowed the disappointment and jealousy burning in her throat. "I understand," she said as sweetly as she could. "I hope we can still be friends." She meant it.

They got to the bench, and Brooke sat first. Nate sat strangely close to her, his thigh pressed up against hers. She almost scooted away. The surface area of her side where his touched hers felt like hot coals, but she stayed where she was.

"No," he said. "We can't be friends."

It was worse than she thought.

"I mean, we can't be *just* friends," he said, taking her hand. "I will always need more."

Was he saying—

"I don't want to scare you, but I have to tell you," he said, turning his whole body to face her. "As soon as I saw a future with you, it changed everything. I know it's early, and I suppose it's the risk-taking part of me, but I refuse to lose you again. I know you just got out of a long relationship, and I'm sure you're not ready for another one, but it has been too many years without you. I can't let anything come between us again."

Was she even sitting on the bench? She felt like she was floating above it, blowing in the wind like the moss, dizzy and subsisting on warm air.

"I went to Atlanta, and I canceled escrow on the home I was buying. I'll have to make a lot of trips and hire someone to oversee my business there, but it's doable. And I explained the situation to the girl I'd been seeing."

Brooke fell back to earth with a thud. That was a lot to process. Had she just unwittingly upset all of his future plans? Was that okay? Did she deserve for someone to change so many things in their life for her? What if she disappointed him? What if she wasn't who he thought she was? She must have looked horrified.

"This is my choice, okay?" he said. "One I made without you. I, alone, am responsible for it. You don't owe me anything."

Her hopes and fears puddled together, threatening to run down her cheeks. She remembered her mother's words: *marry the man who loves you more.* Marriage or not, this time, it was the one man she truly wanted. The one she'd dreamed about for years. What if she was the one who loved him more? Was that a recipe for disaster? "Is she okay?" Brooke squeaked, trying her best to hold her voice steady. She was so incredibly happy, but she couldn't forget that someone else just had their heart broken.

"We hadn't been dating long," he said, the tension between them rising. "She'll be fine."

"You told her about me?"

"I did."

"Oh, God." He was slowly invading her personal space, his face closer to hers than it'd been since they were teenagers. She had to look away. "I feel terrible. I need to apologize to her."

He put a hand on her cheek, and she brought her eyes to

meet his. "It's me, Brooke. Not you. Never your fault. I figured no one would ever make me feel like you do, so I settled for someone I liked—someone I got along with. But once you were back in my life, I knew I couldn't do it. Not to her, and not to myself. She wouldn't have been happy with me long-term. She deserves someone who adores her."

"It's weird, isn't it?" Brooke had to look away. Her heart was pounding out of her chest and she wasn't sure she could survive it. She spouted whatever came to mind first. "The whole finding a partner thing. How are you supposed to know when it's right? If you've never had the feeling we have, you might think that marriage, or long-term partnership, is about choosing someone you can tolerate. But it's so much more. Gates was settling for me just as much as I was settling for him." He was still looking directly at her, and she found the bravery to bring her eyes back to his. "With you, my heart feels safe."

"It is," he said. He took both of her hands in his, still intent on her face. "What are you saying?"

"I tried to get on with my life, but I always, always missed you. I felt like I was supposed to be the witness to your future, all of it, good or bad, and that was stolen away. I haven't been the same since."

"So"—his smile was heart-meltingly hopeful—"you want to give us a try?"

She used the back of her hand to wipe the tears from her face, and nodded.

That was all he needed. His right hand moved to tuck a stray piece of hair behind her ear, the fresh, new hair that still held some old memories but was always adding new ones. As his hand slid to the back of her head, he leaned in, and she joined him, breathless, their lips touching gently, finally. They stayed there, unmoving, their lips pressed together. There was urgency, passion, a thousand different emotions, but there was also time. They pulled apart, then immediately came back together. There would never be enough kisses to catch up. It was kiss after kiss after kiss—nothing raw, nothing pressuring, just the closest form of gratitude, tenderness, adoration, and so much perfect bliss that she wanted to sing with the cicadas and wind around him like a honeysuckle vine.

She decided, with her lips pressed up against his, that she would grow her hair out. She would never lose this memory. Just like she would never lose him again.

Nate took her hand and she rested her head on his shoulder like she had on their very first movie date at camp. They sat in silence. She was consumed with everything she'd just said, marveling that she'd had the chance to say it. They sat with the burgeoning night noises and their own thoughts until the sun disappeared into the darkness, the house lights came on, and the bullfrogs joined in the buzzing chorus. "Banana pudding?" she asked.

"Yes, ma'am. We've been carrying these sandwiches around so long we probably ought to eat them too."

The walk to the house was short, and they went straight to the kitchen. With thanks to Fred, they ate like they'd just finished a marathon and been served their favorite celebratory meal. They were giddy and laughing at every funny and unfunny thing the other said, when Trig came walking in holding an empty glass of whiskey.

"Do you remember Nate?" Brooke asked.

"Of course. He was almost my son." The statement felt inappropriate, like it lessened or belittled Nate. But Trig wasn't done. "So, what became of you? How'd you survive?" His words were slurred.

"How'd I survive my childhood?" Nate clarified.

Trig grunted.

"Well, I had a rough time after I got kicked out of camp."

Trig waited for more. Brooke did too. She'd always wondered what happened to him after that terrible day. "Losing the only person I felt a connection with at that time, plus the only place where I felt like I had roots, set me back."

"Are you talking about my daughter?" Trig asked, and Brooke was glad he wasn't holding a rifle this time.

Nate nodded, and Trig's eyes went briefly to Brooke.

"Camp reminded me of who I used to be," Nate said, "and then I was a loser again. Just like that."

Brooke was shocked at how transparent Nate was being. There was no shame, just a matter-of-fact answer to her father's question.

"Then my asshole uncle died. I thought all he had was debt, but when I was cleaning out the trailer, I found some things in an up-high cabinet."

Trig listened like he couldn't decide whether to love him or kick him out of his house. Brooke knew full well that her father had always wanted a son, but she also knew that, in recent years, he'd had his heart set on Gates.

"What did you find?" She so badly wanted Nate to have something that belonged to his parents. Something that his uncle hadn't hawked or thrown out.

"My grandfather's stamp collection. I'm pretty sure my uncle knew it had value, but he had no idea how to sell it, so it sat there in a bunch of shoeboxes along with some old family photos. I'm lucky they weren't used as fire starters. I contacted the philatelic society and had the stamps appraised, then I kept a few as a memento of my grandfather and sold the rest. Anyway, it was enough to give me a start."

Both Brooke and Trig were silent.

"It's what I used to go to college—community college first, and then University of South Carolina. Those stamps kept me alive, got me an education, and helped me launch my business."

Brooke was astounded. Stamps? Thank God.

"And what is your business?" Trig finally asked.

"I buy historical properties that are at risk of demolition, and I renovate them. Sometimes to rent, sometimes to sell."

"And you make a good living?"

Was her dad onto something? He was asking in a way that felt more than just curious. It was like he was vetting him.

"Yes, sir."

"Isn't *Family Feud* on?" Brooke hoped to redirect her father's inquisition. "Where's Cornelia?"

"She and Nana left me with the dishes and ran off to the cottage to watch some no-good reality show." He was clearly displeased. "It's gonna rot their brains into nothing. I'm afraid that if your mother keeps watching that garbage, she's gonna get ideas in her head and stop cooking me dinner." He stood from the table and left the room, mumbling, "I need more whiskey."

"Sorry about that," Brooke said once Trig was out of earshot. They both got up from the table and moved to the kitchen island where Brooke grabbed two bananas and started peeling.

"I loved it," Nate said. "He cares."

"Sometimes he does, I guess." She placed the bananas on a cutting board and handed him a knife. "Slices," she said. "Small ones."

He got to work immediately while she found a large white ceramic bowl.

"I never knew stamps were valuable."

"Some are," he said. "It was like a miracle finding those, and the photos. It was everything I wanted and needed. And it was my senior year. Perfect timing."

Brooke pulled the heavy cream from the refrigerator and added it to the bowl. "You were completely alone your senior year while I was over here hating my folks and picking out colors for my new dorm room."

"Which were…"

"Pink and white." She went to the pantry and picked out vanilla bean paste, gelatin, and sugar. "But there was a splash of black on my throw pillows to match my framed print of Audrey Hepburn in sunglasses."

He chuckled. "Perfect."

"I thought so." She laughed, measuring each ingredient with her heart.

She replayed the evening's events in her head, as she whisked as fast as she could. It was comfortable having Nate in her childhood kitchen, chatting and jumping in to help where he could. It felt like they were an old married couple, like there had never been a gap of nearly a decade in their relationship. "I hope our duck is doing okay," she said.

"He'll be fine. One night in a cage for a lifetime in the wild." Nate had such an agreeable way about him. "If Nana is having you run the place, will you be living in the lighthouse?"

She stopped whisking. Would that bother him? "Is it okay with you?"

He pulled her into a hug and spoke softly in her ear. "There's no one I would rather have living in that lighthouse. Except for maybe both of us. Someday."

She kissed him sweetly on the lips. "Then we'll just have to see how this goes, won't we?"

Chapter Twenty-Six

THE WIND WAS no help for the summertime humidity. By the time Brooke reached Camp Dogwood, the engine of Dottie's little jon boat smelled like burned oil and Brooke's hair was as poofy and knotted as a robin's nest. Nate waited for her on the half-sunk dock, and she barely had time to pull it back into a ponytail before he offered her a hand up and out of the boat. He tied a knot to hold the boat to the dock and led her along the wobbly old structure until they reached solid ground.

"Fred said he'd be here in an hour with the duck," Brooke said, scanning the grounds. Longleaf pines and oaks gave shade to rotting branches that littered the dirt from past storms. Patches of stinging bull nettle settled near dense thickets of wax myrtle, and round pennywort sprawled up toward the main building where the roof sagged into an old bench that had lichen growing between the wooden slats. "This is going to be a lot of work."

"We can do it," Nate said, sounding genuinely excited.

"We'll triage," Brooke began, her mind spinning. "The most important things first. We'll get enough done for

Libby's wedding, and then make this place better than your grandfather ever imagined."

"It's strange to be back here now when I know the owner," he said. "Just as strange as when it was turned into Camp Dogwood and was no longer in my family."

Brooke wasn't sure how to respond. Was he upset? "I'm sorry," she whispered.

He looked at her with such admiration that her heart did a little flip. "Have you ever heard of spilled juice?"

"What?"

He smiled like the thoughtful little boy she once knew. "You spill the juice in the morning, and because of that, you have to clean it up. That causes you to be late for work. But what you didn't know was that there was a three-car pileup and two fatalities at the exact time you would've been at that spot on the freeway. The spilled juice may have saved your life."

"Right. So?"

"I might not have my career and we might not be here together right now if it hadn't been for me getting kicked out of camp."

"You think that was your spill?"

"I do."

By the time Fred approached, Nate and Brooke's triage list was three pages long. He showed up in a dark red state-of-the-art fishing boat, which was in direct opposition to the old brownish houseboat on blocks behind the gas station where he lived. Fred was an enigma. Yet, there was something safe about the bearded Harvard grad who left corporate law for a simple life on Goose Island. He represented strong minds, tough choices, and straight priorities. Plus, he was the kind of guy who would happily save a duck.

On the bow of the boat, a little green head took on the wind like a dog hanging its head from a car window. Brooke watched as he extended his wings and allowed the generated lift to take him airborne. He flew ahead of the boat like he was leading the way. Just as Fred pulled up to the dock, the duck skidded and splashed, coming to a stop near the shore. Clearly, he was fine to be released.

"Hey!" Fred said, waving from behind the wheel. "Nice place you got here."

It wasn't her place. It was Nana's. Yet it felt like it should be hers. She had a connection to the land that filled her with the greatest intrinsic motivation she'd ever felt. She would work day and night to do right by Camp Dogwood. For now, that was going to mean hiring a cleanup crew, architects, a contractor, overseeing months and most likely years of work, and trying to keep everything on schedule. One month of cleaning up the place for Libby's wedding was nothing compared to the mountain of details she would undertake afterward. Her life was about to go from working forty hours a week to every waking second, and she didn't want it any other way.

She looked up at Nate, a happy set to his mouth as he

watched Fred tie the boat to the cleats on the un-sunken side of the dock, and was grateful he was there with her. Her passion for the place would take her a long way, but it was nice to have a professional nearby for questions.

Fred's shiny new trawler parked next to Dottie's old metal flat-bottomed boat seemed like a picture of this season of her life. She had to find a way to make things hers—to stop borrowing a boat from Dottie, living at her parents' house, and even eating meals provided by someone else. She was an adult, and it was time to embrace it. She might be the lowly jon boat in the metaphor before her, but she would work up to being a boat of real value.

Whew, did she ever need a quacking duck in that moment. The little green-headed guy limped up the beach straight toward her.

"Hey there, Zippy," Nate said. His old camp nickname, once meant to be a slur, seemed to fit the happy little waddler perfectly.

Fred ambled up behind him. "I guess he's officially free."

"Fly away, little guy." Brooke flapped her arms like it was a game of Simon Says. Zippy stood staunchly on his flat orange feet and stared at her defiantly. "Go on back to your people. Your duck people. Your kin."

"He may think he's found them." Fred laughed. "If I remember correctly, you said he was trying to break into your mama's vegetable garden."

Brooke immediately clued in. "And you fed him last

night."

"And again this morning," Fred said.

"He's not stupid," Nate laughed. "He's not going any-where if he's getting free food."

"Welcome to Camp Dogwood, Zip," Brooke said. "I guess I'll be buying duck food today."

"You want a tour?" Nate asked Fred.

"A quick one. I've got to get back to the store." He spat pieces of a chewed toothpick onto the dirt. They'd walked a few steps toward the main building when Fred asked, "Your nana okay, Brooke?"

Why was he asking about Nana?

"Fine. Just saw her at breakfast. I believe she was dressed for golf today."

Fred looked at Brooke strangely. "She's golfing?"

"No. Just dressed for it."

"Good to hear. She must be feeling better."

Brooke stopped at the building's double doors. Feeling better? Was she sick?

Fred's face fell, and his eyes shifted to Nate for help. He got none. "Guess I can't say."

"Can't say what?"

"Well, she and Sam were talking in the shop. She wasn't trying to hide anything. Like all the folks around here, she told me that Sam is the only doctor she trusts."

"Sam? The guy with the big dog? He's a doctor?" Nate asked.

"I mean, he's an EMT and he's applying to med school, but we're just happy to have someone on the island with healthcare expertise. Anyway—" Fred opened the door and walked into the dark, musty space, but Brooke wouldn't budge. "Nothing to worry about, I'm sure," he said. "Just typical old folks stuff. I'm probably on the verge of it myself."

Nate shot Fred a look that said, *You brought it up, dude. Now you have to tell her.*

Fred dramatically looked around the old cafeteria. "This is a wedding venue right here!" He sounded far too chipper. "Clean this place up and that friend of yours is gonna be a happy little bride monster. Are you gonna add chandeliers? A bar? I mean, you gotta get the roof fixed, but—"

It was a failed attempt at distraction. "Fred. What is wrong with my nana?"

He moved to the nearest table and sat his tall body on the attached round stool. "It could be nothing, but the reports say she's been having TIAs."

"Reports? And what's a TIA?"

"She said Duke took her in for an MRI. She's been getting it all figured out. So far, they're just ministrokes."

Brooke felt like she'd been sucker punched. "Does my mother know?"

"I should do better than to make assumptions," Fred said. "I thought your whole family knew."

"Well, if they did, they didn't tell me." She felt her face

flush. *Nana.* It shouldn't be a surprise, Nana was no spring chicken, but she was such a force, so free and full of life, she was supposed to be invincible. "I'm sorry, but I think I need to get home. If Nana's talking about this all around town, and my parents don't know, it's gonna be bad."

There was nothing Trigger and Cornelia hated more than their private family business being aired, especially if it was something they were not yet aware of. "Do you mind if we head out soon?" she said to Nate. She had to get to Nana before word spread. She had to get to Nana before—She couldn't even think it. But the word *stroke* was busy fueling fear in her heart. Strokes could happen at any time.

Chapter Twenty-Seven

"**I** AM NOT dying." Nana sounded exasperated. It was practically a family intervention on the front porch of her little backyard house, and Nana wasn't having any of it. Trigger's face matched the colorless white of the summer-time clouds and Cornelia looked like she'd just had her big toe smashed by a rock. Nana, almost half their size and wearing a short white skirt and bright blue collared golf shirt, pointed a crooked finger at all of them. "Now you listen here, you start dying when you stop living. Got that? I am not dying."

Trig grunted like the statement not only resembled a movie quote, but was obvious. Nate threw an arm around Brooke's shoulders and gave her a quick squeeze of encouragement. He'd left Fred and his car behind at Camp Dogwood, and Brooke couldn't help but feel awe at the fact that he was standing beside her during a family-only discussion. Especially since no one said a word about him being there. "Nana, what did the scans show?" Brooke asked.

"You know what? I do not care. I'm not going to let some scan tell me how I'm going to die. *I* decide." She leaned in toward Brooke and dropped her voice. "And I'll tell you a little something else. I don't need a scan to tell me that I'm old—the mirror reminds me every day." Her eyes were filled with sass as she addressed the half circle of family at her front door. "Y'all don't have to stand there all pale-faced with worry over me. We all know damn well that if I have any time left, it's only a handful of years. Maybe a couple more if Cornelia doesn't smother me in my sleep."

Cornelia gasped in horror, but Nana was quick to give her a wink.

"Cornelia, honey," Nana said. "Why don't you give being a crazy old bitty a try? Dress up when you're feeling pretty. Scream when you're mad. You're so busy worrying about what other people think. Manners this and manners that. Stop letting all these young folks with their silly opinions decide for you how you're gonna live your life." She smirked unapologetically at Brooke and Nate.

Cornelia opened her mouth to argue, but Nana held up a hand to stop her. "Hush." She yelled backward into the house, "Duke! Duke, come out here."

Round-shouldered Duke with his gray combover came shuffling from the bedroom in a plaid bathrobe. He'd clearly spent the night. Nana grabbed his hand and pulled him forward. "If I feel love for someone, I am going to pounce on it like a cat. I am going to give my heart and what is left of my worn-out soul to that person, because you know what? The chance may never come around again." She patted his hand in hers. "Right, sweetheart?"

Duke nodded with a little boy's smile, then pulled his shoulders back to stand taller.

"And I don't give a frog's butthole what rumors people spread or what judgments they heap on me. This is my life. You get me? Mine. And I am not hurting anybody."

Trig sighed loudly. "Are you getting good care, Mother? Are you doing what the doctors say?"

"I am doing exactly what I should be doing for my age. Now, if y'all will excuse me, my *boyfriend* and I were just about to take a nap." She stepped back inside the house and closed the door.

"Well, there you have it," Trig said, turning to go.

"Have what?" Cornelia quickly overtook him and led the way back to the main house spouting a stream of consciousness at him while Nate and Brooke followed behind. "We will be getting her the best doctors immediately. And we have to make sure she is on that blood-thinning medication that keeps her from getting clots. We will call Sam as soon as we get inside and get his help to set up a comprehensive plan of care. It doesn't matter how much it costs. Should I reach out to my old friend who had that natural person who did those new-agey types of things? Yes, I think I should. And Nana should be exercising. And do we know if she is taking her vitamins?"

Nate and Brooke grabbed a bag of bread from Cornelia's pantry before making their way back to Dottie's little boat for their return trip to Camp Dogwood to get Nate's car. In case Zippy was still there, they wanted to have a snack for him.

Nate steered by the outboard motor and Brooke took a moment to appreciate the welcome splashes of water that hit her face and tasted like salt as they worked with the wind to cool them from the late afternoon heat. Seeing Nana had made her feel better. No one that sassy would just keel over and die. It felt like an impossibility. She breathed in the seaweedy smell and smiled back at Nate. Now that she'd been away from Gates for a while, she was actually beginning to feel like a person again. It had felt good to be the chosen one, the lucky one, the how-did-a-girl-like-that-get-a-guy-like-him girl. But she was beginning to see, despite her circumstances, that it was so much better to be the one doing the choosing. There really was a difference between settling and making an active choice. Finally, thanks to God or fate or the universe or maybe just pure luck, she got to choose Nate.

"Hey, Nate," she yelled over the wind and the loud motor.

"Yeah?" He turned his head so his right ear was directed toward her.

"Never mind," she yelled.

"Tell me later!" he said. When the engine was going full-bore, it was almost impossible to hear over it.

She wanted to ask him if he thought she was sweet, and

if he liked her as much as people liked Jessa. Maybe it was good that he couldn't hear her. It was probably a needy question, or at least a self-centered one. She thought about the question until she couldn't remember why she decided that sweet was what she needed to be. Was sweet really the way to happiness? Nana didn't care about being sweet and that woman sure seemed happy. Cornelia cared, but simply didn't have it in her to be completely genuine. She could pretend to be nice all day long, but a sweet disposition toward others wasn't in her personality. And, go figure, it was Cornelia's and Nana's DNA that lived inside Brooke's body.

She turned her head into the wind, feeling a bit like the green-headed duck at the bow of Fred's boat. She pulled out her hair tie and it felt good to set her hair free. It lifted from her shoulders and blew with the wind and she shook her head to loosen every strand.

Maybe trying to be sweet was like that hair tie—holding her back.

Screw trying to be someone she wasn't. She was fine the way she was. She didn't need to be Jessa, or Cornelia, or Nana. And she certainly didn't need to be anything like Libby. What was wrong with just being herself? She was the girl who'd smiled at the boy with the Walmart bag. She had immediately liked the guy who climbed out of the loud grungy pickup truck wearing an ill-fitting blazer and tie to summer camp. She'd smiled at him because she liked him.

Screw sweet. She was going for real. No more people-pleasing. That's when she realized that she was already there. She'd never really changed. Trying to be someone she wasn't hadn't worked. Except maybe for the fact that now she was stuck as a bridesmaid in Libby's wedding.

She turned back to smile at Nate and her hair whacked her in the face and stuck in her mouth. Through the brown strands, she saw him grinning at her.

Life was miraculous.

If she'd stayed with Gates, she would probably never have seen Nate again, or gone back to Camp Dogwood, Nana wouldn't own it, and Brooke wouldn't be in charge of reviving it. If she hadn't gone back to Goose Island, her mother might still feel unappreciated, and Nana might never have met Duke. One little decision could lead to so many good things. Her mind spun with thoughts about decisions and ripples and timing and a million possibilities for the future.

Brooke held on to her new understanding, and it colored her dreams for Camp Dogwood with the brightest hope. She was going back to marketing, back to social media ad campaigns, back to organizing events and using her expertise. Nana's purchase brought back a part of who she used to be. She wasn't all wrong, she wasn't all bad. She was just a girl in her twenties figuring out how to live her best life.

Zippy magically appeared as they tied up the boat, and Brooke was so happy they'd thought to bring along some bread. "I'll get you healthier food soon," she promised as she tore off pieces and threw them to him.

The mallard followed as Brooke and Nate walked the property making lists of to-dos. Brooke was so overcome with the strangest supernatural feeling of being right where she was supposed to be that she almost got lightheaded. Anything was possible. Life was just a series of choices. It was then that she had an idea. One that she would keep to herself for the time being.

Every now and then, a wave of shock overtook her that she was actually there with Nate, making plans for the place where they'd met. The old jumping rock, the creek bridge, swimmin' hole, and horse corrals—they all felt so full of potential. Camp Dogwood deserved for people who cared about it to return and bring it back to life. But what made her stomach tickle and twist with joy and anticipation was the fact that Nathan Daugherty held her hand, stole little kisses, and looked at her like his eyes couldn't get enough of her face, like he'd been starving for her for years.

They were saying goodbye next to the jon boat, with the water spreading wide before them, and it wasn't lost on Brooke that they were near the place where Nate's parents' lives had ended. She felt compelled to ask, "Do you think your parents would approve of our plans?"

"I'm pretty sure my parents have something to do with them."

And that's when she remembered the one little point

she'd forgotten—she could make perfect choices every day, but in the end, no one truly had control. There were always the spiritual factors—the surprises, the uncontrollable events. Horrible ones like plane crashes and TIAs and beautiful ones like green-headed ducks and old loves reunited.

If she was going to take on Camp Dogwood and move forward with Nate, she would have to accept the twists and turns. And yes, there would always be choices—mainly, how to make the best of whatever was coming.

Chapter Twenty-Eight

THURSDAY EVENING, BROOKE walked across the wide backyard and knocked on Nana's door. "Nana, I have a business proposal for you."

"I figured you would," Nana said with a puffy-eyed smile. "Come on in." Everything in her little back house was navy blue or white—the blue velvet couch, the white damask curtains, and the big blue vase of dogwood branches artistically spilling over in the middle of the round dining table.

"Now, I know that you had a reason for purchasing Camp Dogwood, and I don't want to step on any toes, but—"

Nana interrupted. "Anna Brooke, I have no patience for this preamble. What is your proposition?"

"I can get a small business loan, and—"

"And you want to buy the place from me."

"That's what I was thinking, yes."

There was a curious twinkle in her eyes. "And why do you think I purchased that old plot of land to begin with?"

"Well, you have emotional ties to it, and in a business sense, a place to stay near Duke's winery works nicely."

"Honey. Have yourself a seat." Nana cleared a magazine from the blue couch and gestured for Brooke to sit. She remained standing like an angel with her white hair, white bathrobe, and white slippers. "You are aware that business decisions should never be made out of emotion, correct?"

Brooke nodded.

"But I tell you what…time passes. And I don't care how much time—ten years, thirty years, eighty, one hundred, it doesn't matter. People are not forgotten and feelings do not disappear like the danged morning fog. Mark my words, as long as I am alive, I will always hold love for your grandfather and for my best friends. Sometimes we have to tamp down those memories because they are so very hard to bear. But they are there. They live in our souls."

"When you and Mother were swimming, it seemed—"

"I remembered," Nana interrupted. She sat beside Brooke and put a small, cold hand on her knee. "I remembered them all so well. It was like they were right there with me."

"Is that when you decided to buy it?"

"That's when I decided that it would stay in our family. And by *our* family, I am including your young man, Nathan Daugherty. I bought it for both of you."

"Nana, what are you saying?"

"I am saying that at my age I can do whatever I damn well please. The place has been yours all along."

"No, Nana. I will take out this loan and I will buy it

from you."

"The hell you will." Nana stood and turned her back to Brooke. "Do you think your mother has started preparing our breakfast? Duke made me too many gin and tonics last night and my stomach is telling me all about it." She led the way to the front door, no qualms about going outside in her bathrobe and slippers. "Damn wet grass. I'm going to have your father make me a concrete walkway to the house."

"Good idea." Brooke tiptoed alongside her.

"Now," Nana began, "don't you think it's special that you have a connection to that place just like I do? These things should not be ignored. We'll get the paperwork together and I'll sign it over to you. You can consider it an early inheritance, but I see it as part of my legacy. Use that loan you're getting to fix it up and pay the taxes. It's in your hands now. I made it possible, but with hard work, you can turn it into something."

Trigger was sitting on the screened-in back porch drinking whiskey when they approached. He stood and opened the door for them. "What are you two up to?"

"I thought it would take her longer to ask, but our girl knows her mind," Nana said.

"The land," Trig said with a knowing smile. "Cornelia's in the kitchen."

"She did it!" Nana announced as they walked into the oversized kitchen where Cornelia stood flipping oatcakes. "She asked."

"Well, I'll be. Good on you, Anna Brooke. And you didn't even say a word about it."

"I was figuring things out—the loan, the rest of the renovations. I think Nate is going to help as an investor."

"I am a genius," Nana said, picking pieces from the plate and stuffing bites into her mouth. "I saw it all coming."

"As much as I hate to say it, Dottie Boone had something to do with all this," Cornelia said.

"Hush your mouth!" Nana accidentally spat a mouthful of oaty cake onto the counter.

"What are you talking about?" Brooke asked.

"Dottie Boone had some sort of vision about a duck," Cornelia said, "and she was so sure of whatever it was she saw that she called up your grandmother."

Brooke remembered Dottie saying that symbols were hard to interpret. "She called you, Nana?"

"It wasn't just the duck. It was also the boy."

Cornelia flipped another cake before adding, "Dottie said you left camp with the wrong thing—which presumably was Gates Lancaster. According to her, you were supposed to leave camp with my Nathan."

"Your Nathan, Mother?"

Cornelia grinned and shrugged. "That's what I said."

Brooke shook her head. *Cornelia's Nathan*, what a strange and beautiful development. "Is that what she saw coming? Me and Nathan?"

"She saw a yellow duck, rubber or plastic, I think, blocking the way of something."

"It was stolen. It had his phone number on it, and it was my only way to find him."

Cornelia stepped back from the stovetop. "My word. That actually makes sense."

"And now he's back," Nana said.

"Yeah." It was a delicious thing to admit.

Cornelia stacked more oat cakes onto a pile that was becoming wobbly with the height as she spoke. "I cannot for the life of me understand all of this nonsense. Ducks, visions. I declare, it must all be some sort of strange happenstance."

Trigger joined the women at the kitchen island after putting his coffee cup in the sink. "Y'all talking about ducks?"

Cornelia nodded.

"Gun's still ready if you need me to take care of that injured one."

"Trig!" Brooke shouted. "Zippy's mine, he's healthy, and I love him."

Trigger chuckled.

"That's it," Nana said with a frown. "Not another word about ducks, or I will take that rifle and shut you up for good. This is about family, and business, and futures."

THE FRIDAY NIGHT band played riffs into the evening summer air, and groups of people swayed and sipped wine all over the grounds of the Saltwater Winery. Brooke set up a table and chairs to the side of the stage, far enough away that she could talk to Nate over the music and avoid the swell of the crowd. Dottie's food truck was in full force selling Lowcountry Boil in rectangular paper bowls. Jessa and Tulip stacked the corn, pork sausage, shrimp, and potatoes, added extra butter and Old Bay seasoning, then handed it to customers through the truck window. Nana was dancing with Duke, dressed like a flapper in a fringed skirt and a sparkly headband complete with huge black feather. It was the golden hour, and the setting sun cast shades of yellow and orange on everyone as Brooke waited for Nate at their table. She passed the time watching Nana shimmy and Duke beam like she was pure happiness shining onto him like a spotlight.

Brooke felt an overwhelming sense of pride. That was her grandmother out there dancing joyfully, unencumbered by rules and the judgment of others. How liberating it must be to let go of societal expectations and free yourself to dance loose and wide open to the rhythm and magic of the music. Nana kicked her leg out like she was about to do the Charleston, and Brooke smiled at the entertaining old moves. But when Nana went to put her foot down, her ankle bent sideways, limp and useless. Duke tried to catch her, but she was on the ground in a blink. First her hip, then her head. She never even put an arm out to catch herself. The crowd around them echoed Brooke's gasp.

Brooke couldn't remember running to Nana or holding her bleeding head in her lap. She recalled Duke looking frightened, seated in the ambulance next to Nana on the gurney as the doors closed. She ran to her car to follow them and quickly texted Nate to let him know he could find her at the hospital rather than the winery. Duke now sat stiffly on the purple hospital waiting-room chair staring into space. As far as she knew, he hadn't spoken a word since it happened. If she didn't know better, she would have thought it was Duke who'd had the stroke, not Nana. She tried to hug the old man, but he turned away. She offered him water and food from the vending machine, but he wouldn't so much as make eye contact with her. His body may be waiting for news, but his soul was either with Nana or back with Amelia at her Patch of Happiness. Brooke didn't know which.

Life came slamming back into technicolor once Trigger and Cornelia arrived at the hospital. "Mother!" Brooke jumped up and hugged her tightly. Trig stood behind them as expressionless and stiff as a Christmas nutcracker. Brooke worked her way underneath Trig's arm to hug him from the side. "Are you okay?"

"Where are the doctors?"

"They'll be out in a minute," Brooke said. "They're trying to stabilize her."

"So she's not dead?" Cornelia sounded like a squirrel.

Brooke shook her head. "No, but I think Duke might need some help."

Both parents looked his way. Cornelia sighed deeply and whispered, "The poor man. He probably sat in that very spot when his wife died."

"No wonder he's not talking."

Trig made his way to the nurses' station and Cornelia seemed torn between following him and tending to Duke. She opted to rush over to the nurses' station, push Trig aside, and animatedly discuss the merits of the doctors on staff, trying her best to take control. Was there a specialist in the hospital? Were they aware that Grace was a Warter? She must have the absolute best care possible. Additionally, the family must be allowed to see her immediately or they would be in contact with hospital management.

Brooke took the seat across from Duke. "Nana taught them well," she said.

Duke turned and fixed his watery eyes on her.

"I mean, Nana would do the same thing for you, right? Demand the best care, insist on seeing you."

Duke nodded sadly.

"It's what we do when we love someone."

"I held Amelia's hand as she died," he uttered.

Brooke could barely hear him. "What a beautiful thing to do for her."

"I should've stayed alone."

"Mr. Bradley. I apologize if my timing is bad," Brooke began, "but I've always believed that it's worth the pain to have had the love."

"I was supposed to die first. The man dies first." Duke abruptly stood. "Please tell Grace…" he began, but he didn't finish. Instead, he shuffled as fast as he could through the automatic doors leading outside of the hospital. Brooke watched him go and wondered how he planned to get home.

Chapter Twenty-Nine

NATE SHOWED UP just as Duke was walking out of the automatic front doors. He took the spot next to Brooke and sat vigil with the Warter family in the waiting room. Brooke was grateful she had Nate's strong shoulder as a pillow, and it seemed like Cornelia felt a similar gratitude for Trig's. They stayed that way all night. It wasn't until nine A.M. that they were finally allowed to see Nana. She would need to remain hospitalized for at least another three days to monitor her for brain swelling. The doctor warned them that she looked a bit different and had mild aphasia, so she might be difficult to understand.

Even with the warning, it was a shock to see Nana looking so tiny and gray in the long hospital bed. "Go away," she tried to say when they all moved as a mass into her room. Only half of her mouth moved. The rest of her face looked like clay that had been smashed downward, closing half of her eye and making the corner of her mouth droop. The words came out jumbled, like her tongue didn't work.

"Mama," Trig sighed, pulling a chair up next to her bed while Cornelia grabbed the poor woman's hand and kissed it.

"Mama"—his voice sounded strangely young—"are you okay?"

It was hard to make out the words, but Brooke was pretty sure that Nana called her son stupid. Not much progress was made from that point on. After forty-five minutes, Nana was sound asleep and they all decided to go home.

It was already humid when they walked out of the main entrance to the hospital. After sitting on a chair all night, Brooke could hardly wait to be horizontal underneath a set of soft cotton sheets. She was looking for her car when she saw a hunched figure sitting on a bench next to the road. She would recognize the combover anywhere.

"Mr. Bradley!" Brooke said. "You're still here!"

He looked up, his face pale and drawn.

"Duke Bradley!" Cornelia exclaimed, jogging toward him. She had both of the man's hands in hers before Brooke could say another word. "Have you been here all night? For heaven's sake. You have got to be plumb wiped out."

He hunched over even more, like his spine had turned to jelly. His light blue button-down shirt pressed against their combined hands. "Is she dead?" he asked in the saddest, most pitiful voice.

"No, sir." Cornelia patted his hands. "She's gonna be okay. They just need to keep her for a bit longer for observation."

Immediately, the tide shifted. Duke's head lifted, and then his chest. Soon, he was patting Cornelia's hands instead of the other way around. "Can I see her?"

"Of course you can." With a quick goodbye to Brooke and Nate, Cornelia and Trigger each took an arm and guided Duke back inside the hospital.

"Are you as tired as I am?" Brooke asked Nate.

"Pretty sure I could sleep underneath that bush right there." He pointed to the hospital landscaping. "But I'm glad we were here. It was nice feeling like part of your family," he said. "I can barely remember what it was like to feel that kind of belonging."

Brooke linked her arm in his and leaned her head against his chest.

"You drove here?" he asked.

"My car's over there." In the parking lot was a huge yellow truck with SALTY DOT'S in blue curlicue writing. People began exiting the truck like it was a school bus dropping off kids. First Jessa, then Tulip, Fred, and finally Dottie came around the front. The group spotted Brooke and Nate immediately.

"We're here!" Dottie yelled from about fifteen parking spaces away.

All of the Boones waved enthusiastically, but none of them had a smile on their face. Jessa ran straight to Brooke and took her in an aggressive hug. "We're sorry, Brooke. So, so sorry. We know how much your nana meant to you."

Meant?

"We brought it all," Dottie said. "Everything that y'all

asked for."

"Did Cornelia call you?"

"No, honey," Dottie said. "We got the email."

"What email?"

"From the winery," Jessa said.

Brooke made a confused face at Jessa. "Did Duke send it?"

"It came from the main outreach account, the one we use for customers. It went to the entire list. It had to be either Duke or Libby."

"Anyhoo," Dottie interrupted, "like I said, we've got the biscuits with tomato gravy, the baked beans, and the corn. Fred made the pork ribs and brought the bourbon. I believe Allie will be here soon with the RC Colas and the wine."

"Are y'all holding the funeral in the hospital chapel? If I remember correctly, they don't allow food in there, so we'll have to find a spot in the cafeteria."

"Duke arranged a funeral?" Brooke asked.

"It's okay," Jessa said. "No one minds that it happened so fast. We just want to be here in support of you and your family."

It was Nate who started laughing first.

Brooke joined in. "She's not dead."

It took a few seconds to sink in, then Fred joined in, chuckling louder than Nate. Jessa looked as shocked as Brooke probably did. "Well, thank the Lord," Dottie said.

"Can I see that email?" Brooke asked.

Jessa quickly pulled it up.

The title of the email was POTLUCK FUNERAL. And the rest of it didn't sound like it was written by Duke or Libby. It sounded like it was written by Nana herself.

We regret to inform you that our beloved employee and former Miss South Carolina, Grace Sharon Beauregard Warter, has passed on to the highest realm of peace and tranquility. If she were here, she would tell you herself that she has wished for peace for many years, yet no one would give it to her. Finally, God has answered her most fervent prayers and delivered her from this ungrateful earth. In remembrance of our beloved Grace, please bring a food offering to the Charleston Memorial Hospital tomorrow by 10 A.M. Most appreciated would be pork ribs with Carolina BBQ sauce, baked beans, corn, Dottie Boone's biscuits with tomato gravy, RC Cola, wine, and a large bottle of bourbon. Desserts of all sorts are welcome, except for ice cream cakes. Any woman of stature knows that ice cream should only be served on the side and never in cake form. We look forward to your attendance.

—The Saltwater Winery

Now Brooke joined in the laughter. Nana may have trouble speaking, but the sly old fox's brain was working just fine.

It was almost ten o'clock, and cars were streaming into

the parking lot. Trig and Cornelia were in conversation with someone in a black Mercedes, probably figuring out what Nana had done in the same way Brooke just had. A small crowd was beginning to form by the hospital entrance.

For a full twenty minutes, the crowd kept growing inside and outside of the glass front doors. At least seventy-five people had arrived. Cornelia was red-faced at this point. How did a classy woman explain to folks that her dead mother-in-law was in fact not dead, and furthermore, managed to send an email to every wine lover near and far requesting her favorite foods?

Sheet pans, drink cans, and wine bottles were piled up on every bench outside and every chair and table in the waiting room inside. The whole place smelled like a BBQ restaurant. Hospital staff ran interference and tried to keep the crowd noise low until finally, Nana was wheeled out wearing two blue hospital gowns. One as a dress, and another one open in the front and tied around her waist like a dressing jacket. Her hair was slicked back into her signature black-ribboned low ponytail and she wore red lipstick and a pair of enormous round sunglasses. A nurse or two must have been complicit in her makeover.

Only half of her face smiled when she was wheeled into the room, but even so, it was clear that not only was she not at all embarrassed by what she'd done. In truth, she appeared quite pleased. Cornelia was immediately by her side doing her best to appear calm and nonplussed. The crowd instantly became silent and turned toward the lady of the hour.

Nana took Cornelia's hand and squeezed it. "Welcome them," she slurred.

"Welcome, everyone," Cornelia began, her neck red and splotchy with embarrassment. "Grace is so pleased that you're here. We do apologize for the—ouch!"

Nana pressed her fingernails into Cornelia's hand. "No apologies, Cornelia."

"As you can see," Cornelia tried again. "Grace is alive and"—she paused to choose her word carefully—"recovering."

"Where's Duke?" Nana asked.

Cornelia asked the crowd, "Mr. Bradley?"

Duke raised his hand like a schoolboy at the back of the class. "Here."

"Tell him to come here." Cornelia repeated the request since Nana's tongue was still thick and uncooperative.

The crowd parted for Duke like the Red Sea as he shuffled his way to the front. Nana pointed to a spot next to her and dropped Cornelia's hand for his.

"Trigger," Nana called out. "There." She pointed to a spot next to Cornelia. "Anna Brooke," she demanded, pointing to a spot next to Duke. "Nathan."

Both Nate and Brooke went wide-eyed when his name was called. Nana pointed to a spot that would have them all lined up together as couples. Then she waved back toward the door she'd just come from like she was the Queen of

England. Out walked a man carrying a leather Bible.

"Tell them," Nana said to the man. "Welcome friends, and family," he began. "I am Pastor Thompson and you are gathered here today not for a funeral but for a wedding."

Cornelia first looked at Brooke, then at Duke. Brooke shrugged at her mother and whispered to Nate, "This can't be legally binding. Do you want to walk away? We can watch them instead of standing up here."

"Let's stay," Nate whispered back, standing tall and sure beside her. "If it's okay with you."

She nodded and moved closer to him. He put his arm around her shoulders.

Duke looked like the happiest of the seven dwarves with his gnarled hand firmly holding on to Nana's.

Trig looked like he was about to kill someone, and Cornelia's eyes kept going to Brooke and Nate with serious questions.

"It's okay," Brooke mouthed to her parents. As soon as she said it, she noticed a tall figure moving toward the exit from the back of the room. Everyone's attention shifted to the person who was leaving. Brooke's heart fell to her knees. It was Gates, and he looked like he'd just walked into a wasp's nest and had to run for his life.

Between Gates and the panic on her mother's face, Brooke felt more and more alarmed. Surely, her mother was sick with the thought that her one and only daughter was getting married in such a manner. The woman had been dreaming about and planning for Brooke's wedding since the day she was born. Actually, Brooke herself had been dreaming about her wedding for as long as she could remember. Even if Nate was the right guy, this was not the way she wanted to do it.

Brooke felt like her feet were rooted to the ground. Should she run after Gates? Should she stay here and say God only knew what to Nate in front of their friends, a great portion of the residents of Goose Island, and a whole bunch of other people she didn't recognize? Trig and Cornelia looked like marble statues, and Brooke was pretty sure she did too.

Nana had really done it this time. She'd embarrassed them all so much that she had rendered them immobile.

Chapter Thirty

NANA MUST HAVE noticed the collective distress of her family, because she said in her new drawn-out way, "Hush. It's a vow, not a real marriage."

That seemed to help all of them. Except for Duke. He bent down and whispered into her ear, "This is real to me, my love." Who knew how much time Nana had left? If this was what she wanted, this was what she'd get.

The pastor continued. "Grace and I spent time together early this morning, and she has some words she would like to share with you. They are simple, but hold great wisdom. And it begins with the reality that life on earth is short." He pulled a piece of paper from his Bible and cleared his throat. "Hold the door for others. Wear the costume and the fancy dress. Kiss the boy. Buy the island. Say the kind words—not just to others, but most importantly, to yourself. Wear the cheap plastic rings and your inherited diamonds at the same time. Bring soup to your sick neighbors, but not the soup that you've had in your freezer for two years. Apologize when you hurt someone. Admit when you're wrong. And stop judging yourself. Do you know who is the meanest when it comes to judging you? You are. Stop focusing on everything you did wrong in your life and focus on what you did right. And go to the funerals, because they're not an ending. They're a beginning. You're more important than you think you are." The pastor paused for effect.

"Now," he began, "you are all welcome to join in this next part. If you are here with a loved one, feel free to hold their hands and look into their eyes."

There was movement in the crowd, and he gave them a moment before he proceeded. "If you love someone, love them like you're the only two people in a raft together. There will be rocks to get past. And the water will be cold. There is a waterfall up ahead—it could be a big one, it could be a little one. Love your person like you're about to go over the edge together. What does that mean? It means you don't take them for granted. You use every God-given sense to show your love—tell them, touch them, look into their eyes, breathe in who they are, and most of all, appreciate them. Then, when the time comes, take turns holding each other above the water. Why? Because they're the person with whom you chose to share your raft. For better or for worse. If you're lucky, the waterfall will be a long way off, your waters will be calm, and your raft will hold air. During those times, enjoy the sounds and the view together. When those moments happen, hold each other close and be thankful."

Nana and Duke never took their eyes off each other, and Brooke wondered how Nana didn't have a crick in her neck.

"Grace Warter and Duke Bradley." He turned to face them instead of the crowd. "Do you agree to be in the raft together?"

"We do," they said.

The pastor turned to Cornelia and Trigger. "And you?"

"I do," Cornelia said.

"I do," Trig said. It wasn't time yet, but Trig leaned in for a kiss. Cornelia started to deny him, but then softened and kissed him back.

"Brooke and Nathan." The pastor faced them. "Grace informed me that the Warters have a family saying when it comes to choosing a life partner."

Brooke knew exactly what was coming.

"Marry the man who loves you more." Pastor Thompson cleared his throat. "This may not be biblical, but I can see where it might work."

Cornelia interrupted. "It is designed to keep the woman safe, and it is what we hope for when it comes to our daughter. A woman can learn to love a man, but a man must be wholeheartedly in love with a woman in order for her to be happy." The words sounded a bit defensive, but she tried to ease them by adding, "And it is possible that Nathan might be that fine gentleman."

Brooke was instantly infuriated. "No," she said. Adrenaline shot through her as she addressed the crowd. She didn't mean for her voice to be so loud. "Sorry, everyone. But, *no*."

Cornelia's face turned bright red, and Brooke saw her

dad slip his arm around her mother's waist to hold her up.

"Sorry, Mother," Brooke said. "But Nate doesn't love me more, and I don't think he should."

Cornelia made the face that had become very familiar over the course of Brooke's life. The one that said *shut up immediately or there will be hell to pay.*

"Why would anyone get married to someone they don't love as deeply as possible?" Brooke went on.

Cornelia managed to speak in a sing-songy twang despite her pinched lips. "I'm not saying you won't have love for him, I am simply saying that he should love you more."

"I do love her more," Nathan spoke up. "Maybe more than she loves me, and maybe not. We're still working on that." He squeezed Brooke's hands. "What I am happy for everyone in this room to know is that I love her more than enough."

Brooke instantly relaxed. She trusted that whatever he said was exactly what was needed in the moment.

"I love her more than enough to get in that raft with her," he continued, looking at her instead of the crowd. "I know Brooke. I've known her since middle school. And I know that if that raft has a hole, we'll plug it together. We'll work together to reinforce that raft and make it stronger. And I know, without a doubt, that the relationship we are building now, this newfound old love, will be more than enough to handle whatever lies ahead."

Pastor Thompson took control again. "And do you, Anna Brooke, agree to be in a raft with Nathan?"

"I do," she said, her eyes still glued to him, his words zooming back and forth, forging a speedway between her heart and mind.

Nana waited a few seconds before snapping her fingers at the pastor. "Tell the folks it's time to eat."

"A quick prayer, and then we will retire to the cafeteria where I have taken the liberty of reserving several tables for this delicious-smelling food." He prayed for good health and smooth sailing for the couples, and he thanked the crowd for showing up when they thought they were coming to a sad event. "God always brings good from the bad if you work with him," he reminded them. "This unusual ceremony is a prime example."

WHEN BROOKE WALKED downstairs a week later, there sat Nana in Trig's recliner watching *The Price Is Right*. She was skinnier than before the stroke, and the wrinkles in her face were more pronounced, but the fire in her eyes was still flaming hot.

"Hey, Nana," Brooke said.

Nana held up a bony hand to wave but never took her eyes from the television.

"Did you have breakfast already?"

"Yes," Nana said, still not looking at her granddaughter.

For the few days Nana had been home, Duke had joined them at the breakfast table every morning. Despite the fact that he had a huge house on a vineyard, he appeared to have moved into Nana's little cottage.

"Are you okay?" Brooke asked.

"Fine," Nana said.

"Nana." Brooke scooted as close as she could to her. "I want to know how you really are."

Nana looked at her like Brooke was a fire ant that needed to be sprayed with poison. "Don't bother kissing up to me, Anna Brooke. Oh, Nana this, and oh, Nana that. How are you doing, Nana? Do you need me to wipe your butt, Nana? Just pretend like I'm not here." She looked like a furious little elf engulfed by the big leather chair. Her words were still a bit slurred, and her face slightly drooped, but all in all, she'd made a remarkable recovery.

"Do you want to tell me what's wrong?" Brooke asked.

Nana grunted. "Duke's gone into the winery today, and he won't let me go with him. I told him that I work there, too, but he wasn't having it. Said I'm supposed to rest and regain my strength. Well, I'll tell you how I regain my strength—by *doing*! Not by sitting here like some old shell of a cicada stuck to a tree."

"I'm meeting some folks at Camp Dogwood today if you want to come along," Brooke said.

Nana was off the chair and scooting toward the back door faster than the wheel on *The Price Is Right*. "Wait for me. I've got to get out of my slippers and house dress." She stopped for a second. "And with whom is our appointment?"

"Our contractor and some subs."

"What are we working on?" She stopped again. "Oh, hell. I forgot. Duke's trying to appease me by taking us all out to supper."

"Oh, right!" Brooke said. "I almost forgot. The big *Grace is out of the hospital* celebration."

"I mean, I do like a celebration." She smiled. "That man bothers the tar out of me." She took a few steps into the kitchen to check for Cornelia. "I'm surprised your mother has not been in here bugging me six ways to Sunday about what I'm going to wear and what she's going to wear and all of that hooey. How much time do we have?"

"I believe he said three o'clock."

"And you have the time to do that whole meeting?"

Brooke nodded. "Now that I bought a boat, I do."

"Good girl. And you're bringing our boy, right?"

Brooke smiled at how her family always referred to Nate as *theirs*. "I am."

The meeting took several hours, and Nana asked many surprisingly astute questions. Brooke was grateful she was there. Nana was tired afterward, so she waited in the boat while Brooke ran up the winding iron stairs of the lighthouse to her brand-new bedroom, stopping at the top to appreciate the scene. The place was barely inhabitable—there was still so much to do. But the windows had been replaced and the utilities were hooked up. She'd cleaned it herself, wiping deep into every corner and crack and vacuuming up years' worth of dirt, dust, and spider webs. It gave her a feeling of pride to see her big bed with fluffy white comforter and sink-into-it mattress taking up space in the circular room. The afghan Nana knitted some twenty or more years ago lay folded at the foot, and the nightstands she'd bought secondhand and refinished herself held tall silver lamps. Next to the lamp on the right side was a framed photo of her and Nate. She had on a pink backpack and held a large wheeled suitcase. He had on an ill-fitting suit jacket with a tie and wrinkly, too-short khaki pants. In his hand was a Walmart bag. She'd found the photo in one of the old stalls by the horse paddock. It had been filled with bins of craft supplies and at least twenty years of camp pictures. One of the counselors, God only knew which one, must have gotten a shot of them on the day they met. It never made it onto the camp bulletin board, but it found a much better home now.

Chapter Thirty-One

BROOKE HAD JUST finished changing into a flirty white sundress when she heard someone calling her name outside. She was in the middle of the lighthouse tower, and since none of the windows opened, she could go up to the balcony that circled the light, or she could go down to the door on the main floor. She opted to go up, practically giggling as she ran up the stairs. She knew it was Nate coming to pick her up for what were becoming weekly suppers with Nana and Duke. Finally, she was finally going to get her romantic balcony scene.

She swung open the heavy reinforced door and leaned over the iron railing, careful not to get rust on her white dress. "Hello! I'm up here!" she yelled. She heard footsteps on the concrete down below and the sound instantly raised her hackles. The steps were even and precise. There was no limp.

A tall man with dark hair came into view, and Brooke's balcony dream was once again dashed. "Come down here!" Gates yelled. "Why are you up there?"

"Be right there!" she yelled. This time, she took her time

on the stairs. Why hadn't Gates texted her that he was coming? What was left to say? It was made perfectly clear to him that she was now with Nate. Him coming to her home unannounced when he knew she lived alone on an island was downright creepy.

When she pushed open the heavy front door, he was standing there waiting. "Hey," he said.

"What are you doing here?" She didn't invite him in or step outside.

He stood there wringing his hands and didn't even attempt to smile. "I can still track you."

"Shoot." She looked around for her phone. It was upstairs in her bedroom. "I need to turn that off."

"I went to the funeral," he said. "Or wedding, or whatever it was. I know it's been a while since then, but I can't seem to shake it."

She nodded. "I saw you."

He was agitated and fidgety. "You moved on pretty fast."

"I did."

"And your family seems to like him."

"They do."

He nodded gravely. "Did you marry that guy?"

"It wasn't a wedding."

His nervous movements stopped abruptly. "Good."

"Gates. Why are you here? I have to leave any minute now."

He looked down at the pathway leading to the lighthouse. "Is he coming?"

"He is."

"I don't know." He ran his right hand through his hair like he was in agony. "I don't know why I'm here."

Brooke waited. He was clearly there for a reason.

"I ruined so much, Brooke. So much more than you know."

She stepped outside to join him, leaving the lighthouse door open.

"Libby told me what you said," he said.

Brooke racked her brain trying to remember what that might be. She'd never shared anything personal with Libby, and she probably never would. "What did she say?"

"That you were only with Nate because you felt sorry for him."

"Sorry for Nate?" She laughed out loud, then stopped when the full force of what he said hit her. "Wait. Now, let me get this straight," Brooke began. This time she didn't try to keep the anger from her voice. "I'm going to be in Libby's wedding as a favor, right? A favor to the girl who *bullied* me. I'm wearing a dress that costs more than my entire wardrobe for her. I have been stressing myself out trying to get Camp Dogwood ready for her dumb wedding, and let's not forget, she had this great idea to buy vintage china dishes and stemware her guests could use and then take home. Beautiful. Fabulous. We've all spent hours shopping for that stuff. And what did Libby just think of? What just suddenly occurred to her? Oh, that the guests can't take home dirty dishes. So who gets assigned the job of washing them?" She pointed at herself. "This girl. I will be stuck inside washing dishes while you are all dancing under the moonlight." She inhaled deeply before continuing. "And she has the audacity to tell you lies about me? She has the gall to say I feel sorry for Nate when she has no clue about me or about—"

"Brooke." Gates touched her on the arm. "Calm down. I was just asking."

"But can you see how she makes me so mad? She's doing it again! She's trying to ruin my life."

"Well, we just cleared it up, didn't we? The rumor ends here and now."

"Does it, though? Who else is she telling? Who else thinks that I'm pity-dating Nate? He doesn't deserve that. He's the best guy, he's..." As words kept flying out of her mouth, she realized she might be seriously hurting Gates's feelings. "I'm sorry."

"Why?" He seemed genuinely curious.

"I don't know. I guess because I shouldn't say things that might be hurtful. I should be *sweeter*." She said the word with clear bitterness. He was the one who'd put the whole *sweet* and *nice* thought in her brain to begin with.

"I don't think you should be sweeter."

"You said I should be when we broke up."

"I never said that."

"You said that Jessa was sweet and I was nice."

"She *is* sweet, and you *are* nice."

"But you made it sound like sweet was better, that it was genuine. You said nice was all an act."

"I never said that, Brooke. I don't even believe that."

"Well, it screwed me up for a while." Brooke sat on the edge of the concrete platform and tucked her dress under her legs. Gates sat beside her. "I can't be someone that I wasn't made to be. I don't want to be."

"Yeah. Poor Jessa. She's overly kind. Too sweet."

"You think so?"

"I do." He pressed his lips together and looked at her a beat too long. "That's why I chose you instead."

"What do you mean?" She didn't need to ask the question. She knew exactly what he meant. She'd always suspected that Jessa had been his first choice.

"I know I'm a downer. I know I can be hard to handle. How could a person like me ever deserve a woman like her?"

That stung. "And I wasn't as great, so you settled for me."

"No, that's not what I'm saying at all. You were as great. You are as great. Better in some ways. You have really good boundaries, and you're not afraid to stand up for what you believe in. You don't give up on people. It's just that Nathan was the one who saw those things in you first. Not me." He turned to face her. "I know what I did, Brooke. You liked him, and I pushed and pushed until I won you over."

Brooke didn't mention that he might never have won her

over if she'd had a way to get in touch with Nathan. Gates had been her second choice too.

"But I want you to know that it's me who's hurting now. I deserve it. I know I do. I fell in love with you over the years we were together. I will always love you."

They both turned as they heard footsteps approaching. This time, with Nate's signature heavy step, light step cadence.

Brooke placed her hand on Gates's knee. "And I will always have love for you too."

When Nate appeared, Brooke ran over and hugged him. "Look who came to visit," she said. "Our old camp buddy."

"Hey, Gates," Nate said, taking stock of the situation. "All good?"

Gates walked over and shook Nate's hand. "Yeah. Fine. Hey, uh, sorry about the camp stuff all those years ago."

"It's all good now," Nate said.

Gates took a few steps down the pathway. There was something in the back pocket of his jeans. Maybe he had overstuffed his wallet, or maybe he'd picked up a rock that he wanted to keep.

Brooke yelled out, "Hey, Gates. It's okay with me, you know."

He stopped and turned around. "What is?"

"You and Jessa."

"She has no interest in dating me," he said.

"You never know until you try."

He nodded, and walked on.

"Gates wants to go out with Jessa?" Nate asked.

"He always has. I'll tell you all about it in the car."

"Are you going to tell Jessa too?"

"Of course I'm going to tell Jessa! Should I call her, or should we stop by after supper?"

"Depends on if Duke buys us dessert."

"Right. Dottie's always got something."

"Do you think Jessa likes him back?" he asked.

"I have no idea. She pretends to be anti-men, but I don't believe her."

Nate waited as she ran inside to get her phone and purse. She excitedly reached for his hand as they walked to his car. "I can hardly wait to hear what she says."

"GROSS," JESSA SAID. "No way. I'd rather have food poisoning. Honestly, I never understood how you could stand him."

"Doesn't get any clearer than that," Nate joked.

Brooke, Nate, Jessa, and Tulip were all sitting around Dottie's kitchen table with bowls of peach cobbler topped with vanilla ice cream. Jessa hadn't touched hers. "Jess, are you sure you don't like him?" Brooke asked. "There was a time back at camp when I thought you two might have something. I promise, I *swear*, if you do, it is absolutely okay with me."

"Listen, you and Nate were able to turn back time because you never let go of each other. I don't even remember if I had feelings for Gates back then, but if I did, those feelings have been dead and gone for years. They will never be resurrected."

Dottie joined the group with her bowl of dessert and a heaping side of prognostication. "I tell you what," she said. "I knew something was off all those years ago."

"Mama. Stop it, please," Jessa said.

"I didn't say he was supposed to be yours, baby girl," Dottie said. "He just wasn't rightfully hers. He could be meant for Harriet Whatsamadinger way out in Australia for all I know."

"Harriet who?" Jessa asked.

"You know better than to ask that, Carolina Jessamine. I just plucked that name from the air." Dottie pulled off her blue knit cap and placed it on the table before taking a huge bite of the warm cobbler with cold ice cream topper. Her dark hair was salted with grays. Parts of her were beautiful, like Jessa. Mainly her large blue eyes and soft, delicate chin. The rest of her looked like an overworked sun-lover. "I've been on the hamster wheel all day," she said. "And that damn wedding is coming up so quick. I mixed up remoulade sauce for two hundred people, I made the yeast bread and the coleslaw, and then I sliced open every one of those damned crab legs. Thank God she didn't ask me to make the cake. My hands are going to smell like crab and horseradish for the rest of my days."

"I'll be glad when this wedding is over," Brooke said. "It's been tons of work getting Camp Dogwood ready too."

"Well, sweetheart, I'm proud of you for sticking to your word," Dottie said. "You committed to doing that wedding and you're seeing it through."

"Not happily."

"Now, lookie here. That might be a little bit my fault. I've been telling you all about my visions and making you feel like you had to do certain things. I apologize for that. I do. This wedding might be the biggest disaster in the Northern Hemisphere. It might go so bad that people leave crying. Libby's a real wild card, ya know?" Dottie took a big bite of dessert and chewed carefully while she thought. "Here's my final piece of advice. And I want you to really hear me on this, okay?" She turned to her daughters. "Carolina Jessamine and Tulip, I want you to hear this too." She aggressively wiped her mouth with her napkin and looked back and forth at the three of them with intensity. "Just believe that everything will work out, and let the universe surprise you."

Chapter Thirty-Two

CAMP DOGWOOD HAD been resuscitated. Once again its heart beat with human footfalls, water flowed through its veins, and electricity ran like nerves through every building and outdoor light fixture. On that particular day, it had been adorned with twinkle lights, summertime pastel flowers, white folding chairs, and bows made of pink tulle. At the end of the brand-new wooden dock was an archway covered in flowers. Mason jars hung in varying lengths lighting up the space beneath peonies, roses, and eucalyptus leaves. "The Dog" was as pretty as a bride.

Two of Libby's bridesmaids had come back on board, so, along with two cousins who clearly did not want to be there, plus Brooke and Jessa, there were six bridesmaids in total—respectable for a Southern wedding if the bride was naturally careful and prudent. But in Libby's case, it was obvious that she'd worn out her bridal privileges. No one treated her as special anymore. There had been a bridal shower thrown by a cousin at a park outside of Charleston with uncovered picnic tables, fading balloons, one lukewarm casserole, hot dogs, and too many grocery-store-bought desserts. Jessa had done her best to follow Libby's explicit instructions for a bachelorette party in Charleston. But the bride forced her bridesmaids to wear the most unflattering shade of yellow T-shirts with ironed-on letters stating FRIEND OF THE BRIDE while she wore a short white sundress with a golden BRIDE-TO-BE sash and extra-large crown. Libby didn't pay for a single cocktail or for the appetizer, salad, main course, and dessert she ordered at dinner.

By the end of the night, the bride-to-be stumbled around like a woman who had just consumed four top-shelf mixed drinks and two shots of tequila. Which she had. Brooke offered to help Jessa with the bill, not because she had any extra money, but because she knew what it felt like to be walked all over.

If it hadn't been for Dottie seeing that there was some sort of supernatural reason for Brooke to be in the wedding, she would have backed out long ago. She did have to admit, though, that she was curious to see how it would go. Plus, she'd already bought the dress.

Brooke's first real introduction to Libby's family had been years ago. When parents dropped their kids at camp, there was always a moment during the goodbye where people took stock. What kind of car did the camper come in? What did their parents look like? Who got extra-long hugs and tears? Who was only waved at from the driver's seat? Libby's mother was the heavily made-up, hair-sprayed woman who gushed and doted, hugged too long, and said goodbye 217 times. Even so, Brooke was not prepared for what awaited them in the bridal suite, previously known as The Doghouse's storage room.

The lady was wonderful.

She greeted each bridesmaid with a hug like she'd known them since they were three years old and loved them like her own. Each hug lasted just a beat longer than usual, and sweet words of appreciation were generously whispered to them during the embrace. She was a pretty lady, barely taller than the four-tiered wedding cake, yet somehow stately in her beige sequined dress.

"I am just so thrilled y'all are here to celebrate with us," she announced to the group fawning over her daughter in the makeup chair. "I am Mrs. Melba Trotter, Libby's proud mama. Yes, Melba like the toast, if you can remember that far back," she giggled. "But I do not answer to that name anymore—no, sir. Y'all can all call me Mama Trotter." Her eyes kept going to her daughter. "I speak for Elizabeth and for the whole family when I say just how happy we are to be sharing this special day. Isn't my daughter just the most gorgeous thing you've ever seen in a white dress?" Melba forced a kiss onto Libby's cheek. "Now, if y'all don't mind, I'm gonna shoo y'all out of here. Don't want to keep you from all of the other good things outside, now do we?"

"No, ma'am," one of the cousins answered for all of them. Brooke was last in line for the side hugs, air kisses, and well wishes for the bride before exiting the room. She shut the door behind her, but before it latched, she heard Melba's voice. It had a completely different tone.

"You look like a harlot," she said to her daughter. "That lipstick is far too dark. And who are those people? Do they even have jobs? They're going to ruin our wedding. Not that it isn't ruined already. This place is an embarrassment. I have half a mind to just go on back home right now."

"Mama, please," Libby pleaded like her mother's biting words were a common occurrence. Brooke quickly caught up with the rest of the group, singling out Jessa. She pulled her aside, into the trees where no one else would hear them.

"I think I understand better why Libby is the way she is," Brooke said.

"Why?" Jessa was immediately invested.

"Because her mother is awful."

"That sweet lady? Melba toast?"

"She was sweet to our faces, but as soon as we left, she turned terrible."

"Oh," Jessa said. "She's one of those."

Brooke nodded. "At least Libby doesn't try to hide her meanness. At least she comes right out with it."

"Mama says that people choose who they're gonna be. Libby probably thought she only had two choices: victim or perpetrator," Jessa said. "She didn't want to be a victim, so she became the perpetrator."

"Well, I'm still mad at her." Brooke pulled at the thick pink taffeta band around her waist that ended in a big bow on her behind. "This is too tight."

Jessa, in a matching pink dress and freshly curled hair, helped retie the bow.

"But I guess knowing she's got a crappy mother will make it easier to walk down the aisle and pretend to be her friend," Brooke said.

"We're showing her that there's another way to be."

Brooke thought about that simple concept. Maybe that was it. Maybe Libby or one of her cousins or maybe even several people there needed to see that there was another way to be. "Love conquers all, right?"

Jessa shrugged and smiled. "Only if it's true and real."

It didn't escape Brooke that Jessa was the one who'd never actually been *in love*.

Gates was there as a guest, and that wasn't a surprise, although Brooke never imagined he'd be an entire hour early. As always, his presence could not be ignored.

"Well, hey there," he said when he saw her. He seemed strangely unaffected by her, like they'd always been casual friends instead of each other's main squeeze for too many years. It was further proof that the breakup was the right thing to do. He gave her a brief hug before squeezing Jessa tight.

"Did you bring a plus-one?" Jessa asked.

"Yeah, she said she'd meet me here." He didn't seem excited at all, but that was classic Gates.

"Someone we know?" Brooke didn't feel jealousy, but

her curiosity was definitely piqued.

"Met her online. She's a Charleston girl."

"And she's afraid you might be a serial killer, so she's driving herself?" Brooke giggled.

"She's gonna get onto this empty old island and figure her fears were right," Jessa said. "Your date's about to turn tail and run, Gates. You might as well hang with us."

The hired staff was putting out the champagne glasses at the greeting table, so they all grabbed one. As soon as the green-headed mallard saw Brooke, he was immediately at her side. He was her constant companion every time she was there. His leg was healing, but there was still a little orange hiccup in his waddle, which made his nickname feel like redemption. The name had taken on a new meaning. Everybody loved Zippy. He was a friendly little duck who had made Camp Dogwood his home. He had a nest by the swimmin' hole and was apparently quite a hit with the ladies. Little brown ducks followed him around like groupies.

Nate was taking a shower at the lighthouse. He drove in from Charleston that morning and went for a swim while Brooke had her hair and makeup done with the other bridesmaids. She'd made sure to install Wi-Fi in her little round house so not only could Nate work while he was there, but they could always be in touch with each other. It was one of the many things she'd gotten up and running in a very short time.

Nana had been proven right. Brooke was the right person for the job. She'd been running the cleanup and fix-up while working on a website and marketing materials. As soon as the wedding was over, the real work would begin. Camp Dogwood was going to be like an updated version of the old *Dirty Dancing* movie, with family entertainment, outdoorsy things to do, and a little ferry to take guests back and forth from the Saltwater Winery.

Gates wasn't the only one who showed up early. Car after car drove down the old dogwood-lined drop-off lane and parked in the brand-new asphalt parking lot. The white stripes had barely dried in time. People were beginning to mill around—some walked down to the new floating dock where chairs had been set up for the ceremony, others appreciated all of the freshly planted flowers, and some held their champagne glasses while taking a short stroll through the cleared pathways in the woods. The bridge over the creek was freshly painted white, and signs had been made to guide people toward all of the important areas: the horse paddock, the kayak launch, the beach, The Doghouse, the jumping rock, the swimmin' hole, and each of the yet-to-be-transformed cabins, which were named after flowers.

Trig and Cornelia looked like movie stars. Trig still fit into his specially tailored tux, and Cornelia had her hair done in the most flattering updo. Surely, Libby's mother was not going to be happy about it. The groom's mother, on the other hand, appeared to be a genuinely kind person. That gave Brooke hope for Libby's future. Once again, Libby would have an opportunity to see that there was another way to do things. She didn't have to protect herself by putting others down. She could elevate herself by lifting others up. So many things about Libby's wedding had been a gut punch for her that it might be the catalyst she needed in order to change.

The great humbling of Libby Trotter had begun, and it was her recent gratitude for Brooke and Jessa that proved it. She'd written them each a heartfelt note of thanks for the bachelorette party and included a gift card for dinner at the Peninsula Grill. For the first time ever, Brooke saw a glimmer of a chance that they might actually remain friends after the ceremony.

Just as people were beginning to find their seats, a loud horn came from offshore and a white-haired woman waved from a speedboat as it made its way toward the lighthouse beach. Nana and Duke were making an entrance.

Jessa walked down the aisle first, then Brooke, then Libby's two other friends, and her cousins. Their matching cotton-candy-pink dresses coordinated with the pink bow ties and sweaty pink faces of the six groomsmen who stood in a line next to James. It was four in the afternoon, and the guests who got a spot in the shade were the lucky ones. Most champagne glasses had been switched out for water bottles by then, and James kept wiping his forehead with a hanky. But the bride appeared cool and fresh in her lace-bottomed white ball gown dress. The faux diamonds on the strapless top shimmered in the sun, and her smile looked certain. Maybe she really was in love.

When it was Libby's turn to deliver her vows, she actually began by thanking her bridesmaids. Brooke made eye contact with Nate in the audience, and everything good and happy in the world bubbled inside of her all at once. She still hadn't gotten over the awe that he was finally back in her life and they were back where it all began. It felt like everything she'd always wanted was hers. Trig and Cornelia were holding hands, and Nana and Duke were no longer lonely. Nana had literally and figuratively added color to that man's life. He wore a royal blue tie to match her dress and a feather in his breast pocket from her hat made of peacock plumes.

The ceremony was half over when Gates's date showed up. Everyone had given up on her, but all of a sudden, there she was, standing at the back looking over the heads of a sea of people for a guy she knew only from a photo. Brooke knew the minute she saw her that it wasn't going to last. First of all, she broke the cardinal rule of wedding etiquette and wore white, and second, the dress looked more like lingerie and barely covered her behind. Even in stilettos, she was scarcely five feet tall. Not Gates's type at all. And she was from Charleston? Certainly, she didn't grow up there.

When Brooke realized she was staring at the poor girl, she forced her attention back to the wedding. She was being horribly judgmental. Gates's date might be a very nice person, and Brooke should treat her that way.

Dinner was inside The Doghouse. Candles flickered on the rented round tables with white tablecloths and pastel flower centerpieces, and the air-conditioning was doing its job well. Finally, Brooke and Nate could sit together. They shared a table with Jessa, Dottie, and Tootie, and Gates and his date, Juls. The girl's personality was the opposite of her outfit. She was so shy, she could barely speak. When dinner was over and the dancing began, Gates asked Jessa to take Juls to the bathroom. Brooke watched the whole thing, and was surprised when he walked straight back to her and Nate. He took something from his pocket and handed it to her.

It was yellow with a big number two, and on its side was a phone number written in black ink.

The stolen duck, the one with Nate's phone number was finally Brooke's again. She held it to her chest.

"You've had it this whole time?" she asked, the gravity of his betrayal setting in.

Gates nodded.

"You stole it?" she asked. He'd stolen the duck and stolen her. How dare he.

He nodded again, looking sheepish.

Nate didn't appear mad. Maybe it was because things had worked out. But what if they hadn't? What if she'd never seen him again, and Gates had been hiding the one way she could find him? "Why?" she asked.

"I was stupid," he said. "There was that movie night..." He shrugged at both of them. "I saw y'all kiss out there on the dock and I guess it got my competitive juices going."

"That's why you led that charge and tore down the movie screen?" She knew it. She knew back then that the interruption was directed at her.

Gates nodded. "That's when I decided that I wanted you."

"Not much of a bro code." There was no malice in Nate's voice, but it needed to be pointed out.

"I'm apologizing to both of you now and trying to set things right. Brooke didn't act like she was interested in me back then, and that made me want her even more."

"But you still stayed with me all of these years. Just to keep me away from Nate?"

"No. No, of course not. I told you. I really did love you. But I've always known I wasn't right for you." He didn't say it like a man with a broken heart, he said it like a man who had healed from one.

Brooke took a deep breath, and Nate reached for her hand under the table, giving it a squeeze. The fact was, Gates was already forgiven. As soon as Nate kissed her again, as soon as she knew that Nate had always thought she was the girl for him, nothing that happened before mattered.

Maybe she had some sweetness in her after all, because she was genuinely not upset. She was just happy to have the little plastic duck again.

The DJ made an announcement that the sun was setting and those who wanted to watch fireworks should move outside. He played "The Star-Spangled Banner" while the crowd made their way back to the swimmin' hole and the floating dock where Libby and James had said their vows. Gates helped his date navigate the uneven ground in high heels, and Jessa walked with them while Tulip ran ahead. Brooke and Nate took a seat on the slatted wood of the dock in the spot where they had their first kiss as fire lit up the sky with cracks and shimmers. Zippy came out of the water and ambled over to join them, unfazed by the bright lights and loud sounds. He snuggled his football-shaped body into Brooke's side, and she felt like they were a little family of three on vacation enjoying a perfect summer night.

There was movement in the woods off the right. Two people stood together watching the fireworks from the private spot on a small patch of beach. Each time a shower of white sparks hit the sky, their smiles glowed in the light. The tall man in the tux, Brooke's father, had his arm around his wife's shoulders, and she leaned her head into his chest. They looked like they were young and newly in love.

"I think my parents are actually happy again," she whispered.

Nate had been watching them too. "It looks that way."

"What do you think ducks symbolize?" Brooke asked, peacefully stroking Zippy's soft green head.

Nate pulled out his phone and looked it up. "Emotional balance, strong bonds, perspective, good luck, and love."

She patted Zippy next to her and laid her head on Nate's

shoulder. The sky exploded colors in quick succession. "I think they represent all of that, plus hope and resilience."

"Our duck sure does." He kissed her on the forehead. "Didn't you tell me that Dottie saw fireworks in one of her visions?" he asked.

Instead of answering, Brooke lifted her chin. Nate leaned over and kissed her and she soaked in his lips, his nearness, his presence.

"Dottie was right," she said. "There are definitely fireworks."

Epilogue

B ROOKE WAS USED to her lighthouse home. It was a favorite sleepover destination for Jessa, and surprisingly, for the good-time team of Cornelia and Grace. But mostly, it was her happy place, her castle turret where her prince came to visit after long days spent building careers. The Dogwood Resort was up and running. They had great reviews online and even a shout-out in a prominent Southern magazine. Each flower-named cabin was reserved twelve months out, and more than fifty new jobs were created for nearby residents. The best part, though, was the Grace Warter Pavilion. From dances to karaoke to fashion shows, concerts, and art classes, there was something for everyone. Grace herself made sure of it.

On Fridays, while a ferry boat called *Daugherty's Destiny* shuttled visitors back and forth from the winery, music floated across the water like magic, plucking strings and striking notes that sounded like abundance and joy. People sat by the old swimming hole with glasses of wine and gourmet sandwiches wrapped in crisp white paper. A green-headed mallard milled about fearlessly as if he were the true owner and proprietor. Fireworks would be added soon.

With all of the challenges and chaos of the past year, it was no wonder that she had completely forgotten about the little bag she'd seen hanging underneath a second-story outcropping on the lighthouse. But she happened to remember it while Nate was there that weekend for his regular visit. He lifted her up to retrieve it.

The bag had been hung on a nail and tied tightly. Judging from the dingy state of the material, it had been there quite some time. Inside was a rock. Just a plain gray river rock, like the ones scattered around the property. But this one had been painted with a small red heart and the words LOOK IN THE OYSTER PILE.

They both stared at it until a dawning light came over Nate's face. "Do you think—My parents died on their anniversary. Do you think he planned a scavenger hunt for her?"

"You think this is from your dad?" She held the precious stone. It felt like a link to the life that Nate should have had. To the parents who loved him.

"Let's go check the oyster pile," he said.

It didn't take much digging to find another canvas bag and another painted rock. LOOK FOR THE WOODPECKER TREE.

"I think I know," Nate said.

They ran to a white birch tree several yards away, barely alive, with little black holes throughout its white trunk.

Hanging from one of the thickest branches was another canvas bag, and another rock. MEET ME UNDER THE BRIDGE, it said.

Brooke ran as fast as she could to keep up with Nate. When they got to the bridge, they both went directly to the spot where she'd dreamed about a white plastic duck long ago. Nate picked her up, and she used the flashlight on her cell phone to look deeper into the spot underneath the trestle. Zippy must have heard them; he appeared from the sky, quacking loudly before landing on the empty creek bed and fast-waddling, limp-free, to join them. They took a moment to greet him, then went back to work. Sure enough, the spot from her dream held another canvas bag. The way it was stuffed into the spot resembled a little white duck. She reached in and handed the bag to Nate.

Inside was a note wrapped around a little square box.

Brooke had never seen Nate cry before. Not while talking about his parents or his grandfather, not while recalling the trauma with his uncle. Grief, loneliness, poverty, abuse, judgment, hatred—for him, it had all simply been a part of life. But as he read the note aloud, tears streamed down his face.

For my beautiful wife on our fifteenth anniversary.
You have given me more than I deserve. More than I
ever hoped. You alone have shown me what it means to
be truly happy. We have every good thing that life
offers—our Nathan, and each other. Your love fills my

*soul. It is you who has made this world tolerable, and
my life worth living. The diamond in this necklace
comes from my grandmother's engagement ring and the
surrounding diamonds were curated just for you. I
designed it with the help of my father, and I hope that
every time you look at it, you know that you are fully,
completely, and infinitely loved and appreciated. The
greatest joy, the greatest gift of my life has been the honor
of loving and being loved by you.*

As he came to the end of the note, Nate turned to
Brooke.

She could see on his face what he was about to do. "No,"
she whispered. "No, Nate. This is yours."

He opened the box and immediately held it up to her.
"This is ours," he said, his voice thick with emotion. "None
of this is a coincidence. I knew it from the first time I saw
you smile. I finally have something to give you—something
from my past for the girl who is my future."

His eyes welled with tears, and hers were just as blurry
with the heft of the moment and the beautiful turn their
hunt had taken.

"Anna Brooke Sharon Warter," he whispered. "It's always been you for me."

"And it's always been you for me."

He gently clasped the necklace behind her neck. Miracu-
lously, their quacky little mallard had managed to keep quiet
until they kissed, then his raucous noise-making began.

"We're happy too, Zip," Nate said. "We're going to have so many great days here together."

"We rewrote the past," Brooke said, leaning into his embrace. "And now I get to be in my favorite place in the world. With my favorite person." She laughed. "And a duck."

The End

Acknowledgements

First, I have some heartfelt appreciation to extend to the person who just read this book. My writing journey has opened the door to a world I've never experienced from this viewpoint before. I've always been a reader, and now I get to be on the other side. I can tell you that I have so much admiration for the generosity and kindness of "book people." I've seen the studies about how reading builds empathy and emotional intelligence, how it expands knowledge and critical thinking, improves focus and mental resilience, and so many other great things. But I would like to add that, from where I sit today, every time you read a book (and leave a review if you're so compelled) an author gets her wings. Okay, maybe it just feels that way.

Thank you for picking up a book from a new-ish author. Thank you for supporting bookstores. Thank you for your willingness to expand your mind and explore.

I also owe a truckload of gratitude to Jane Porter, Julie Sturgeon, Kelly Hunter, Nan Reinhardt, Beth Attwood, Cyndi Parent, Mia Gleason, Lee Hyat, and the entire team at Tule Publishing. This book would A) not exist, B) would be full of a million comma errors, a plot hole or two, and varying degrees of grammatical mistakes, C) would not have a cover or professional marketing, and D) would not have a math-brained person to do the tracking and accounting, without the Tule group. Not to mention, they are easy to work with and really nice people.

My incredibly supportive husband, Bryan Reese, encouraged me to start writing years ago, and I wish I could say that I didn't need his permission, but writing can seem like a massive waste of time if you're unsure whether you can actually do it. Thank you, Bryan, for reminding me that it's important to make time for myself. I have come to believe that a person probably won't have a strong desire to do something unless they also have the ability. I also believe that most readers are wholly capable of being writers. If you feel like I'm talking to you, I am. Just get something on the page because the real work comes with the revisions.

I won't go through my list of kids, family, and friends to thank because I hope they already know that they are absolutely the most important parts of my life. They are the core, the special sauce, and the icing on the cake.

I hope you are enjoying this new series! *Chasing Carolina Jessamine* is up next, with two more to follow.

Please connect with me online!

Facebook:
Laurie Beach

Instagram and TikTok: @beachauthor

If you enjoyed *The Dogwood Days of Summer*, you'll love the other books in....

The Southern Isles series

Book 1: *A Saltwater Christmas*

Book 2: *The Dogwood Days of Summer*

Available now at your favorite online retailer!

More Books by Laurie Beach

Book 1: *The Firefly Jar*

Book 2: *Blink Twice If You Love Me*

Book 3: *Christmas in Crickley Creek*

Available now at your favorite online retailer!

About the Author

Photographer: Stephanie Lynn Co

Laurie Beach writes about small southern beach towns, quirky friendships, and true love. When she's not holding down the couch and typing out words, she stays busy keeping track of her husband and four children. A graduate of Auburn University with degrees in Mass Communications and Psychology, she worked as a television news reporter, an advertising producer, and a political press secretary. She now writes full-time.

Thank you for reading

The Dogwood Days of Summer

If you enjoyed this book, you can find more from all our great authors at TulePublishing.com, or from your favorite online retailer.